BLUEPRINT FOR FALLING IN LOVE

CARRIE CLARKE

eBook Format: 978-0-6456982-2-0

Print Format: 978-0-6456982-3-7

Cover Design: Akapit Ryan Alexander Gilchrist

This book is written using Australian English. You might find unfamiliar spelling or phrases. If anything in particular perplexes or interests you, please contact me at hello@carrieclarkeauthor.com.au. I'd love to hear from you.

 A catalogue record for this book is available from the National Library of Australia

CONTENTS

To my Pop, for whom I have so much love and admiration. A brilliant mind, a kind soul and a wicked sense of humour.

CHAPTER ONE

JOSH

Hiking my battered leather laptop bag over my shoulder, I check the area around my seat to make sure I haven't missed anything before turning towards the exit. The old lady in front of me is still gathering her belongings, so I entertain myself by gazing down the long corridor of poor souls who travelled cattle class. It's a tangle of cramped bodies struggling out of tiny seats, bags falling from overhead lockers and people jockeying to get off the plane as fast as possible.

Flights to Australia are interminable. Especially from London. This one was blessed with the added entertainment of not one but two storms. The turbulence was so bad dinner was delayed, and the smell of airsickness wafted through the plane for hours. I don't envy the economy passengers right now. At least the pointy end provides a little extra space and comfort.

A swirling curtain of glowing red hair catches my eye a few rows down in the economy section. Not Ron Weasley red. A rich, deep, coppery red. Framing an elegant profile, tipped up to search the overhead luggage bins. Long slender arms pull out a small backpack. I'm mesmerised by the grace of her movements as she slips it over her back, highlighting small yet spectacular breasts, which bounce under a clingy t-shirt printed with Frida Kahlo's face, as she settles the straps. My body reacts of its own accord. Worn-out old jeans tightening as my pulse picks up. What a shame she wasn't sitting next to me on this long and boring flight. She's not my usual type—I tend to go for curvier women—but there's no getting away from the fact she's piqued my interest.

"Excuse me." The tone belies the sentiment as I hear a throat clearing behind me. Someone's in a hurry to get off. "How about you get moving?"

It's the buttoned-up, business-suited guy who was in the seat across the aisle from me. Who wears a business suit on a twenty-hour flight? He gave me the stink eye when I boarded and turned left instead of right. Like he thought I didn't belong there. I get that a lot. I think it's the hair. Or maybe the tattoos. Then again, it could be the biker boots. Sure, I could tone it down for flying, but I get a kick out of irritating the entitled arseholes who fly business. Even though I'm one of them.

I realise the little old lady has gone and I'm free to make my way to the exit.

"Yeah, sure, man. You go ahead." I step aside and let the dickhead pass me, which earns me nothing more than a slight shove and an eye roll. I don't care. If I linger long enough, I might be able to meet up with the owner of the hair on the jetway. Maybe we can share a taxi and get to know one another.

No such luck. I'm pushed along by the stream of people eager to get wherever they're going. Or at least eager to get out of the cramped and smelly torture chamber we've all been trapped in. I'm in no rush. I'm happy just to be here, breathing the Sydney air.

Even in the airport, where the stench of jet fuel, unwashed travellers and cleaning products is strong, I can smell the familiar scent I think of as distinctly Sydney. Eucalyptus mixed with sea air and humidity. It smells like home. Only now do I realise how much I've missed it. It was a conscious decision to stay away all those years, but I wish I'd at least made an effort to visit once or twice.

I wander aimlessly through the booze and perfume-filled duty-free shops for a while, happy to stretch my legs, keeping an eye on the walkway. I don't spot the amazing hair again until I get to passport control, where it's organised chaos. It seems the automatic passport scanning system has been fried by a direct hit during a lightning storm last night and we're back to old-school systems of officers eyeballing you and stamping your passport. Luckily, we're the first plane in, so the wait won't be too long. I pity anyone on the ten o'clock from LA.

The delays work in my favour because there she is, in the queue next to me. I can't see her face, which is hidden by a waterfall of incredible hair, while she taps at her phone. Until she tucks her mobile in the back pocket of her faded jeans and looks up. Our eyes connect over the lane dividers keeping us in our neat little lines, and I feel like someone's hit me with a taser. Only in a good way.

The face matches the hair for beauty. This woman is drop-dead, kick-you-in-the-balls gorgeous. Her eyes are dark blue, almost navy, framed by curved brows and high cheek-bones. Freckles dance across a delicate nose, which leads to a full, lush mouth. I can think of many, many things to do with that mouth.

Her face lights up like Sydney Harbour on New Year's Eve when she notices me.

"Hey." I tip my chin at her.

"Hi." She's Australian, and her expression is more friendly than you'd expect from a stranger, even an Aussie. Her smile is blinding, and for a second or two, I'm spellbound by those navy eyes. "It's great to see you." She leans across as if to hug me and is brought up short by the rope barrier.

That seems like a weird reaction. She doesn't know me. Does she? Okay, I do sleep with a lot of women, and usually only once, but I think I'd remember her. The hair alone is not something you would easily forget. Although she does seem vaguely familiar.

I'm not sure how to respond. "Yeah ... ah ...you too." It comes out as almost a question.

Elegant brows draw together at my response. She looks slightly confused and opens her mouth as though she's about to speak when the guy behind her gives her a not-so-gentle nudge. There's no time for patience in an airport.

"Ooh. Sorry. Sorry." She smiles at him before turning to me and pointing at the counter. "My turn. Catch you on the other side, I guess."

I watch as she chats with the officer. She's beautiful. No doubt. And maybe a little crazy? He chats right back, clearly attempting to flirt before he stamps her passport and waves her through. She turns again and gives me a wave that's way too cheerful for someone coming off the back of twenty hours in economy, before heading down the stairs to the baggage claim.

I get the distinct impression she's as interested as I am. Looks like my welcome home just got a whole lot more interesting.

My line stalls thanks to the guy in front of me, who seems to be arguing the point with the passport security officer. Airports really do bring out the worst in people. Eventually, they come to an agreement, and I move forward.

I've travelled all over the world, and it's not an exaggeration to say Australia has the friendliest border force officers of anywhere I've been. But don't be fooled. They will drop on you from a great height if they get a whiff of something dodgy.

My officer rolls his eyes and cocks his head towards his previous customer who is stomping down the wide stairs, face red and sweaty. I shrug a 'What can you do?' and he smiles. "Welcome home. Sorry for the delays. Technology. Great when it works." He checks my passport and sends me on my way.

The baggage claim is packed with cranky travellers impatient to get through this last torturous hoop of international travel. I scan the sea of bodies. Lucky for me it's not hard to pick out such bright and shiny hair. I spot my bag and edge through the crowd to lean in and snag it. Most of my belongings are being shipped, so there's only the one case.

This woman is breathtaking, and she's aroused my curiosity, not to mention something a little lower. I drift towards her. Bags are starting to come down the chute thick and fast. I arrive at her side and am about to make my move when a guy way too old to be wearing a wanna-be-a-lad tracksuit in look-at-me-day-glow, drags his bag off the belt, swings it around and hits Red square in the hip. Taken by surprise, she lurches left, and I'm there to catch her. Full-frontal on my chest. My hands come up instinctively, supporting her back.

"Hey man, watch what you're doing." I give the guy a glare, which has no impact on his self-involved arse. I look back at Red. "Are you okay?"

She's leaning against my chest and rubbing her hip, which moves her breasts against me. They're small, firm and perfect. My hands move to her arms, where I find the skin smooth and warm, and I have to resist the temptation to circle my fingers. Taking a deep breath, I try to calm my body's response. The reverse happens as a dose of perfume and pheromones heads straight to my boxers. How does a woman get off such a long flight smelling so good? Like cinnamon rolls. Spicy and sweet and buttery. Delicious.

"Yeah. I'm okay. Thanks." She casts a glare at the disappearing back of the dickhead who whacked her with his bag, making no move to step back from my hold. Without pulling out of my arms, she turns her head towards the luggage parade.

"My bag." With a gasp, she lunges for a huge red suitcase about to lumber out of her reach.

"Let me help you there." I reach for the bag and heft it off the conveyor belt with a grunt. It weighs a ton. "Travelling light, I see."

"Never. Thanks again," she says with a laugh.

"Is this it?"

"What, you don't think that's enough?"

"I wasn't sure if I should wait for the kitchen sink." I look her in the eyes, and there's definitely a vibe between us. I don't miss the way her gaze drifts to my lips, continuing on to my chest. Maybe she's not crazy, just flirty. I think about getting her number, but she's already wheeling her New-York-apartment-sized bag towards the queue for customs. I hurry to catch up and fall into step beside her. Close beside her. Our shoulders brush and heat ignites between us.

"Oh no, I had the sink shipped on ahead. Saves on excess baggage fees."

I can't hold back a laugh. "Good thinking." A good sense of humour is sexy AF.

"I didn't see you on the flight. I guess you were luxuriating in business class?"

I wonder why she would assume that. Especially given the way I'm dressed.

"Guilty. It's quite unfortunate turbulence doesn't discriminate. It was a pretty shit flight."

"It wasn't great. Regardless, I still love flying. Even in economy. It means you're going places, which can't be a bad thing." Despite the long flight and the slight purple shadows under her eyes, she's glowing with some kind of inner joy. It's incredibly appealing. "How have you been? Are you happy to be home?"

I've been away a long time, and although I still have traces of an Australian accent it's been buried under years in America and Britain. How does she know this is home? That feeling of familiarity stirs, but I can't quite latch onto it.

"Yeah. Always. You?"

"Yes and no. You know how it is."

Now's my chance. "Where are you headed? Maybe we could share a taxi?"

"Oh, that would've been good, but I think I'm being picked up by the fam."

I check her left hand, which is resting on the handle of her bag. Nope. Bare. Good.

"Right. Well, maybe we could catch up sometime, grab a drink or a meal?"

Her eyes lock on my mouth as she rubs her pillowy lips together. Yeah, she's interested, for sure.

"That would be great."

I hand her my phone, trailing my fingers across hers as she takes it from me. "Excellent. I'm Josh. Give me your number, and I'll give you a call." Maybe if I get her name, my brain will twig to whether or not I know her.

She starts typing, a cheeky smirk on her face, handing the phone back as we get to the head of the queue. I look down and see she's entered her details as *Airport Pickup*.

"Hey, wait. What's your name?" I call as she's herded forward to one of the customs desks. She turns, continuing to walk backwards, and with a grin, makes the universal sign for call me with her fingers before waving and handing her declaration to the customs guy. He unzips her bag and begins to paw through her stuff. No doubt he wants to get a look at her knickers. Pervert.

The guy at my desk takes one look at my declaration, and I get waved straight through. Guess my jocks are not anywhere near as interesting.

The stream of impatient people behind me keeps me moving towards the door, and I wonder whether to wait for her in the arrivals hall or to give her a call in a day or two. It's entirely possible she's given me a bogus number. Nah. Unlikely. There was a distinct whiff of interest there. Something about her has got under my skin. I really want to see her again. And I don't even know her name.

The doors open, and I'm met with chatter and screams of excitement from the waiting crowd. I can hardly believe my eyes when I find my oldest friend Will and his parents, Harry and Stella, waiting. Their eyes light up, and they're waving with delight.

"Hey guys, I didn't expect you to be here to meet me." I can't even remember telling them what flight I was on. Will looks confused as I go in for our customary man hug. His eyes are darting from my face to over my shoulder. Harry and Stella are not even looking at me. They're looking past me. I'm missing something. I turn, and there she is. The redhead from the plane. And Harry is sweeping her off her feet.

Fuck. No wonder she seemed familiar. I know her. It's Greer. Will's little sister.

CHAPTER TWO

GREER

"No need to crack a rib, Dad," I wheeze as he nearly crushes me before dropping me to the floor in the middle of the terminal, oblivious to all the travellers trying to get out the door past his giant self.

"We're so happy to have you home, Gee." He takes a moment to wipe away a tear before I'm in the customary Carter family headlock.

"Cut it out, Harry," Mum says with a shove. He lets me go and Mum goes in for the hug. It's complete pandemonium. Anyone would think I'd been away for years, not six short months.

As I come up for air, I catch the gobsmacked expression on Josh's gorgeous face, Will's arm draped over his shoulder. I'd like to take my time and drink him in like a strawberry margarita. I didn't get much of a chance in customs. But there's too much going on, everyone talking over one another and claiming my attention and his.

"You didn't recognise me, did you?" I give him a slight nudge in the ribs. It's rhetorical really. I know he didn't. Although it wasn't until I was waiting for my bag that I realised he thought he'd been hitting on a stranger in the passport line. I couldn't resist playing it up. Especially when he caught me after I was clobbered with the suitcase. Let's just say it was no hardship being pressed against such a delicious wall of muscle. It was all I could do not to climb him like a tree. And the look on his face when I put my number in his phone as *Airport Pickup*? Priceless.

"I ... ah ... Well, no, I didn't."

I grin so wide my cheeks hurt. "I thought not." As Mum and Dad turn their attention to Josh, I turn to my brother, who, it has to be said, looks like he's been dragged through a hedge backwards. "Wee, I wasn't expecting you to be here." He wraps an arm around my neck and rubs his knuckles across the top of my head like the obnoxious big brother he is.

"Don't call me that." He hates it when we use his child-hood nickname. Which, of course, makes us do it more. The funny thing is, he gave himself the nickname when, as a tod-dler, he couldn't wrap his tongue around William. It came out Wee-yam. Which, at some point, became Wee. And now the rest of us are stuck with our own versions of it—Gee for me and Bee and Eee for my brothers.

"Mum guilted you into it, didn't she?"

"No. Well, maybe a bit." I'm guessing he hasn't been to bed yet. At least not his own. He ruffles my hair before turning to Josh. "You guys were on the same flight?"

I answer because Josh still looks like someone has punched him in the junk. "Apparently. But only one of us was in the pointy end."

"I gave you my points. Did you not get an upgrade?" Dad starts to bluster, incensed to discover his little girl wasn't travel-ling in style.

"Nope. Fully booked flight. But it was okay. I slept most of the way."

Although, if an upgrade had come through, I might've spent the flight with Josh, which adds a layer of disappointment I didn't feel earlier.

They spend a few more minutes fussing over me and Josh before Dad grabs my bag and we start to make our way to the carpark. Josh stands where we left him, hands on hips, expression blank, until Will turns and waves him on.

"Well, come on, dickhead. Did you think we'd leave you stranded here? There's plenty of room."

Shaking himself out of his fugue state, Josh grabs the handle of his suitcase and legs it to catch us up.

Luggage safely stowed in the boot of Dad's obnoxiously over-sized Range Rover, I, as usual, end up in the middle of the back seat, sandwiched between Will and Josh. Will, I can ignore. The solid warmth of Josh's thigh pressed against mine, not so much. My pulse is quicker than it should be, and I can feel my nipples tightening under my t-shirt.

Josh clutches his laptop bag over his lap. Interesting. He was very flirty with me before he realised who I was. I didn't miss the way his body reacted when I accidentally fell into him. And you'd have to be an idiot not to know what grabbing a drink or a meal meant. But all the flirtiness came to a screeching halt when I was outed by the waiting family. Shame. Still, it was fun while it lasted.

Now he's looking out the window with great concentration while carrying on a conversation with Will and Mum about what he's been up to since he left. His jaw is tight, and I can see the pulse thrumming at the base of his throat. In time with my own.

My eyes drift to his beautiful hands, gripping the laptop bag like his life depends on it. The long, strong fingers. The neat nails. The raised blue veins pulsing under the skin. And the dusting of dark hair peeking out from under the sleeve of his jacket and whispering across his wrist.

"Where can we drop you, Josh?" Dad asks as we hit the Eastern Distributor, which is thankfully almost empty this early on a Sunday morning.

"The agency has put me up in a serviced apartment at Milson's Point if it's not too much trouble, Harry."

"Not at all. It's on the way. Will tells me you have a high-powered new job."

"I don't know about high-powered. It's definitely a step up, though."

Will snorts. "Don't sell yourself short. I did some digging. Parachute is the fastest-growing agency in Sydney. And you're their new wunderkind creative director. Sounds pretty high-powered to me."

"Oh, how wonderful for you, Josh. You deserve it. We know how hard you've worked. We couldn't be prouder of you," Mum gushes, twisting in her seat to pat Josh on the knee. She adores Josh. As does Dad. Although they didn't always. I can see the blush creeping along Josh's sharp cheekbones.

"You've certainly turned yourself around since you nearly got William expelled from school for sneaking off to the adult entertainment shop at lunchtime," Dad roars, laughing at the memory of their first encounter with Josh. Dad wasn't laughing then, that's for sure.

Will winces and gives me the side eye.

"Yeah. Right. As though I didn't know about your little excursion. You could hear Dad yelling from two suburbs away." I jab him in the ribs.

The blush on Josh's cheeks goes from pink to deep red as he rolls his extraordinary, mismatched eyes. "Don't remind me."

"Water under the bridge now, Josh. And we're all so happy to have you home. Ten years is too long to be away from family, son." And when Dad says family, I know he means us. Not Josh's biological family, who more or less left him to his own devices from a very young age.

"It is. But the experience I got in New York and London was incredible. I would never have landed this job without it."

Since he isn't looking at me, I have a chance to study Josh's profile and take in the small changes ten years have wrought. Last time I saw him, he was still a boy, really. Now he's a man. There's a new sharpness to his jaw. And tiny lines fanning out from the corners of his eyes. He's paler than he was as a teenager, and his wavy hair is darker, almost the colour of bitter chocolate, with a surprising scatter of silver hairs at his temple. It's still long, pulled back in a messy bun, exposing a broad forehead and those perfect cheekbones.

If it weren't for his short, scruffy beard and full soft lips, his face would be all hard planes and angles. But his eyes are his standout feature. His left eye is a beautiful warm, tawny amber, while the pupil of his right eye is half amber and half silvery-green. It looks as though the hands of a clock have stopped at two and eight, creating a slightly lopsided divide in the colours. Despite the disconcerting effect, both eyes are full of fierce intelligence and sharp wit, balanced occasionally with a hint of softness.

"I can't believe you didn't recognise Greer at the airport," Will chips in.

"In my defence, she has changed quite a bit since I last saw her." Josh shoots me a sideways glance.

This makes Mum laugh. "She was a late bloomer, that's for sure."

And I was. My love of ballet probably had something to do with it. Then I hit sixteen and seemingly overnight, I went from a skinny kid with a flat chest to a slightly less skinny kid with boobs. I'll never be curvy, but I'm comfortable with my shape. And judging by Josh's flirting in the airport, he seems to like it.

"Well, this is handy. Greer's flat is right around the corner." Dad pulls up outside the address Josh gave him, and we all pile out of the car into the soft morning sunshine.

"She's not living at home?"

"*She's* standing right here, you know." Being the 'baby' of the family, I've often been talked about rather than to, and it drives me nuts.

Josh has the good grace to look a little sheepish. "Sorry. You're not living at home?"

"I bought a place at Kirribilli not long before I left for my internship." And I can't wait to get back into my own space and do some nesting. "Jess—you remember my friend Jess?— was living there taking care of it while I was away."

"That's fantastic. I'm not looking forward to a serviced apartment, I have to say." Josh manages to direct his eyes to somewhere over my shoulder rather than look me in the eye, which makes me smile.

"You know you're always welcome to stay with us, Josh. It would do you good to have some home-cooked meals," Mum fusses as he hefts his suitcase onto the pavement.

"I know, Mama C. And thanks for the offer. But I'll be working crazy hours, and from here, the office is walking distance, which will make life easier."

"Well, don't be a stranger. In fact, if you're not too jet-lagged, why don't you come for dinner tonight? Will can pick you up. Or Greer." Yes. Thanks, Mum. Giving Josh a lift sounds perfect.

"That would be great. But I think I should probably get an early night. I start work tomorrow, and I want to be on point. No time for jetlag."

I can't say I'm not disappointed.

"Of course. If you change your mind, you know the door is always open." My tiny mother barely reaches his shoulder, and Josh has to stoop to accept the fierce hug she gives him. "It's good to have you home, darling boy."

I catch Josh's eye over Mum's shoulder. His gaze flicks away quickly before he turns and wheels his suitcase off through the door of the building. We all pile back in the car, and I'm busy planning our next meeting and wondering whether I'm bold enough to make the first move, when Will interrupts my thoughts.

"You were on a plane with Josh and didn't even know it, Gee. Shame. You could've had twenty hours to sit and stare at him like a creeper." Will laughs as we settle into our seats. The whole family used to tease me about the crush they thought I had on Josh as a kid.

"Not that again. God you're annoying. I did *not* have a crush on Josh." I smack Will in the stomach with the back of my hand. Hard. I can feel the flames starting up in my jeans. Because that's a liar, liar, pants on fire, bald-faced, great big, nose-growing, tongue-blackening lie.

I've had it bad for that man since the moment I laid eyes on him when I was six and he was fourteen. Before today, I thought I'd moved on. Now I know otherwise.

CHAPTER THREE

JOSH

Unsurprisingly, the serviced apartment feels like a cross between a cheap hotel and a display apartment. Soulless. The building is so quiet I could be forgiven for thinking I'm the sole survivor of an apocalypse. At least I get some harbour views from the tiny balcony and a communal gym, which I spend a couple of hours in, hoping to wear myself out enough to sleep tonight without the three o'clock jetlag monster.

I order take away and eat it in front of the television, thinking about Will, Greer and the rest of the family, sitting around their living room, sharing their regular Sunday night meal. It's been a tradition for as long as I've known them. I guess it's their way of making sure they never lose touch with each other in their busy lives. I've missed that feeling of belonging. I've only ever had it with Will and his family. And I'm here to get it back.

As much as I'd love to be there, I can't bring myself to go to the Carters' tonight. Not because I'm jetlagged, although I am, but because the idea of seeing Greer again so soon makes me a little uncomfortable. And by a little, I mean a lot.

I can't believe I hit on Will's little sister. The last time I saw Greer, she was a sweet but nerdy kid of fourteen with long skinny legs and braces. It's not surprising I didn't recognise her. You'd think I would've seen a picture of her in all that time, on Facebook or Insta maybe, but the whole Carter family avoids social media like the plague.

It started with an online bullying incident with Greer in high school, and then there was Will's naked selfie scandal at uni. Not his finest moment. None of which negates the problem. Or my reaction to her.

Cards on the table, I'm a man whore. There's no other word for it. Always have been, and I expect I always will be. It's in the genes. The problem is, I can't go there with Greer. I don't think I could bear the look of disappointment from Stella, not to mention Harry's booming lecture and Will's right hook when I inevitably broke her heart.

Regardless, there's no denying the way my body reacted to her. And until I can get those thoughts out of my head, it's best I keep my distance. Sadly, early indications are this strategy isn't going to work. The thoughts aren't going away. But if I keep my distance long enough, I'm sure they'll fade. After all, I've never had trouble forgetting a woman in the past.

It's a good thing I walk into chaos in the new job on Monday morning. My team has been leaderless for a while and pulling them back into some sort of shape will take work. Which is why they brought me in from London. I have a reputation as a team player and a strong leader and love nothing better than creating a collaborative working environment.

It also doesn't hurt that I've been on a winning streak with the campaigns I've worked on recently—both from a commercial and an award-winning point of view—because there's also a couple of high-profile pitches coming up, which we need to nail. And perhaps most importantly, the MD's favourite client, a boutique distillery, restaurant and hotel, is threatening to walk away following some recent lacklustre creative. I have a fortnight to pull together something impressive enough to avoid us losing the business. No pressure.

Not that I'm complaining. I thrive on the pressure. And I love my job. Creative writing was always my standout subject at school. I guess inventing alternate realities helped get my head out of my less-than-happy home life. I thought about writing a novel when I left uni. And one day, I will. But at the time, spending too much time inside my head seemed a dangerous thing. The antidote? The fast and unrelenting pace of advertising.

Most of the first couple of weeks are taken up juggling. I split my time between pulling together the pitches and meeting with each member of my team. I need to assess their creative skills and interpersonal relationships to allow me to create a more effective department structure. Unfortunately, I have to let a couple of people go, which is never easy. It's not a task I enjoy, but ultimately the team will be better for it.

I also physically rearrange the entire department. I hate the open-plan format most agencies use, and this one is no exception. Unlike some agencies I've worked in, though, there's plenty of space at Parachute. So I use desks, sofas and bookcases to create zones. It helps provide teams with a bit of privacy and offers nooks for brainstorming and quiet thinking.

The upshot of all this is there's no time for spare thoughts about anything other than work. Specifically, there's no time to think about Greer. During the day at least. It's the middle-of-the-night thoughts that plague me.

I managed to squeeze in a beer and a meal with Will and his brothers on Thursday at the grungy little Mexican restaurant we loved when we were at uni and it was all we could afford. I can't believe it's still open, and the food hasn't changed. It's so good to be spending time with these guys again. Reliving our clichéd misspent youth. It's easy and seamless. Like I've never been away. Except for the ever-present spectre of my inappropriate attraction to Greer, which is always at the back of my mind.

It's a relief that her name doesn't even come up, although they both guilt trip me about not going to Sunday night dinner. I'll have to do it eventually. I want to do it. Stella and Harry are the parents my own couldn't, or wouldn't, be. Which is one of the many reasons the Greer thing is such a problem. Because to avoid her, I have to avoid them. Which I don't want to do. I'll work through it, but for the time being, I settle for calling in on them unexpectedly when I have the chance, hoping she won't be there.

My luck runs out on the Friday of my second week on the job.

"There's someone here to see you, Josh. She says it's your airport pickup? I didn't know you were going somewhere." The receptionist's voice calls through the hands-free set on my desk. "I told her you're in a meeting. She said she'd wait. Is that okay?" She sounds all kinds of confused and I don't blame her.

"Oh. Ah, yeah. That's okay, Ingrid. And no, I'm not going anywhere. It's a joke." Suddenly it feels like my stomach is up somewhere near my tonsils.

"Lunch date, boss?" One of the copywriters sends me a smirk from where he's stretched out on the floor in my office, back propped against the glass wall. It hasn't taken the team long to gel. We're already on pretty familiar terms.

"Not exactly. Okay, have we cracked the concept, guys?" I stand up, signalling the meeting is over. "I know it's a big ask, but I'd like to see, say, three or four rough executions for discussion after the WIP meeting on Monday?" I stretch my arms over my head, trying to appear calm whilst at the same time getting them out of my office. Fast.

Hoping to appear cool, I buzz Ingrid to send Greer in. She waltzes through the open-plan creative department, which moments ago was buzzing with activity and has now fallen silent.

Wearing a sharp, cherry red pants suit, she somehow manages to look professional and sexy at the same time, trailing red hair and, no doubt, her delectable spicy cinnamon scent. Mouths are left hanging open in her wake. With a playful rap on the glass wall of my office—as creative director, I'm the only one afforded the privilege—Greer swings in through the door. She lifts on her toes to peck my cheek, which pulls her silky cream top tight across those perfectly formed breasts and delivers a lungful of the scent that's been haunting me. Shit.

"I know we didn't have a date, but I had an interview with a recruiter up the road, and I thought why not call in and see if you can spare an hour for lunch?" Greer perches on the arm of the sofa in front of me.

Date? Not a word I want to hear from Greer. Because we can't be doing that. But all the blood has effectively drained out of my head and is making its presence felt in my jeans, and I'm struggling to come up with a reasonable excuse.

"Yeah, umm, I don't know, Greer. I'm pretty busy—" The disappointment on her face stops me. It's only lunch, I guess. What harm can it do? It'll be like exposure therapy. "I guess I could spare forty-five minutes." Her face lights up, which doesn't help the situation in my jeans. Too late now, bigmouth.

Which is how I find myself heading for the lift with Greer. Thank God I'm in the habit of wearing long, loose t-shirts to work when I don't have a client meeting. I can feel every eye in the office on me. I'll have some explaining to do later.

"I haven't had much spare time to get to know the area yet. Do you have any idea where you'd like to go?" Awkward small talk it is then. Anyone would think I'd never been in a lift with a beautiful woman before. And therein lies the rub. I'm not sure

I know how to interact with a beautiful woman without hitting on her.

"There's a little bar round the corner that does a great counter lunch, and they're quick," she replies, stepping out into the winter sunshine and turning left. I usually have to shorten my steps when walking anywhere with a woman, but Greer's long legs eat up the pavement as we head along the street to a tiny bar set right on a corner. Greer slides her perfect arse onto one of the last two free stools at the bustling bar and gives the bartender a dazzling smile. "Hi there. Lemon lime and bitters for me, thanks. Josh?"

"Asahi, thanks." I'm going to need a beer to get through the next half-hour or so. I can feel myself scowling at the bartender, who seems to be enjoying his view of Greer's cleavage as she shrugs out of her business-like jacket, while simultaneously chanting 'don't flirt, don't flirt, don't flirt' in my head. Because I know what I'm like.

"We didn't get much of a chance to talk the other day. I thought it would be fun to catch up. I'm glad you're free." Greer swings around on her stool, and our knees brush. Even through two layers of cloth, I feel the buzz of electricity between us. I start to swing my stool back and forth, trying to break the connection without being obvious. Jesus, I'm beginning to understand what guys mean when they say they have a case of blue balls. When Greer is around, I feel like I'm on high alert, ready to come to full attention any minute. Meanwhile, she's looking over the menu as though she hasn't a care in the world. Maybe she didn't feel that hit of electricity, but I doubt it.

"You said you were at an interview this morning?" I try looking anywhere but at her, which is hard, because there's a mirror behind the bar, reflecting her gorgeous red hair perfectly. "I thought you'd still be at uni. What is it you're doing? Did Will tell me architecture?"

"That's right. Although, it wasn't so much an interview as a preliminary chat with a recruitment agency. I've just finished my master's." Greer runs her finger down the side of her tall glass, collecting the gathering condensation. Fuck. I gulp my beer to clear my throat. "My last semester was an internship, which I was lucky enough to do in New York. I'm looking for a job now and thinking about starting my PhD."

"PhD, huh?" I always knew she was smart. All the Carters are, with the possible exception of Benedict, and that's a long story.

"I think I'll have the chicken caesar salad, please," she responds to the barman's enquiry.

"Medium rare burger, thanks," I haven't even looked at the menu, but a guy down the bar is tucking into a burger, and it looks great.

"I didn't get a chance to congratulate you on your new job." Greer smiles with genuine warmth. "Everyone is so proud of you. Especially Will. He's been telling everyone his friend is creative director of the hottest agency in town."

I feel a thump of pride. There was a time when nobody, including me, thought I'd ever amount to anything, yet here I am.

"Well, hopefully, we will be. That's what they brought me in for. The London and New York experience got me the job. Now I have to prove myself."

"We all have complete faith in you. I'm guessing you've got the whole five-year plan mapped out?"

I laugh at how right she is. I do have a five-year plan.

"Of course. It's great to be creative director, but ultimately, I want my own agency. All I need to do is get a little local experience and exposure under my belt, make some connections, and find a suit I can work with."

"A suit?"

"Yeah. Ahh, a suit is an account handler—someone who manages the business side of things. In an ideal world, you need good suits and good creative for a successful agency. I need to find one I can work well with, who sees things the way I do, and hopefully, we can set up an agency of our own."

"Here's to world domination, then." Greer holds up her glass in a toast and laughs. And it's husky and sexy and all kinds of right. I mean, wrong. It's wrong.

"How are you liking the apartment they put you up in?" She takes a sip of her drink, and I have trouble taking my eyes off the plump lips on the side of her glass.

"It's fine for the moment. Finding a place is on the to-do list. The problem is, I haven't quite decided whether to rent or buy—or even where I want to live yet." Thinking about it gives me a headache. Right now, there's too much on my plate. Once the pitches we're working on are done, I plan on making it a priority. "So, you've moved out on your own. That must have broken Harry's heart."

"He'll get over it. Eventually. Although he and Mum use every opportunity to suggest I move home."

That makes me laugh.

"I can imagine."

"I used the money Granny left me to buy this great flat in a really old building in Kirribilli. It was in a pretty bad way, but I've been able to do it up how I want it, and it has a great feel—big rooms, high ceilings. Took a bit of convincing when Dad first saw it, and he wouldn't let me move in until all the renovating was done. His excuse was it would be inconvenient, but I think he wanted to keep me at home as long as possible."

"I'm surprised he didn't chain you up in the basement."

Greer laughs out loud. "If we had one, he would've tried." She takes another sip of her drink and unwraps the serviette from her cutlery as her salad is put in front of her. "But I can match him for stubbornness. And I fell in love with the place. The ad said *harbour glimpses*, and if you stand in the kitchen sink, you do actually get a glimpse of the harbour."

"I'm not sure I want to know what you were doing standing in the kitchen sink."

My burger is dropped in front of me with a definite thunk by the bartender, who only has eyes for Greer, and the conversation moves on to less personal topics. Travel. Skiing. Music. After a while, I lose track of the fact that this is Greer. My best friend's little sister. A girl I've known since she was six years old. And by the time we're leaving, I realise I've really enjoyed myself.

Lunch has felt like a combination between a date and a meal with a good friend. Which is weird in itself. Apart from at work, or the partners of friends, I don't have many female friends. It's not as if I don't like women. I do. Typically, though, sex gets in the way pretty early, and it's all downhill from there. And that can't happen here. Under no circumstances can I give even a passing thought to hooking up with Greer Carter. I ignore those hits of electricity from earlier and focus on the feelings of friendship we managed to create. I can do this. I can be her friend. And nothing more.

"You look happy, Josh." The comment from a senior copywriter interrupts my thoughts as I stroll back into the office. "I guess I would too if I'd just spent an hour with a woman who looked like that. Are you considering her for the haircare campaign?"

"What? No. No, she's an old friend." And maybe it comes out as a snap. It's not okay to be caught daydreaming. Especially about Greer. Even if they can't read my thoughts.

"Huh, wish I could find a friend like her," one of the art directors pipes up.

"If she's *just* a friend, you're doing something wrong, boss," someone else calls out. I glare at the lot of them, who have apparently spent most of the preceding hour gossiping and speculating on who Greer is and exactly what we were doing.

"Okay, guys. My private life is off limits—got it?" And that was definitely a bark.

"Fifty says she's more than a *friend* by the end of the month," I hear seconds before I snap my office door shut behind me.

Fuck. If I can't even convince my team, who barely know me, there's nothing going on, how am I going to convince anyone else? How am I going to convince *myself*?

CHAPTER FOUR

GREER

I head home after lunch with Josh on a bit of a high. Sure, there wasn't any overt flirting, but there were definitely some *moments*. Those schoolgirl crush feelings I had for him all those years ago have morphed into something ... well, something adult. I've never felt so attracted to a man. Physically, mentally and emotionally. It's a rare trifecta I've never experienced before. And I know he felt it too.

And here we are, weeks later, and I haven't seen him again. According to Will, he's busy sorting out his new team and getting new clients. I'd been hoping he would call or I would run into him at the family dinner, which it seems he's been deliberately avoiding, because I hear he's popped in on Mum and Dad more than once. Always at late notice, so there's no time to organise the rest of the family.

He's also managed to catch up with Will, Ethan and Ben. More than once. It was hard not to take it personally until I had a bit of a lightbulb moment. When Josh saw me in the airport, there was definite interest, which I think intensified during lunch. But the reality is, I'm his best friend's little sister, which seems to be a no-go zone for men for some reason. Never mind that we're all fully functioning adults. This requires a plan. Which requires a strategy meeting. Which is why I arrange to have a drink with Jess after our weekly ballet class. Not that I need an excuse to spend time with my bestie.

Jess and I went to a bitchy all-girls school together. She was a couple of years ahead of me, so I didn't have much to do with her. Lucky for me, we also went to the same ballet school and bonded over our mutual adoration of our ballet teacher, Miss Robyn. I can honestly say, if it wasn't for Jess watching out for me, I don't know if I would've made it to the end of high school. And then she went and fell for my brother, who fell right back. Which creeped me out a little at first. Now we're sister-friends, and I know one day we'll be sister-sisters. If Ethan ever pulls his finger out.

"Is it wrong to be drinking gin right after a ballet class?" I ask as we settle into a small corner table at the pub down the road from our ballet studio. "I'm sure Miss Robyn would not approve."

"She would definitely not approve. All these empty calories?" Jess laughs. "How can we dance like Fonteyn if we are fat, girls?" she says in a perfect imitation of Miss Robyn's slight, and I suspect fake, French accent.

"Okay, Gee, spill the tea." Jess sniggers at her rhyme.

"So, you know I had lunch with Josh a couple of weeks ago. And we had a moment." I pause for dramatic effect, taking a slug of my drink. "Well, I haven't heard from him or seen him since. It's like he's deliberately avoiding me."

"Are you sure you didn't imagine the *moment*? You know, because of the years of crushing and all?" Jess softens her verbal blow with a squeeze of my hand.

"No." I can hear how petulant I sound. I also know I didn't imagine it.

"Do you want advice, or do you want me to listen and agree?" she asks.

"Advice. Definitely."

"Relax. I know how you feel about Josh, but he's probably still trying to wrap his head around the fact that you're not a kid anymore. Give him a hot minute to work it out."

"You think?" That sounds like good advice. The problem is patience has never been one of my defining characteristics.

"Yep. It was obvious from what happened when you ran into him at the airport that he's interested. Give him a chance for his brain to catch up with his dick." Gin and tonic sprays across the table as I choke and Jess laughs.

"Also, he's got a lot on his plate with this huge new job. Maybe he doesn't want any complications right now."

Damn. Jess makes a lot of sense. I down another good mouthful of G&T and mull it over.

"You think I should give him a bit of time to get himself together? Work wise and everything?"

"Yep. I mean, you've crushed on him this long. Is there any rush?" Jess grins at the waiter who has put a plate of hot chips between us. I can feel Miss Robyn judging, but we need something to line our stomachs.

"Ha. You know what he's always been like. He'll be hooking up with someone in no time." I swipe a chip through the mayo on the side and Jess grimaces. She's a tomato sauce girl.

"Is being a hook-up what you want? Or are you looking for something more?"

"More—obviously. But I don't want him to meet someone while I wait around like a loser."

"No, but like I said, he's got a lot going on right now. If it's going to happen, it'll happen." Jess spreads her hands out like a game show presenter displaying a prize. "Chill out. And you need to get your own shit together too. What's happening with the job situation?"

"Nothing yet. I'm still looking. The recruiter I saw when I had lunch with Josh hasn't come up with anything interesting. I don't want to jump at the first job that comes along, and I don't have to, thanks to Granny's money. Right now, I'm researching until I find the right job and the right company." My bag starts playing the theme song from *Round the Twist*, Will's own special ringtone. Jess makes the signal she's going to the bathroom as I answer.

"Watcha up to?"

"Having a drink with Jess, talking about prospective employers," I answer. Which is not untrue, if not entirely what we've talked about.

"Aww, Gee. Look at you, being all grown-up about looking for a job and everything." There's eight years between Will and me and he's always treated me like a baby.

"Is there ever going to be a time when you don't think of me as a little girl, Wee? Because I've been a grown-up for a while now. I drive a car and vote and do all kinds of grown-up stuff."

He snorts. "Yeah. Nah. Doubt it. You'll always be the baby sister to me. And don't talk about doing grown-up stuff. It creeps me out. Anyway, Josh is thinking about buying a place. He thinks he might've found a beaten-up old Federation cottage in Manly."

"I didn't know there were any left." Pretty much the whole of Manly has been 'gentrified' to within an inch of its life, and not always in a good way, in my professional opinion.

Will chuckles. "The open house is this Saturday. I'm going with because, obviously, my opinion is gold. And I thought since you're in the business, so to speak, you could come along—give him a few ideas on how much it might cost to make it liveable. I gather it needs a lot of work. You free?"

"Yeah, sure, I can come. What time?" I do a little shimmy of excitement in my seat as I open up the calendar on my phone.

This is a great opportunity to spend some time with Josh and maybe show him I'm more than his best friend's little sister.

"I'll pick you up at eleven. Open house is at noon. Maybe we could have lunch and a drink afterwards."

"Perfect. See you then." Yes, perfect.

I fill Jess in when she gets back to the table.

"How convenient. Precisely the opportunity you were looking for," she says, and I don't miss the sarcasm. "Just don't get carried away, yeah?"

The look on Josh's face as I climb out of Will's Jeep on Saturday morning tells me he had no idea I was coming. It was quick, but I didn't miss the way his gaze travelled from my head to toes and back again, his expression going from relaxed to tense in a heartbeat.

Speaking of heartbeats, mine picks up as I take him in. If you didn't know Josh, you'd think he was a bit wild. And, okay, he is in some respects. But even though I haven't seen him for years, I know who he is at his core, and he's kind and honest and a bit squishy in the centre, a fact he would no doubt deny. Which doesn't mean I can't appreciate the rugged look he's got going on. The tattoos, the messy man bun and the chunky boots cause a chain reaction from my eyes, to my lips, to my lady parts. Magnificent is the only word for it.

"Thought I'd bring Gee along," Will explains. "She can maybe help you with what you'd need to do. And how much it might cost. Which, from the looks of it, might be a lot." Will gives the front of the little house a look of thinly veiled disgust. His taste runs much more towards sleek, modern and minimalist.

Josh rolls his eyes. "Thanks for the expert opinion, Wee."

Stepping between Will and Josh, I take their arms in a Dorothy-style grip and start towards the front gate of the run-down old house partially hidden by a huge for sale sign. "I love Manly. The beach, the restaurants. There's always something going on. Investment-wise, you can't go wrong in an area like this."

As I drag the boys up the short path, I enjoy the effect I seem to be having on Josh. His arm is pressed firmly against my right breast, and I can feel his muscles tensing. Unfortunately, the narrow hall forces me to let go of both Josh and Will, but maybe I've made my point.

Josh loosens up as we work our way through the house, dodging other potential buyers. Even though it's in sad repair, it still has most of the original features intact, and the sight of the old bones of the house gets my mind spinning. I'm all business, pointing out opportunities as well as some potential structural issues that look, even at first glance, like they might cost quite a bit of money to put right.

"Well? What's the verdict?" Josh asks as we stand under the bare branches of the spectacular jacaranda tree at the back of the overgrown yard.

I can't wipe the grin off my face. I came with Will as an excuse to see Josh. But I adore this place. The little gingerbread-house features at the front, the bay window with the original stained glass still intact, the old trees in the back garden. It even has enough room for a carport in the front yard, which is worth its weight in weedy concrete in an area like Manly.

If Josh buys this place, I hope I get to help him restore it. Because to say it would be a labour of love would be no exaggeration. And it feels good to have Josh ask for my professional opinion.

"Maybe we should talk about this over lunch?" I suggest, not wanting the other buyers wandering around to get wind of the things I have to say.

·♥·♥·♥·♥·♥·

We walk down the hill to the centre of Manly for a meal and a beer at the pub.

Will heads to the bar to order our drinks while Josh and I settle in at a table on the end of the verandah, where we can catch the warmth of the afternoon sun, balanced by the salty sea breeze.

I can't wait for Will to get back to the table before I burst.

"Josh, your house is fantastic. It's got so much going for it. I can't smell any sign of dampness. The rooms are a good size, and it has a north-easterly aspect, which is great. Not to mention space for a carport."

"Slow your roll. It's not mine yet." Josh laughs. "I know it needs a lot of work, but you really think I can do something with it?" His eagerness to hear my professional opinion adds another layer of connection to my feelings for him.

"Absolutely. I think it's got enormous potential." I picture the sagging roof and rotten stairs at the back of the house. "There's a lot to spend, but the bones are great, especially at the front. And there's plenty of room for an extension." I can already see an additional storey, which would possibly get water views, and a massive entertaining area where now there's a patch of half-dead weedy grass, a square of cracked concrete and a rusty, lopsided old Hills Hoist.

"Seems like a lot of hard work to me," Will complains as he brings our drinks and the food menu to the table. "Why don't you buy one of those new apartments in the tower near the wharf—great views and no need to do any work?"

"Great views and zero character." Josh and I shoot back in unison. Will's roar of laughter gets annoyed looks from the middle-aged couple at the table next to us. My gaze connects with Josh's, and I know he feels the frisson as strongly as I do before he drags his eyes away.

After we order lunch, I pull out the research I did during the week and hand the printout to Josh.

"I did a bit of research into the market after Will called. This gives you an overview of what's been sold in Manly recently." I point to the second page. "And there you can see the price difference between renovated and unrenovated properties. Honestly, you'll probably have to spend quite a bit to get the house up to scratch, but you can see from those numbers, it would be almost impossible to overcapitalise on a house in that position. Unless you do something over the top."

"Right. Well, you've seen the place. What would you recommend?" Josh looks impressed by my spreadsheet, which makes my cheeks heat. I turn the page to the floor plan of the existing house, which I printed out from the real estate listing.

"Okay, this is the floorplan of the existing house. Three bedrooms, a living room and not much else. And here"—I turn the page—"I've done a bit of a rough sketch. Very rough, mind you, but it shows what I think you could do. Although now I've seen the house in person, I have even more ideas about how to make it an amazing home."

Josh whistles. "Wow. That's ... wow."

"I know it seems like a lot, but if you're going to spend money to make it liveable, you might as well spend a little more and make it a house with great resale value and appeal." The stunned look on Josh's face is making me a little nervous. "I mean, the roof at the back needs replacing anyway. You might as well raise it and put some bedrooms up there while you're at it."

"No. I mean. Yes. That makes perfect sense. It's just ... it's only me. This seems like a lot."

As I look at my sketches, I realise what I've designed is very much a family home. "Well, it is for now, but you never know. You might, you know, get married. Or something."

Will bursts out laughing. "Yeah. Good one, Gee. I don't think so."

I can feel my cheeks burning as Josh looks up from the sketch.

"No, Gee. This is great. I mean, marriage is not for me. My parents made sure of that. But it makes sense to turn the house into something with good resale value. And this looks great. Really."

Ouch. It takes me a hot second to absorb what he's said. I know Josh has always been a player. I had no idea he was so dead-against marriage. Which hurts. Because growing up, he was always the one I thought of as my future husband, having him around again has brought all those fantasies back to life in my heart.

I mean, I'm not expecting him to declare his undying love and carry me off into the sunset. Well, not right now, at least. And maybe it's romantic nonsense, but I hate to think of him all alone forever. I hate to think of him with someone else, too.

He flicks a scowl at Will, who is still chuckling at the thought of Josh getting married. "And is this figure here how much you think it might cost?"

I take a mouthful of wine to clear the lump of disappointment from my throat before I answer.

"Yeah, that's a ballpark. I just thought, you know, it would give you an idea." I'm embarrassed now. I got carried away. It's overkill if he's never going to get married. I give myself a mental shake. First things first. He needs to decide if he wants this house.

"I can't believe how much work you did on this, Greer. Thank you. This gives me a really solid idea of what I should pay for the place and what I could potentially do with it."

Lunch arrives, and Will turns the talk to more practical matters.

"How do you plan to pay for all this, Josh?"

"Wee," I hiss.

"What?"

"That's none of your business."

"It's okay, Greer." Josh laughs and gives Will a shove. "Don't beat around the bush, man."

"I need to know if I'm going to do the conveyancing." Will gives me a superior big brother smirk.

"I've got the finances lined up to buy the place, and I thought I'd use my trust fund for any renos. The old man has to be good for something, right?"

Josh doesn't have much of a relationship with his father, and I've never even met him, which goes to show how absent he was. All I know is he owns a pretty successful company. Something to do with medical equipment. Money has never been a problem. Lack of it, at least. Just a lack of attention.

"Fair enough. I've got one of my staff looking over the contract you sent me, and I'll let you know if they find any nasties lurking in the small print." Despite his wild personal ways, Will is a really good lawyer.

"Great. Thanks. And if there's any way we can get an expedited settlement, let's go for it. The sooner I can get out of the serviced apartment, the better. The agency has taken a lease through to October. I can extend it if I need to or rent somewhere else. If I could get out earlier, I'd be happy."

"Whoa, whoa, whoa. Renting? Fuck that noise. You can move in with me. I've got a spare room. Think of how much fun we could have." Will is practically bouncing in his seat with excitement. I, on the other hand, have a stomach-sinking dread. Those two together are mischief waiting to happen. Not to mention, the close proximity to my brother will seriously limit any opportunity for privacy.

"I wouldn't want to put you out, man."

"Put me out? Having my best friend on tap for shenanigans? You jest." Will slaps Josh lightly upside the head.

Josh turns to me. "How long would renovations like these"—he points to the sketch still open on the table—"take, do you think?"

"Depending on the weather and how long council approval takes, I'd say three or four months, give or take," I answer.

"Well, if you're sure?" Josh looks at Will, who beams from ear to ear. "Looks like you've got yourself a flatmate." And for some reason, they both crack up.

I already feel sorry for Will's neighbours.

CHAPTER FIVE

JOSH

The amazing work Greer did on the Manly real estate market, and the potential renovations I might do have helped me work out exactly what I'm prepared to pay for the house. By the time the auction comes around the following Saturday, I have a strategy ready.

Will insists on coming to the auction, and after the work she did, I can hardly not invite Greer, so we're all standing in the dilapidated and overgrown back yard as the auction gets underway. I hope I can concentrate. Because I know she didn't mean to do it, but Greer looks like sex on legs in a fitted t-shirt and a flirty little knee-length wrap skirt that keeps getting caught by the breeze and showing far too much of her toned and creamy thigh. And I'm not the only guy who's noticed.

There are four other potential buyers and I keep quiet as four become three. Bidding slows and I still haven't put up my hand. Will keeps throwing me anxious glances. I keep quiet and don't make a move until there are only two bidders, inching the price up with agonising slowness. Finally, when things have stalled and the auctioneer is about to call, it I throw in a bid of five thousand dollars more than the last, causing gasps of surprise from the small crowd.

I want this house. At some point, it's become a symbol of why I'm back in Sydney—to put down roots and reconnect with the people I love. To create a real home for myself, where maybe I can give a little back to Will, Ben, Harry and Stella. I choose not to think about all the things I'd like to give back to Greer. Because that isn't happening.

The hammer comes down for the third and final time, the auctioneer shouting 'SOLD', and before I have time to think, Greer is launching herself at me with a shriek. My reaction is pure instinct. Crushing her against my chest, I spin us around and plant my lips on her lush mouth, oblivious to Will and the crowd around us. Our lips cling and my blood hums for endless seconds before a none-too-gentle slap on the back from Will breaks our trance.

"Put him down, Gee. Out of the way," Will interrupts, shoving Greer aside with a look of disgust as only a brother would do. "Great work, Josh. I was beginning to wonder what you were up to. Then bam. Last minute stealth attack."

I take a long step back from Greer as Will gives me a man hug, without taking my eyes from Greer's face. My body is still vibrating with the energy of our kiss. I know I didn't imagine how intense it was, and the slightly dazed look on Greer's face confirms it. Before anyone has time to think, the real estate agent is dragging me off to sort out the details and sign the contracts. One of his staff pulls out a bottle of cheap bubbly and pours it into little paper cups, offering us all one.

As Will corners the agent to talk about organising a quick settlement, I find a moment to talk to Greer. "Listen, about what happened earlier. I'm sorry. I guess I got carried away with the excitement of bidding and winning."

"There's nothing to apologise for." Her blue eyes lock on my face, and part of me wants to run a mile, while the other wants to grab and kiss her again. And again. But I can't. I soldier on. "I should probably apologise for the airport too. Should have done it at lunch the other day."

"What? For the flirting? Well, that's rude. It's bad manners to tell a girl you regret flirting with her." There's the flirty vibe I got at the airport again.

"It's not that. I shouldn't have—"

"Hit on me?"

"Well, yeah. It was ... inappropriate."

"Because I'm Will's sister?" Greer's expression is somewhere between exasperation and disappointment.

I don't answer. I don't know what to say. My gaze flicks to Will, standing a few feet away, negotiating with the agent.

"I might be Will's sister, but I'm also an adult. What I do is none of Will's business."

I wince, imagining what we might have done had I not found out who she was.

"He's my best friend." Even I can hear the whine in my voice.

"I get that, but—"

"You get what?" Will has snuck up on us, paper cup of the terrible sparkling wine in hand.

I have to think fast because Will is not an idiot, even though he acts like one a lot of the time.

Greer beats me to it. "I was offering to help Josh with blueprints for the renovations."

"And I was saying I couldn't ask her to do that." I jump in to shore up the story. And maybe to avoid spending time with her.

"I think it's a great idea. She's really clever, Josh. You should take her up on it."

The problem is, what I'd be taking her up on might not be what Will is expecting. And the potential fallout scares the shit out of me.

I have mixed feelings as I pull up outside the Carters' on Sunday afternoon for the regular family dinner. When I was a teenager,

I loved getting invited to these dinners. The feeling of family, the laughing and teasing was something I never got at home. It was one of the things I missed the most when I was away.

The closeness the Carters have is something I never had with my family, having been an only child until the ripe old age of sixteen, when my brother was born courtesy of wife number three. In fact, I haven't even called my father since I've been home. Or my mother. And they haven't called me. I did send them both a text before I left London, letting them know when I'd be back in Sydney. All I got was a thumbs-up emoji from my father. Nada from my mother.

Tonight though, I feel uncomfortable. Greer will be there. I've managed to avoid Family Night, as it's called, since I've been home, but after the auction, Will had given me a guilt trip, saying Harry and Stella would want to celebrate with me. So here I am. In reality, what I've been avoiding is spending too much time with Greer. The last thing a woman like her needs is a man like me. She needs someone who will settle down and give her the sort of family life she's used to. And that sure as shit isn't me.

Dinner is served outside, taking advantage of the unseasonably balmy weather, and as cold creeps in, the patio heaters are turned on to keep us warm.

"Tell us about this place you've bought," suggests Harry as he scoops generous amounts of salad onto his plate. "Will says it needs a bit of work?"

"Yeah. A bit might be an understatement. I'd say a lot of work is more accurate. But it's in a great location, and I think it has a lot of potential." I'm happy to talk about my new house and avoid anything too personal. "Since it's a deceased estate, I'm hoping to rush through settlement so I can move in sooner rather than later. I guess timing depends on how much work I decide to do on it."

"What made you buy a renovator's delight, Josh? I thought you'd rent a shiny new apartment to impress the women."

Ethan, who is making a rare appearance at family dinner, waggles his eyebrows and gives me a cheeky leer, which earns him a light slap from his girlfriend, Jessie. Ethan is working on his PhD and always seems to be away at some sort of conference or project to do with his work. It's nice to see him for once, even if he is giving me shit.

"You know, I really don't know. I started out looking for a place to rent. Standing outside the real estate office, I spotted this house in the window and somehow, when I went inside, instead of asking to see some rentals I asked to see the house."

I came home to put down serious roots. I need a life. A real one of my own. Outside of work and partying. Although I took myself a little bit by surprise with the suddenness of my decision, this house feels like the right first step.

"What are you planning on doing with it?" asks Stella, passing a basket of bread.

"I'm not sure. The house is big enough for me, but because of the state it's in I'm going to have to do some structural repairs. Greer suggested I do a bit of an extension while I'm at it for resale value." As Greer rightly pointed out, it makes absolute financial sense, even if I don't need the space. "She even did a preliminary sketch of some ideas, which was great."

"Well, you need to look no further for an architect, you know." Harry beams at his daughter. "Greer can take care of your plans. You won't find anyone better."

"Dad, don't put Josh on the spot. He might not want me to do it. Maybe he wants someone more experienced," Greer interrupts, then turns to me. "Don't feel obliged, Josh."

"Nonsense. Josh is practically family. It would save him a lot of money, which I'm sure would be welcome," Harry blusters.

"You did offer after the auction, Gee." Will reminds her of the white lie she told.

I can feel Greer's embarrassment and her silent begging of Ethan for help.

"Dad's right, you know," Ethan agrees with Harry, "Greer's got a really great eye and lots of ideas. You might as well take advantage of connections if you have them."

"Josh, please. I don't want you to feel ..." I can see Greer is embarrassed by their insistence, but I know from what she said at the open house and the auction that she would love to get her teeth into making it a great piece of real estate. Or a home. And they're probably right. Greer is smart and creative. It's my fault the idea of having to work closely with her hits me right in the boxer briefs.

"I'm sure Greer won't have time to look at a little project like mine. She'll be too busy anyway when she gets a job." I make one final half-hearted attempt, but Harry's having none of it.

"Rubbish. She hasn't found anything she likes yet, so she's got plenty of time on her hands, haven't you, sweetheart?" Harry pats Greer's arm.

"Cut it out, Dad. It's up to Josh."

"Well, that's settled then. I can't wait to see the house and the plans." Harry beams and tucks back into his food with his usual enthusiasm.

Greer gives me an embarrassed frown across the table. We've both been trampled by Harry, who is a force of nature, and used to getting his way. I don't know how she feels, but I'm conflicted. Based on the sketches she's already shown me and what I know to be true of the ability of her whole family, I know she'll do a great job on the house. And a great renovation could make me a big profit when I come to sell. The problem is, being with Greer makes me nervous, and spending time alone together seems like a dangerous idea.

After we finish dinner, Greer catches me in the hallway while everyone else is clearing the plates.

"Look, Josh, about the house. Please don't feel obliged. Dad put you in an awful position. I completely understand if you want to use someone else."

"Yeah, I don't think that would fly with Harry." Which is the lesser of two evils? Upsetting Harry or spending time with Greer?

"Don't worry about Dad. I can handle him."

"I don't want to take advantage—"

"Oh, please. I'd love to do it. I have so many ideas already. It's up to you, though."

"Well, if you're sure? I'd love you to draw something up for me. I've got no idea what I want. I'll probably be a nightmare to work with, but I really liked the sketch you did." The words are out before I even realise what I'm saying. *Shit*. Am I crazy? I had no sooner decided I would call Greer tomorrow and somehow back out of the deal when suddenly I'm saying, 'Yeah, let's go.' I should be jumping at the chance to escape. Too late now. Greer seems thrilled. And damn if it doesn't look good on her. Fuck.

"Okay, great. Well, don't worry about ideas—I have plenty of those. Give me a call when you want to get started. I'll need to take more detailed measurements and photos, and get an idea of budget, so when you're ready ..." Greer is vibrating with excitement.

And there goes my damn imagination again, thinking about her vibrating with a different type of excitement. Double fuck.

CHAPTER SIX

GREER

I don't hear from Josh again till he rings late the following Friday as I'm getting ready for my regular theatre date with Mum and Jess. We buy a subscription to The Sydney Theatre Company and The Australian Ballet every year. It's fun to dress up and have dinner at a nice restaurant first, making a real event of each performance. There's way too much testosterone in a family with three boys, and it's nice for us girls to have time to ourselves.

"Hey, sorry I haven't called. Work's been crazy busy." Gah. That voice. All smooth and deep, with a hint of his old Australian accent starting to creep back in. My thighs clench and my heart lurches. "I wanted to let you know what's happening with the house. Since it's a deceased estate and nobody's living there, the owners have agreed to give me access on the weekend to take some measurements and whatever. I was wondering if you might have some time for a look."

Well, that puts to rest my fears that Josh has changed his mind. And spending some time with him one on one will maybe give me the chance to convince him to at least give us a chance. I put the phone on speaker and drop it on the bed so I can keep getting ready and not run late.

"Of course. I'd love to. Are you going to family dinner Sunday night? Maybe we could go and do a recce sometime after lunch, then go on to Mum and Dad's." My words come out muffled as I bend and twist to do up the buckles on my shoes.

"Works for me. I thought I might go down to Manly for a surf in the morning. I'll hang around till you get there."

I finish with my shoes and am tempted to reach for my laptop and open up the file where I saved all my notes and ideas. But if I go down that rabbit hole now I'll miss dinner, and probably the performance as well. I have a habit of getting lost when I'm working.

"Great. I'll need a couple of hours to do all the measurements and get a feel for it. How about mid-afternoon?" I slide the diamond stud earrings my parents gave me for my twenty first birthday into my ears.

"Perfect. Come over whenever suits. I'll be there from around two. You sure you don't mind giving up your weekend?"

"Nah, it's fine. I'm gainfully unemployed, remember? Any day is good for me. I was thinking I'd try and get the blueprints moving quickly. Maybe even get them finished before I find a job." I do a last check of my makeup in the mirror. Mum will be here any second to pick me up.

"Hey, whatever works for you. And let me know your rate and account details so I can get the money to you."

"Your money is no good to me, mister. Consider it a house-warming present."

"That seems like a pretty pricey housewarming. How about we talk about it on Sunday?" As he hangs up, I hear a knock at the door. Perfect timing. Along with the perfect opportunity to show Josh I'm more than a little sister. I'm a grown-arse woman. And he'd better believe it, because I'm done with waiting for him to get his shit together.

· ♥ · ♥ · ♥ · ♥ · ♥ ·

Josh is already at the house when I arrive right on the dot of two—damn punctuality. He's obviously been to the beach, judging by the brand-new surfboard leaning against the wall and the wetsuit draped over the ancient Hills Hoist in the backyard. His hair, still crusted with sand, is a damp mess around his face and shoulders, for once not tied up in its usual ponytail or man bun. Soft grey sweatpants cling to the muscles in his legs, which are long and lean, his white t-shirt doing nothing to disguise the firm belly and well-toned chest. He's so hot I can feel my tongue sticking to the roof of my mouth and my cheeks getting warm, and it has nothing to do with the afternoon sun streaming through the uncurtained windows.

"It's amazing how your mind plays tricks on you. I had forgotten how much work this place needs. It reminds me of an old movie—Tom Hanks was in it, I think." Josh smiles ruefully as he surveys the kitchen, which is not much more than a collection of old wooden cupboards, a wonky sink and an ancient gas stove that looks like it might blow up if you tried to light it.

"*The Money Pit*. I loved that movie when I was a kid. Let's hope this turns out a little better." Josh can clearly see the problems. Lucky for him I can see the potential.

"Will's done a great job getting them to agree on fast-tracking settlement. I should have complete access to the place by the end of next week. I still have a few months on the lease at the serviced apartment, and once it's up, I'll move in with Will."

"Well, you and Will living together ought to be interesting." I can't control my eye roll at the thought.

"Hey, I saw that." Josh waves his finger towards my eyes. "We're responsible adults now. There'll be no wild parties."

"Uh-huh." We both grin. I wish I could believe it, but I know my brother too well.

For the next couple of hours, I work my way from room to room, measuring, photographing and making pages of notes and rough sketches of ideas. Like most Federation houses, there is a narrow hallway with bedrooms off to either side at the front of the house, which opens up at the end to the lounge room with a tiny, dark kitchen tucked in the corner. The bathroom and laundry are tacked on the back, in what was once maybe the verandah. All three bedrooms are a decent size, and one would make a really good home office with a gorgeous bay window begging for a built-in window seat.

I have so many great ideas running through my head I barely even notice Josh, who pretty much stays out of my way. He sits on the floor, propped against the kitchen cupboards, working on his laptop, answering any questions and helping me with measurements when needed.

"Are you almost finished?" Josh asks as he watches me pack up my tape measure. It's a little after four o'clock. The light is fading fast, thanks to the ugly storm clouds that were on the horizon and have now taken over the sky.

"Almost. I have a few more notes I want to make ..." I'm so busy with a head full of images of the finished job I hardly hear him.

"Okay. Great. I'll be back in a minute." Josh heads out the front door.

Since there's no furniture, I drop onto the rickety back step with my notepad, hoping to catch a bit of fresh air after being cooped up in the dusty old house. It's unnaturally still, as though waiting for something, and I know it won't be long before all hell breaks loose. I take a couple of deep lungfuls of the expectant air. I love thunderstorms. I hope this one's a belter.

Flipping to a clean page in my notebook, I start roughing out some preliminary sketches, taking my original ideas to the next level. I already have a clear idea of how I want the house to look. Of course, I have to keep reminding myself it's Josh's house and he no doubt has ideas of his own—and a budget, of course. I should wait until we've talked these things out before I get too carried away. It's just so tempting. This place is exactly the sort of house I would want if I was buying one.

"I thought you might need one of these after all your hard work." Josh drops soundlessly to the step beside me, handing me a caramel swirl Cornetto.

"My hero." I don't waste any time tearing off the wrapper. "How did you know these were my favourite?" I lick the ice-cream and stray nuts off the inside of the foil wrapper.

Starting on his ice-cream, Josh gives me the side eye. "I didn't. They're my favourite, so I got you one too. I missed these while I was away. These and Twisties."

"I don't know if I could live anywhere without Twisties for too long. Six months in New York was more than enough. Although Dad found an excuse to visit three times, so I got a steady supply. I especially missed them when I went to the movies," I say between licks of the creamy deliciousness Josh has given me.

"It's a dilemma, alright." It doesn't escape my notice that Josh keeps his eyes firmly on his ice-cream while shifting around a bit on the step.

"Okay. I have all the information I need except a brief and a budget from you." I swap my ice-cream to my right hand, to take some notes.

"Huh. You're a lefty too. How did I not know that?" Josh notices before quickly looking away.

"I don't know. Technically, I'm ambidextrous. I can write with either hand. I just prefer the left. Are you left-hand-ed too?" Of course I've always known he was left-handed. When I was eight, I saw it as a sign from the heavens we were *meant to be*.

"Yep. Despite the best efforts of the nuns in primary school." We both laugh, knowing how tough it is to be a lefty in a righty world.

"About the house—to be honest, I don't really have a brief. Like I said, fixing up what's here would be enough for me on my own, but I can see the resale value in making it more of a family home." Josh leans back on his elbow on the step behind him, causing his t-shirt to pull tight across his abs. Gulp. "Which I guess means I'm giving you an open brief."

"Right. And what about budget?"

"Well, without wanting to sound like a tool, like I said, I'm going to dip into the trust fund for the renos. I don't want to overcapitalise, though, so I'd like your advice on how much is too much." Josh screws up his face as though he's smelt something bad at the mention of his trust fund.

"Sounds like you don't like taking money from your dad." I know I'm poking at a sore point based on his comment to Will.

He takes a while to answer.

"It might sound harsh to you, coming from the Australian version of the Bravermans as you do, but I hate the prick. The less I owe him, the happier I am."

"The Bravermans?" I've never heard of them.

"From *Parenthood*. A TV show. Big family. Parents who loved them. And each other. Anyway, the point is, I hate taking anything from him." Josh shifts on the step, uncomfortable with the turn the conversation is taking, so I detour.

"I hear you. Anyway, you'd really have to go all out to over-capitalise on a house in this location. Do you trust me?"

Our gazes connect, and the discomfort of a few moments ago drops away. The heat that always seems to be simmering under the surface whenever I'm with Josh rises to my cheeks and his.

"I trust you completely, Greer."

Metaphorically crossing my fingers, I ask what, for me, is the most important question, "Do you want to gut the place and make it modern, or would you like to retain the old-style character?"

"I don't want to gut it." Josh's eyes snap wide, making his parti-coloured eye pop. "I'd like to retain the character, that's what attracted me to this particular house—the fact it hadn't been buggered up with aluminium windows and such. But I don't want the extension to look like a fake old-style house either—like those hideous project homes you see. Am I making sense?"

"Absolutely." I can feel my mile-wide smile. "What you're looking for is original character with a contemporary twist."

"Exactly." No sooner are the words out of his mouth than a deafening clap of thunder has us jumping out of our skin.

"I think we'd better get ..." Anything else Josh might have said is lost as the torrential rain that's been threatening pounds down around us.

CHAPTER SEVEN

JOSH

We're both laughing and completely soaked as we fall through the back door, despite having only been in the rain for a matter of seconds.

"There's not a lot here to dry off with, I'm afraid." I hand Greer the damp and sandy towel I'd hung over the kitchen door after my surf. "As you've no doubt noticed."

"Thanks anyway." She hands the sand-covered towel back to me with a grimace and lifts the hem of her t-shirt to wipe her face.

My mouth goes dry. It was hard enough to look at Greer when her wet t-shirt was clinging to her. To be confronted with the creamy flesh of her belly and the transparent lace of her skimpy lavender bra is more than a man should have to take. My cock, which has been on high alert since I sat down with the ice-creams—yeah, okay, all afternoon—takes it up another notch and throbs in time with the beating of my heart.

The pull I feel towards this girl—woman—keeps getting stronger and stronger, and no amount of reminding myself who she is or cold showers seems to be making any difference. Maybe even more terrifying is my lack of interest in other women. Even though work has been hectic, I've managed to get out with Will a couple of times, and despite several opportunities, I've gone home alone every time.

Clearing my throat loudly, I turn away as quickly as I can, holding the crusty towel in front of me. "What time are we expected at your mum's?"

"About six. I guess we'll have to wait this storm out, though. You couldn't drive in this rain." Greer smiles in a way I recognise. It's the smile of a woman who knows she's got under a man's skin. Shit. Bugger. Bum. As we used to say when we were kids, and they were the worst words we knew.

"Yeah, well ..." Wiping my face with the sandy towel, I risk a glance back at Greer, relieved to find her t-shirt back in place. It's the colour of ripe watermelon flesh, and I want to sink my teeth into it. Into her. Greer almost always wears warm colours, which is odd for a redhead. But it's as though the colours of her clothes reflect the warmth of her personality, and it works for her. I rack my brain for a topic of conversation to take my mind off my need to touch her perfect breasts and smooth stomach. Although, I don't hold out much hope since it's burnt into my retinas.

Anything would do. Anything at all.

Luckily, Greer unwittingly hits on the one subject guaranteed to calm my raging hormones.

"Mum and Dad are so keen to see your house. They were determined to come with me this afternoon. I managed to convince them they'd be a distraction. I'm not sure how much longer you'll be able to hold them off though."

"I can't wait for them to see it either." My desire for them to be proud of me is as strong as if they were my actual parents. It's no exaggeration that they've been the only constant in my life. The first authority figures to trust me. To not assume the worst of me. Which is one of the long list of reasons Greer is, and always will be, off limits.

"They'd love that. It's made them really happy, you buying a place. I think they see it as a sign you're back to stay."

"Well, that's the plan," I say, mesmerised as I watch Greer gather her hair into a bundle and squeeze the water out onto the floor. It's many shades darker when it's wet but no less beautiful.

"I kind of envy you, being able to pick up and go where you wanted to." A small, wistful sigh escapes as she twists her hair into a knot. "If I tried it, Dad would report me missing to Interpol and I'd be dragged back in handcuffs."

Jesus. Why did she have to mention handcuffs? It's never been a particular fantasy of mine, but an image of her spread out on a bed and tied up with silk scarves slaps me right in the neocortex so hard I need to shake my head to try and dislodge it. Without success.

"You just got through saying you'd miss Twisties too much," I remind her.

"Yeah. I guess so. It's ... sometimes my family can be a lot. You know?"

I'd give my right arm for a family who loved me the way the Carters love Greer. But I can also see how it would sometimes be a little claustrophobic.

I'm still struggling to shake the image of her in restraints. On a bed. Naked. With a sigh, or maybe it's more of a groan, I move to the window to watch the lashing rain and lightning.

"Be careful what you wish for, Greer. They might be a lot, but they love you."

"I know," she whispers from behind me.

"I love storms, the weird light you get before they break, the crack of lightning and thunder ..."

"Me too." Greer moves to stand beside me. "I love the smell of them, and afterwards, the smell of the wet earth and the steam rising off the ground when the sun breaks through."

"Petrichor," I say. Greer gives me a quizzical look. "That's what that smell is called. Petrichor."

Her presence starts to chase away some of the chill the rain brought on.

"Huh. I never knew it had a name."

We stand side by side at the window, looking out at the backyard. At the rain pounding the cracked concrete and the wind whipping the trees. Leaves and small branches are flying thick and fast. There's an ominous creaking in the roof and a whistling accompanied by a cold draft across our feet that tells me somewhere nearby there's a gap in need of filling. What a shock.

I don't know how long we're standing there before I realise I'm no longer looking at the storm. I'm looking at her.

Watching her watch the storm is mesmerising. In the dim light, her eyes are dark and serious. Greer turns, and my heart rate kicks up. She's quivering. I don't know how much of it has to do with the damp chill from the storm and how much from the intensity of our eye contact. I can see what she's feeling as clearly as if it's written on her smooth forehead. Time stands still as we look at one another. Moving in slow motion, my hand comes up to gently cup the side of Greer's face, my fingers skimming her cheekbone before burying themselves in her hair. It's like an out-of-body experience. I'm intensely there in the moment. At the same time, I'm observing from outside. I'm not conscious of moving, but my head lowers and our mouths draw together as if controlled by some outside force. Her eyelids flutter closed, and I hesitate, my lips a breath from hers.

A sudden deafening crack behind me has us both crashing to the floor.

CHAPTER EIGHT

GREER

"Oh, my God." Josh is flattened over the top of me. At any other time, I would be ecstatic, but right now, his hard body is shielding me from the worst of the rain. With a quick look over his shoulder, he turns back to me, taking my arms and helping me to sit up.

"Are you alright? Are you hurt?" He runs his hands over my head, across my shoulders and down my arms.

I stare in horror at the enormous old gum tree that has smashed through the roof at the back of the house, less than a metre behind Josh, and hangs suspended centimetres above the floor. The room is littered with plaster, wood, branches and roof tiles. Rain is pouring through the hole the tree has gouged.

I take a moment to assess how my body feels. Apart from being chilled, and a trembling, which could be from cold or maybe adrenaline, I seem to be okay. "No. No, I'm not hurt. Are you okay?"

"Yeah, I'm fine. Jesus, what a mess." Josh slides me across the worn wooden floor to where the rain isn't reaching and sits next to me, resting his forearms on his bent knees. Which is when I see it. Blood. Lots of it.

"No, you're not. You're not fine. Look at your arm." I gently take hold of Josh's hand as we look at the jagged gash on his right arm.

"It's okay. It's only a scratch." He tries to draw his arm away. I keep a firm hold, trying to see how bad it is, but the gloom is too deep to get a good look. Blood is mixing with the rain, making it hard to tell exactly how much it's bleeding.

"No, it's not. I think it might need stitches. I've got a first-aid kit in the car. I can clean it up and bandage it until we can get you to a doctor." Without waiting for an answer, I scramble to my feet, slipping on the wet floorboards, dash down the hall and out into the rain. Luckily, my car is parked right outside, but I'm already soaked, so it doesn't matter. By the time I get back into the house, Josh is already on the phone with emergency services, listening to hold music while he waits to give details of the damage to the operator.

"Give me your arm. Good grief, it's bloody dark in here." I push Josh onto a rickety old kitchen chair left behind by the previous owner. The emergency services operator comes on the line, and Josh gives her the details of the house while I unpack what I need from my little first-aid kit. It's pretty basic, but it'll do the job for the moment.

I flip the light switch. Nothing. "Powers out." I swipe on the torch on my phone.

"Emergency services will be here as soon as they can, but it could take a while. The storm has caused a fair bit of damage." Josh studies the gash under the bright light and winces. It looks a mess.

"Okay. You'll need to hold the phone for me. Can you manage?" I hand him the phone and tear open some gauze to clean the wound. As I bend closer, I notice blood trickling down his temple and into the scruff on his jaw.

"What's that on your head? Oh, Josh, why didn't you say you'd been hit on the head?" As gently as I can, I probe the bleeding lump on his scalp. His hair is too thick to get a good look, and the sand left on his scalp from his surf doesn't help. I'm no expert, but I wouldn't be surprised if it needed a few stitches too.

I get to work quickly, and it's not long before I've cleaned and dressed Josh's wounded arm. There's not much I can do for the cut on his head other than clean it. I'm more worried about the large lump coming up under the cut. There's a definite risk of concussion, and I want to get him to a doctor quickly.

"You're not just a pretty face, are you, Florence Nightingale?" Josh jokes, watching me pack up my kit. His face is pale, and his eyes are pinched with pain.

"You can call me Flo." My grin is more than a little wobbly. Now that I've taken care of the practicalities, realisation is starting to set in. "My God, Josh, you could have been killed. If you'd been standing a little further back …" Tears threaten to spill over and run down my face.

"But I wasn't, and we're both okay," Josh soothes, taking my hands. Internally, I want to take his comfort. To hurl myself onto his lap and sob into his shoulder, even though he's the one who's hurt. I should be the one comforting him. I take a couple of deep, steadying breaths and think about the next steps.

"Well, I guess the next thing is to get you stitched up. We can leave a note for emergency services in case they come while we're gone. No arguments," I add as I see the belligerent look on Josh's face.

I tear a page from my notebook, scrawl a message for the SES and slide it under the old-fashioned knocker on the front door before I help Josh down the path. He's a little unsteady on his feet, but it's not far, and in no time, he's buckled in.

· ♥ · ♥ · ♥ · ♥ · ♥ ·

The storm is already beginning to ease as I make the short drive to the medical centre. Although the rain is still heavy, the wind has dropped. The gutters are running over with water and deep lakes are forming at the sides of the roads, which are littered with leaves and branches. I check the clock in my car and can't believe less than an hour has passed since we were sitting on the back step discussing the merits of Twisties. Luckily, the waiting room is almost deserted because only an idiot would go out in this weather, and Josh gets seen straight away.

"Someone did a great job of patching you up," the doctor notes as he cleans up Josh's arm and checks his head. "Looks like you have a mild concussion. Nothing too serious. No driving. Take it easy for a few days and come back to get the stitches out in about seven days."

A tetanus shot, some painkillers and eight stitches later, we're back at the house, where there's no sign of emergency services.

"I guess we'll have to wait." Exhausted, I flop down on the floor in the front bedroom, where the roof is still intact, preparing to wait.

"You don't have to stay." Josh slides to the floor next to me, nursing his stitched and bandaged arm in his lap. "It could be hours before they get here."

"Well, I'm not leaving you here by yourself. For one thing, you can't drive home with a concussion or that arm—and there's no way you can stay here tonight. It looks like you're stuck with me."

He would never admit it, but I can see Josh is relieved I'm staying. He's looking quite out of it from the combination of concussion and the painkillers, and I can see by the way he's nursing his arm how uncomfortable it must be.

"You know what you need? Food. How about I order some pizza, and we have a little indoor picnic while we wait?"

I google the nearest pizza place and order a large meat lovers, along with a cappuccino for Josh, then spread a picnic rug from my car on the floor for us to sit on, rolling up my jumper and the damp towel as pillows so Josh can lie down.

I call Mum and Dad to let them know what happened and have to talk them out of getting in their car and charging to the rescue. The last thing we need is them navigating the treacherous post-storm roads. After a brief debate and a short chat with Josh, they agree, on the promise we'll keep them posted and call if we need them. I love them to bits, but sometimes they need to back off a little.

"First-aid kits. Rugs. What else do you carry in that tiny little car of yours? It's like the Tardis. More stuff just keeps coming out." Josh's voice sounds a little woozy.

"I always like to be prepared," I answer, folding my hands primly in my lap. "And I prefer to think of it as Mary Poppins' carpet bag."

Laughing, Josh settles himself more comfortably on the rug and closes his eyes. "Okay, Flo. What are we going to do while we wait?"

"I guess arm wrestling is out of the question." I kick my shoes off and lie down, pressing up next to Josh and flick the corner of the rug over our legs. There's not much we can do about our wet clothes, but a bit of shared body heat will at least help combat the cold from settling in our limbs.

"You should get yourself a spot at the Comedy Club. You're hilarious," Josh replies dryly, cracking one eye open. Despite the pain he must be in, there's a smirk lurking on those plush lips. "You know, I've never had stitches before."

"Really? I have." Lifting my hair, I point to a faint scar on the top right-hand corner of my forehead, almost in the hairline. "Water skiing. The ski didn't come off when I fell. And I've broken my arm. Snow skiing."

"Are you accident-prone or reckless?"

"Both, I think," I answer with a grin.

As the storm finally passes and the rain slows to a heavy drizzle, we talk about childhood accidents and illnesses until we're interrupted by a knock at the door.

Josh struggles to sit up. I beat him to it and answer the door for the pizza guy, giving him a hefty tip for coming out in this weather.

It's pretty dark, so I use our phones as torches, put the pizza box between us, and take a long appreciative sniff before selecting a piece. We eat for a while in silence. We're both enjoying the food and the comfortable atmosphere that seems to have sprung up. Not to mention Josh is struggling to stay awake.

"Is it just me, or was that pizza exceptional?" I sigh as I lick the last of the pizza sauce from my finger.

"No, it was definitely exceptional. And so is the coffee. Thanks for thinking of it, by the way. It's good to know the local pizza place is a winner. I expect they'll be getting a lot of business from me once I move in."

Conversation slides seamlessly into food, and we're both surprised when we hear the doorknocker again and realise it's fully dark outside.

Josh staggers a little as he gets up from the floor to let the SES workers in, and I take hold of his elbow to steady him. For a moment, we both stand silent, gazes clinging in the dim hallway before he turns to open the door. He doesn't say it, but I can feel how grateful Josh is not to be alone right now.

"Well, this is one hell of a mess," the guy supervising the team says. "By the look of this place, maybe the storm did you a favour. You could knock it down and build a nice townhouse or two on this block."

Josh and I exchange eye rolls.

It takes quite a few hours for the guys to remove the tree and secure the roof with a tarp. I can tell by the strained look around his eyes by the time the SES leave that the whine of chain-saws and the throaty rattle of the generator they used for their lights have given Josh a pounding headache. I know my head is throbbing and I don't have a concussion. As he closes the door behind them, I hand him a couple of the painkillers the doctor gave him and my water bottle.

"How did you know?" He seems surprised I've noticed his discomfort.

"Psychic." I smile as I fold up our picnic blanket. "Come on, let's get you home. It's nearly midnight."

The rain stopped long ago, leaving behind ample evidence of the storm. The drive back to Kirribilli is littered with downed trees, flooded roads and several roofless houses.

"I guess we got off lucky," murmurs Josh, his voice weary.

Without further discussion, I head straight for my flat.

"You're staying with me tonight, Josh. I don't want any argument." I expect him to object, and when he doesn't answer, I glance over to see him sound asleep, his head resting on the window.

Josh makes a token protest about staying at my place when we arrive, which I ignore as I help him up the stairs to my flat. Steering him down the hall and into the spare room, I lay him on the bed as gently as I can and take off his shoes. His eyelids drop shut, and his even breathing tells me he's almost asleep. Trying not to disturb him, I slide off his still-damp sweatpants and, without a hint of guilt, take a moment to admire him in his boxer briefs. After a short debate with myself, I take scissors to his t-shirt, which is torn, covered in blood and still damp. Tucking a couple of soft blankets over him, I leave him to sleep. Utterly exhausted, I strip and fall into my bed without even bothering to shower.

CHAPTER NINE

JOSH

I'm not sure whether it's the pounding in my head or the ache in my arm that wakes me up. Closing my eyes, I take a few deep breaths, drinking in the lavender scent of the crisp cool sheets, trying to piece together what happened yesterday.

Why, after all the events of yesterday, is my clearest memory the feel of Greer's skin under my fingertips? The moment when our lips had been a whisper apart? Okay, maybe it isn't the throbbing of my injuries, but it's definitely the throbbing of something that woke me.

Easing out of bed I can't hold back a groan when I check the time and realise the morning is half over. My t-shirt is nowhere to be seen, and reaching for the tattered trackpants I'd been wearing yesterday makes my head spin. I sit for a minute to settle before stepping into the hall and following the quiet hum of indie rock music into a large airy living room flooded with light. The room is very Greer. Warm and welcoming, and yet elegant and stylish and a little bit quirky. The walls are covered in an eclectic arrangement of photos and artwork, all of which clearly mean something to her. The sofa is big and squashy, with a tumble of richly coloured cushions in velvets and linens and embroidered silks.

Greer sits at the dining table in front of a laptop, surrounded by notes and sketches, a pencil tapping against those full, luscious lips.

"Morning." My voice comes out as a croak.

"Josh, you're up. I was hoping you'd sleep a little longer. Ooh, don't look, don't look," she squeaks, slamming the laptop shut and shuffling papers together, turning them over.

"Sleep a little longer? It's half past ten. I need to get to work." Everything hurts as I ease onto the plush linen sofa, and close my eyes against the pounding in my head.

"It's okay. I've called your office and told them what happened. They're not expecting you back in until Wednesday. Would you like something to eat or drink? I have some great herbal tea. It will help with your headache."

"Yeah, thanks, Flo. That would be great. What about you? I'm sure you've got things to do. You can't hang around here all day nursing me."

"Sure I can. I have things to work on. It's no problem." Greer returns from the tiny kitchen with a glass of cool water and drops a couple of pills into my palm.

I want to argue, but being looked after sounds like bliss right now. I swallow the tablets and close my eyes again, willing them to work fast, as she disappears back into the kitchen to make the tea.

"What is it I'm not allowed to look at?" I ask, opening one eye and peering at the document-strewn table as curiosity gets the better of me.

"I've made a start on your plans. They're preliminary ideas, so I don't want you to look at them until they're finished."

"That was quick. I wasn't expecting you to get onto it so soon." I contemplate getting up to look at what she's done but don't quite trust my body to move fast enough not to get caught.

"I like to work when inspiration strikes, and inspiration struck. I called Manly Council this morning and had a chat with them about the tree situation, and they said if I can get plans submitted to them in the next couple of weeks, they'll fast-track them for you, so you won't have to repair the tree damage to the existing structure before you start work on the extension. As long as you've completed settlement."

My stomach rumbles as Greer hands me a mug of fragrant tea and a plate of hot Vegemite toast dripping with slabs of melting butter.

"You must be psychic. You seem to know exactly what I need before I do, and now you manage to sweet-talk a council into fast-tracking building plans. The purchase should be through in the next week or so, according to Will."

Yesterday she was all calm, practicality and thoughtfulness in the face of chaos, and I realise I don't know the adult Greer. Only the little girl Greer, who was sweet and a little bit shy. Getting to know grown-up Greer is dangerous but oh-so enticing.

"Yes, well. Talk is cheap. Let's see if they actually *do* fast-track approval before we get too excited." Greer pulls a sceptical face. "When you've finished your breakfast, feel free to have a shower. If you give me your keys, I can run over to your place and pick up whatever you need."

"Really, I'm fine to go home. I've been taking care of myself for years."

"Not with concussion you haven't. Stay here tonight, and tomorrow if you're feeling better, you can go home." The look of determination on Greer's face makes it clear arguing is not worth the effort. And if I'm honest, I really don't have the energy. Or the will.

"Okay, but tomorrow I'm going to work," I mutter like a five-year-old as I finish my tea. A snort of derision is her reply.

Greer collects some clothes and my wash kit from my apartment before helping me get organised for a shower. It's not easy showering without getting your arm wet. But Greer wraps it up in a plastic bag and I feel marginally better once I'm clean and changed out of the grubby pants I was wearing when the tree came down.

Greer insists I take a nap. I want to argue, except I'm actually feeling too weary, so I give in, although with very little grace. Turns out I'm not a good patient.

"I'll lie down for half an hour. Then I need to call the office." I'm still arguing as I slide onto Greer's obscenely comfortable spare bed.

It's two hours before I surface again, groggy and starving, and with considerably less pain in both my arm and my head. Judging by the state of the table in the living room, Greer has spent the hours I slept working feverishly on the plans for the house. She doesn't even register I'm there until I speak.

"That has to be the most comfortable bed I have ever slept in."

Her head snaps up and she smiles. "You slept well? Good. You look a lot better." Greer is out of the chair and taking my good arm to help me to the sofa before I can even think of protesting. "Would you like something to eat?"

"Yes, thanks. Point me in the right direction and I can get it."

"No patients in the kitchen. You sit down there and watch the afternoon soaps. I made us a salad earlier. I was waiting for you to wake up." Gently Greer pushes me down on the sofa and heads for the kitchen, tossing me the TV remote as she goes.

By the time she returns to the living room with two large bowls of salad loaded with chicken, I've found an afternoon movie. Handing me my bowl, she settles on the couch next to me and props her feet on the coffee table, looking prepared to relax for the afternoon.

"That was truly dreadful," she huffs as the credits roll. "Not one of those characters were believable. She would never have gone to that house alone. She was too scared. Scary movie rules 101. Never go out alone."

"Aw, come on, it was great. Had you glued to your seat." I laugh at her review, even though she's not wrong. I stack our bowls a bit awkwardly with one hand and head for the kitchen.

Greer's reply is cut off by the ringing of my phone. It's Sean from the office. They need my help.

"Hey, Greer, they're having problems with a couple of the concepts we're working on for a pitch. I told them to bring them over and I'd take a look. I hope that's okay with you?"

"Sure, as long as you're up to it. I'll move all this stuff so you have somewhere to work." Greer begins to gather up papers before my hand on her arm stops her.

"No, don't worry about it. We can use the coffee table." It's the first real physical contact, apart from Greer's first aid, we've had since our almost-kiss yesterday, and it sends a buzz up my arm. Suddenly the air is thick with unspoken feelings, and I can't seem to pull my hand from her warm skin. "Greer—"

I'm not sure what I'm about to say, but this time we're interrupted by Greer's phone ringing. We both sigh with frustration.

"How's the patient?" Will's voice comes through loud and clear.

"Oh, Will, hi. He's much better this afternoon. Do you want a word with him?"

Greer hands me the phone and heads for the kitchen where she puts on the kettle. I try to focus on my conversation with Will, but I'm distracted by Greer moving around the kitchen. It's hard not to look at her. Constantly. No sooner have I hung up the phone than the doorbell rings.

"That'll be the guys," I call and head slowly down the hallway on slightly wobbly legs to open the door, feeling equal parts irritation and relief at the constant interruptions to my time with Greer.

"Hey, boss, you look terrible," Sean greets me as I usher them into Greer's living room carrying laptops and notebooks. I roll my eyes, only to discover it hurts.

"Guys, this is Greer. Greer, this is Sean and Fiona."

"Hi. Would you like some tea or coffee?" Greer offers, shaking their hands.

"Yeah, sure. Coffee thanks." Fiona jabs Sean in the ribs as he stares at Greer. I hope it hurt. Lecherous fucker.

When Greer disappears into the kitchen, Sean pulls himself together enough to sit down and flip open his laptop.

"Try not to drool all over the sofa Sean. It's not a good look," quips Fiona.

"Man, she's hot. You're a lucky guy, boss." Sean shakes his head with envy.

"She's not ... we're not ..." I start to explain, but I'm stopped by the look of disbelief on both their faces and the memory of the moment before the phone rang.

"Wow, you really are in a bad way!" Fiona laughs.

"Yeah, you don't know the half of it." I scrub my hands over my face, trying to restart my brain, wincing as my fingers connect with the emu-sized egg at the top of my forehead. "Okay, let's have a look at what you've got."

In the end, Sean and Fiona stay for more than an hour. Greer sits at the dining table working on her laptop, and I can sense her watching and listening from time to time.

What's left of the afternoon passes into evening with Greer beavering away on the plans for the house as I work on some copy Sean and Fiona left behind. It's late when we notice how hungry we are and decide to put together a spicy stir-fry to eat on the tiny balcony, which Greer has decorated with fairy lights and candles.

"So, you're not only a great nurse, you're a bit of a Nigella Lawson in the kitchen as well." The food is delicious, and I've managed to polish off a second bowl.

"Yep. I'm a regular domestic goddess," Greer replies, smiling.

After a brief tussle during which Greer makes it clear I'm less than useful in my current state, she clears up in the kitchen while I search the streaming services for something we might both like to watch. Settling down on the sofa with tea and chocolate biscuits for dessert, I think about how much we've been enjoying each other's company. I've been careful not to touch her. Every time I do, the tension between us, always simmering under the surface, rises like steam off a hot spring and spoils the developing atmosphere of friendship. And friends are all we can ever be. It's a concept I need to get through my thick head. Or my thick something else.

"Well, I think it's my bedtime." I yawn and stretch as the credits roll. "Do you need the bathroom?"

"No, you go ahead." Greer turns off the TV and heads back to the pile of notes on the dining table. "I'll be up for a while yet." I can almost see her fingers itching to get back to her drawings, which kicks up my excitement to get the project started.

"Okay. Thanks for today. I don't know what I would've done without you."

Her answering smile is soft, and my heart kicks in my chest at the thought that in another world, maybe I could watch her smile at me like that again, and again. "Well, it's a good thing you'll never have to find out then, isn't it?"

Next morning, I'm up and about early, determined to get to the office. There's so much to do, and it's too early in my tenure to be taking my hands off the wheel, even for a couple of days.

Greer wanders into the kitchen in a silky singlet and pyjama shorts as I'm trying to fill the kettle for tea. Sadly, there's no sign of any kind of coffee machine. Looking at her dressed —or more to the point, undressed—in pyjamas is perilous, yet I can't look away from all her creamy skin. She takes the kettle from me, fills it and switches it on.

"I'm going to call an Uber to get me down to Manly and pick up my car. I feel fine, and I really do want to get to the office today. We've got a pitch I'm determined to win on Friday and another on Monday. I can't afford not to be on top of it." I know enough of Greer to expect an argument, but I can be just as stubborn.

"As much as I'm against it, I can see I'm not going to change your mind. But I really don't think you should drive. How about I drop you at work instead, and you could pick up your car later in the week?" Greer challenges. I'll take it for the win.

"It's not an inconvenience? Taking me to work?" I know I'm not up to walking, even though it's not far.

"I wouldn't have offered if it was. It's only up the road."

"Okay. Deal. Do you want first shower?"

"Sure. You can make breakfast since you're feeling so much better."

It's disturbing how natural running through a morning routine with Greer is. I imagine doing this every morning, and for the first time in my life, my blood doesn't run cold at the thought. Christ. I'm screwed.

The best I can manage with my bandaged arm is cereal and tea, which we eat leaning against the kitchen bench. I'd give my injured arm for a proper coffee.

Greer smells mouth-wateringly of her soap and shampoo. At least she's covered up by jeans and a long-sleeved t-shirt now, because despite my aches and pains I'm having trouble keeping my response to her under control.

I squeeze myself into Greer's little electric clown car. The trip to my office is short, but not so short that Greer doesn't have time to bring up the unwelcome subject of my mother. Out of nowhere.

"Have you called your mum yet about the accident?"

I snort in distaste. "No. Why would I?"

"Because she's your *mother*. And she'd want to know." Greer glances at me while we wait for the stragglers to cross the road at the lights.

"Experience would suggest not. But whatever." I don't tell her I haven't even called my mother since I've been home.

"Please promise me you'll call her today. Let her know? She might surprise you."

If anyone else asked this of me, they'd get a short sharp fuck off. But this is Greer. And after all she's done for me in the past twenty-four hours alone, it's the least I can do. If only to prove to her, and myself for the thousandth time, that Mum really doesn't care.

"Okay, fine. I'll call her," I concede, as she pulls to the side of the road in front of my office.

"Good. And promise me you'll take it easy." She rests her hand against my cheek. "Call me to come and get you if you start to feel sick or dizzy."

With a mind of its own, my hand comes up to cover hers. "I promise. Thanks for everything, Flo." Our eyes meet and the strange sensation I felt when I saw her at the airport washes over me again. Bringing her hand to my mouth, I kiss her palm before I think better of it and climb quickly from the car, waving as I head into the building.

The sense I have of wading into quicksand is not improved by the reception I get as I walk into the creative department.

"Hey, Josh. You look much better." Fiona calls as I walk past her cubicle.

"So would I if I'd spent the night with Red," Sean pipes up. "I'm surprised you've got the strength to stand up!"

I love how relaxed and familiar the team already are with me, even if sometimes they do take it a step or three too far.

"I'll say it once more for the dummies—Greer and I are just friends."

"Yeah. Sure. I could tell. There was absolutely no sexual tension between you at all." Leering, Sean rolls his eyes.

Which stops me short. "What are you talking about?" Despite myself, I'm curious.

"She couldn't take her eyes off you. And you looked like the wolf when he was about to eat Red Riding Hood." Sean smirks.

"The wolf ate the granny, not Red Riding Hood. Get your fairy tales straight, you tool," Fiona corrects with an exaggerated eye roll of her own. These two talk about the chemistry between Greer and me. I wonder if they've ever taken a look in the mirror. Their constant bickering is an office romance waiting to happen.

"Whatever. Greer is no granny. And he looked like he wanted to take a bite of her. That's all I know."

Taking advantage of their already familiar squabbling, I leave them to it, disappear into my office and close the door. Dropping into my chair, I lay my forehead on the desk, careful of my arm and the lump, which has now turned purple, blue and green and seems to be spreading all the way past my eyebrow and down my temple to my cheekbone. I don't have the mindspace for this right now. Despite what I told Greer, my head is still pounding, and my arm is throbbing. I fish the painkillers the doctor gave me out of my pocket and throw a couple back.

I'm already feeling like shit. I might as well get the call to my mother over with. Then I can get on with my day.

"Hello, Helen. It's Josh. How are you?" I haven't called my mother 'Mum' for years. It doesn't seem to bother her, and it's a more accurate reflection of our relationship to call her by her first name. I really don't need this right now, but I promised Greer. At least I know the conversation will be quick.

"I'm well. I thought perhaps you'd changed your mind about coming back to Sydney since I haven't heard from you."

I pick up a pencil and start twirling it to distract myself. Like a home-made fidget spinner.

"I'm sorry." I'm really not. "It's been crazy here at the office. I haven't had a chance to call."

"I see. Well, perhaps you could make some time to come up and see me." Helen lives in an isolated little house in the Blue Mountains. Tucked away from the world. Which suits her down to the ground.

"I don't suppose you're ever in Sydney? You could come and have lunch with me?"

"I avoid the city at all costs. You should come up here. Have a relaxing weekend. See what I've been working on. I think you'll like it. What about this weekend?"

My jaw tightens. The pencil spins faster. A weekend with my mother will be the opposite of relaxing.

"Not this weekend. We have a pitch on Monday. How about next weekend?" Visiting either of my parents falls somewhere between root canal therapy and a colonoscopy on my list of favourite things, but I guess it has to be done, even though it feels like beating my head against a wall. I wonder if I'll ever be able to entirely free myself of the deep-seated need for parental approval they have never, not once, bestowed.

"Next weekend it is, then. Drive up on Friday night and we can have dinner. Let me know when you're leaving so I know what time to expect you. I'll see you then, Joshua."

It's not until I hang up the phone that I realise she didn't ask one question about me or my life—not even how I'm doing. The pencil snaps.

I shouldn't be surprised. It's always all about her. Nothing ever changes.

CHAPTER TEN

GREER

By four o'clock, I haven't heard from Josh and I figure it might be a good time to check in on him.

"Hey, how are you feeling? I thought I'd see how you're doing. If you're about ready to go home."

"Well, that's spooky. Not two seconds ago, I was thinking I've had about enough for today."

"Huh, I must've picked up the home-time vibes. Want me to pick you up?"

I can tell he's torn between soldiering on and getting out of there. I give him some thinking time. It doesn't take long.

"You would be saving my life," he groans.

"Okay. I'll be out the front of your office in fifteen minutes."

Josh is waiting at the curb, and I can see how pale he is before I even pull up. I'm guessing he feels pretty terrible, even though he'll never admit it.

As he gets into the car, he leans over to put his laptop bag on the floor.

"What's with the bags?" He nods towards the shopping bags on the back seat.

"I thought you might be a bit shattered, so I picked up some things for your dinner. I'll cook while you have a power nap and then I'll get out of your hair and let you get a good night's sleep."

The look on Josh's face makes me smile. It's triangulated somewhere between relieved, guilty and nervous.

I bulldoze a reluctant Josh into bed with a couple of painkillers as soon as we arrive at his apartment, then get to work in the tiny kitchen, pulling together some dinner. He's convinced he won't sleep, but when I check on him a few minutes later, he's out like a light. I take this rare opportunity to absorb the lines and planes of the face I love. I'm sure my feelings, which are hard to keep off my face, must be showing, but he's asleep, so it's safe to indulge myself for a few minutes.

He sleeps so soundly, I have to wake him when the food is ready.

"Josh, wake up. You need to eat. And you don't want to sleep too long, or you'll be awake all night." I shake him gently and smooth his tangled hair back off his forehead.

Josh sits up, groggy and disoriented. "I'm sorry. I must have fallen asleep after all," he croaks, looking towards the window. "Shit. It's dark already. What time is it?"

"It's time for dinner, Sleeping Beauty. Get comfy, and I'll bring it in. Then, as promised, I'll get out of your way."

"Aren't you going to stay and eat with me?" He looks crestfallen, and I can't resist.

"Are you sure you're up to it? I thought you might like a tray in bed. It's easy one-handed eating."

"Come on. I can't let you go home without eating some of the food you've slaved over. And I do feel a lot better after my nap."

We settle at the little dining table and tuck into the chicken pesto pasta I threw together.

"I called my mother today, as requested," Josh says as he reaches for his water.

"Really? That's great. It must've been good to talk to her when you were feeling so battered. What did she say about your accident?"

"Nothing."

"Nothing?" I squeak.

"I didn't tell her."

"What?" Gobsmacked, to say the least, I put down my fork and stare at him. "Why not?"

"She didn't ask. She didn't even ask how I was. The subject didn't come up."

I know Josh has a broken relationship with both his parents. But this is beyond anything I could imagine. Having been helicopter parented my whole life and all.

"Oh, Josh. I'm sorry. I know you're not close, but ..." I don't quite know how to finish my sentence.

"Yeah, well. She's not what you'd call a motherly type. Never has been. The complete opposite of your mother. Anyway, I agreed to go up there next weekend. She wants me to see what she's working on." He rolls his eyes, clearly unenthused with the idea.

"Wait a minute. Have you not gone to see her yet?"

"No. I haven't had time to go up to her place, and she'd never put herself out and come down here to see me. So ..." He shrugs and goes back to eating his dinner.

I hardly know what to say. "Well, maybe things will improve if you spend a bit of time together?"

"No, they won't." His relaxed body language of earlier has morphed into a stiffened spine and clenched hands.

"It might be what you both need. A bit of time together."

He snorts, scowling at his bowl of pasta.

"Greer, I'm thirty-two years old, and she has never shown the slightest interest in me yet. I doubt she's going to start now."

It's on the tip of my tongue to argue with him. And if he wasn't injured maybe I would. But now isn't the time to stir him up, so I go back to eating my pasta, which suddenly tastes like cardboard and disappointment.

"That's my family, Greer. Not just Mum. Dad too. Nobody cares about anyone except themselves. It's always been the same, and it's not going to change now. I'm no different. Selfish and self-absorbed to the end."

This is absolutely not true. He's been there for all three of my brothers, always, and has never been anything but appreciative of my parents. Despite having been away for such a long time. I don't think he missed a card or a call for even one birthday or Christmas.

"You ..." One look at his face has me swallowing my words. His jaw is set and his beautiful lips have almost disappeared into a thin, grim line. He's convinced himself and nothing I can say right now will change his mind.

We finish our dinner in strained silence, and once we've cleared the table, I make my excuses and leave. I can't shake the image of the look on his face—a little boy lashing out in hurt at the person nearest him. It just sucks it happened to be me. It felt like he was trying to hurt me, maybe before I hurt him. Or to push me away, warn me to keep my distance. Regardless, if he thinks he's scared me off, he's got another thing coming. At least now I have an idea where his head is at. Not to mention his heart. Which is much more vulnerable than I imagined.

The next morning when I'm getting my yoga mat out of the spare room, I realise Josh has left his car keys on the bedside table. Rather than stew on the argument Josh and I had last night, I decide to hop on a bus and head down to Manly after my class.

I'm relieved to see the tarp is still secure over the roof of the house from the front, and I pick my way down the overgrown side path to check it from the back. Josh's wetsuit is in a soggy heap under the clothesline. I shake off as much water as I can manage and bundle it up into the boot of Josh's car. The surf-board is safe inside, miraculously unscathed by the falling tree.

There's a car park access card in the console, so I drive the car back to Josh's place and put it in his spot in the communal garage under the apartment block. I toss up what to do with the key and decide since it's a nice day, I'll walk up to North Sydney.

I planned to drop the keys and go, but the receptionist remembers me from the day we had lunch and insists on letting Josh know I'm there.

"Hey, Greer. What are you doing here?" He's a little hesitant as he comes out into reception, dressed in his usual long t-shirt and jeans. He has a lot more colour in his face today, and I don't mean the wicked bruise that's now spread across the whole right side of his forehead and down his cheek.

For a moment, we both stand awkwardly. I'm remembering the cross words we had last night. By the look on Josh's face, and the tentative way he greeted me, he's remembering too.

"You left your car keys at my place." I hold the keys out to him.

"Oh, thanks. I'll go down tonight and pick it up." He takes the key, careful not to touch my fingers as he does.

"No need. I picked it up this morning. It's in the garage at your building. Oh, and your wetsuit is in the boot. You'll need to hang it up. It's still pretty soggy."

"You picked up my car?" His surprise is obvious, and it makes me a little sad that he doesn't expect anyone to do anything nice for him.

"Yeah. Well, you'll need it to go and see your mother, and I thought maybe you wouldn't be up to driving yet. Anyway, it's there when you need it. I hope that's okay?"

"I can't believe you went to so much trouble. No, wait. I can. That's exactly the kind of thing you'd do. Thank you."

"No problem."

Josh puts his hand on my arm and steers me away from the reception desk, away from flapping ears. "Greer, listen. I'm sorry about last night. I was feeling shitty, and I took it out on you. And that's not okay. I'm sorry."

I can't help myself. I lean over and hug him. "It's okay, Josh. I know you weren't feeling great. I get cranky when I've got a headache too. I get it."

His whole body stiffens at my touch. But it only takes a second before I feel him relax and hug me back, burying his face in my hair and breathing deeply. He feels so good I can't bring myself to let go, despite the fact we're in the reception area of his work. Eventually he pulls back, and his eyes are sad.

"I don't deserve how kind you are to me. You know that, right?"

"Well, I think you're wrong, Josh. You deserve all the kindness." And I know we both mean what we say.

The problem will be getting him to believe me.

CHAPTER ELEVEN

JOSH

Branches scrape at the sides of my car as it bounces and jolts down the narrow, rutted dirt track, causing me to wince more than once. I'm not particularly car-proud, except this one is only a few weeks old, and I can almost feel the scratches on the paintwork.

If I didn't know better, I'd assume this was an unused trail leading nowhere. But within a few hundred metres, the track opens out to a small clearing in the centre of which sits a tiny, slightly dilapidated timber cottage. The back of the house faces the track, seeming to tell anyone inadvertently stumbling upon it *visitors are not welcome*. Which is, in fact, true, although I imagine the original reason for placing the cottage this way was to maximise the breathtaking view of the Jamison Valley, which opens up beyond the clearing.

I sit in the car for a few minutes studying the house, which apart from the occasional paint job, hasn't changed much in the twenty odd years my mother has lived here. Even though she must certainly have heard the car approach, it wouldn't occur to her to rush to the door to greet her son. Most likely she's too absorbed in her work. As usual. It's an interesting contrast to Greer, who seems to be able to manage being absorbed in her work, yet still have time for the people she loves. Maybe I've hit on the difference there. Love. I'm not sure if it's a word my mother understands.

I left work early to drive up here, and the late afternoon light is golden and warm, in counterpoint to the welcome I expect.

The old screen door screeches with rust and bangs woodenly against its frame when I enter the house and head down the shotgun hallway to the covered verandah at the front, which is my mother's studio. Totally absorbed in her work, she barely glances up, angling her cheek slightly for my kiss and murmuring what might have been, 'hello Joshua'. By my reckoning, we haven't seen each other in over three years, when she happened to visit London for an artist's retreat and she spared me time for a coffee. Three years, and this is all she can manage. There really is no hope for me with the genetic legacy my parents have handed down. Whether it's nature or nurture, I missed out on both fronts.

"What do you think?" she finally asks, sitting back from her work and tipping her head to the side, considering. My mother is tall and rail thin with porcelain skin and cropped, dark brown hair. She's beautiful and looks nowhere near old enough to have a son my age. She's wearing her trademark black pants and shirt under an ancient, clay-smeared calico smock.

"It's excellent, Helen." I don't know what else to say. It's a lump of wet clay on a wheel. It does have an elegant shape, I suppose.

"I'm trying some new techniques. You can make some tea while I clean myself up if you like."

Finally, she spares a glance for me. Noting the still-fading bruises around my eye caused by my brush with the tree, she lets out a deep sigh I recognise right away as disappointment.

"Aren't you a little old to be getting into fights?" It's amazing how with one sentence she can reduce me to a small boy again.

Alone and unloved. I focus on the shark cage I've spent my whole adult life building around myself and let it deflect the barb.

"Actually, not that it matters, but it wasn't a fight. A tree fell on me. It's a long story. I won't bore you with it." I know full well she won't ask for details, and I'm not disappointed as she turns away and begins soaping her hands and arms in the clay-stained sink mounted in the far corner of the verandah.

Tea mugs in hand, I find my mother perched on the bush rock steps leading down from the verandah, the Jamison Valley spread out in blue-grey splendour before her. From this spot you can neither see nor hear any signs of human habitation. No power poles, no drone of cars, no roads scarring the bush. Nothing but the heavy stillness of the waiting air, cracked by the occasional cry of a bird. Filled with the hum of the cicadas and the earthy scents of eucalyptus and sun-warmed fallen leaves.

"Now you're back in Australia, do you plan to stay, or are you going to wander off again?" As if she cares either way, which her disinterested tone underlines. Helen takes the mug from me, and her gaze flicks briefly, without comment, to the bandage on my arm.

"No. I think this time I'll be staying." I settle on the step below my mother. "I have plans to start up my own agency. And I've bought a house." Any other mother would probably express happiness, or even surprise, given what a nomad I've been for the past ten years. Helen sips her tea and nods.

I don't mention Greer or my growing fears about our ... what? Feelings? Relationship? She'd tell me not to involve myself. The only person you can rely on is yourself. Yet I'm beginning to feel I can rely on Greer. The problem is, she shouldn't rely on me. I'm a bad risk.

We talk about things of no consequence as the sun lowers in the sky and the shadows deepen.

Dinner is a spartan meal. Helen became a vegetarian a long time ago and eats like a sparrow. A bowl of steamed vegetables with a sprinkle of pepper and a pot of green tea is all that's on offer.

Lying on the rock-hard spare bed, my stomach growling with hunger, I can't help comparing the life my mother leads with that of Greer and her family. It's not about money. Mum's divorce settlement was more than generous, and she makes a good living from her pottery. It's about nurture. I don't think my mother ever possessed the ability and nurture, to care for and comfort others. Not even her son. It shows in the small things. The discomfort of the bed, the thin and scratchy towel, the austere meal. And it shows in the big things. Her complete lack of interest in my life, the inability to show affection, the withdrawal from human contact. I'm not sure if it's always been her nature or if her marriage to my father broke her so badly she was unable to get past it. A bit of both, I suspect.

Which all leads me to contemplate my own inability to maintain a romantic relationship. Nature or nurture? Do I have trouble connecting because of my childhood or because that's the way I am? Either way, the outcome's the same.

I'm dragged from bed at dawn the next morning for a walk along the valley rim. The combination of lingering hunger and lack of sleep has worked on my temper, and I'm not the most pleasant of companions as we set out, but it's not long before the beauty of the misty morning, dew glittering on the hundreds of new spider webs built during the night, improves my spirits and gets my blood pumping. By the time we get back to the little house,

I'm in a sufficiently good mood to offer to make breakfast. At least there's a chance I'll get enough to eat.

Predictably, Helen has green tea and unbuttered wholemeal toast. At least she has some eggs in the fridge, no doubt a concession to my visit, which I scramble for myself. Unfortunately, coffee isn't on the cards. It's a good thing I don't hate green tea.

I know my mother well enough not to expect her to change her routine for me, and I'm not surprised when she leaves the table without a word, grabbing her work smock off the hook by the door as she heads for her studio. I take the opportunity to rifle through the garden shed, find the shears and walk back along the track, chopping back the branches blocking the way and stacking them neatly beside the woodpile. Once they dry out, they'll make good kindling for next winter. It makes my arm ache, but at least I'll be able to get out of here without any more damage to my car.

After a pathetically lukewarm shower in the tiny trickle of water available, I hop in the car aiming for somewhere to get a decent coffee.

The little villages closest to Helen's house have changed considerably since my last visit, and I'm pleasantly surprised to see a couple of well-curated art galleries and several small antique stores. Pulling into a vacant car space, I decide to while away a couple of hours browsing before heading back to the cottage. Browsing becomes buying as I wander from shop to shop. First is an enormous and stunning modern nude in shades of rich red, deep pink and burning orange that reminds me of Greer.

In the antique shop, I find an enormous four-poster bed taking up a good third of the floor space. The polished mahogany gleams like satin, and I can't resist running my hands over the smooth, aged wood.

"It's a beautiful piece, isn't it? Only came in this week. It's not often we find a bed like this. Most antique beds are smaller. This one must have been custom made. We've measured it, and it will take a standard king-size mattress." The salesman watches me like a hawk, gauging my intent as my hand glides over the beautiful inlaid panels of flowers.

"I don't think it will fit in my car." I know they can ship it. I'm just messing with him. But the salesman takes it all very seriously. Clearly, he smells a sale in the air.

"We can ship it for you, sir," he says, all earnest enthusiasm.

I have no intention of buying the bed. "No, I really—"

"I'm sure we could move a little on the price if you're interested?"

This is a serious bed. A bed for a couple. A family. A lifetime. That's not ever going to be me.

"It's not that, it's … " Why do I sound so wistful? I think about the house I'm about to renovate. There's no doubt I'm putting down roots. What does it matter if I'm the only one who ever sleeps in it?

"You know what? I'll take it."

"Excellent choice, may I say. You won't regret it. That bed will become a family heirloom," twitters the salesman as he heads back to the counter to complete the paperwork. "Is there anything else I can interest you in today, sir?"

"No, I don't think so." I'm about to hand over my credit card when I notice the jewellery displayed in a tall glass cabinet beside the counter.

"Actually, those earrings." I point to a pair of warm gold drop earrings. "Are they sapphires?"

"Yes, sir, sapphire and seed pearls. A fine example of art deco jewellery." Fumbling with the keys in his haste to open the cabinet, the salesman takes the worn velvet box and places it on the counter. "Of course, they come with a certificate of authenticity and a full valuation. For your, er … wife?" He tilts the box, allowing the light to play over the sapphires.

"No, a—um—a friend." They're beautiful. The blue of the sapphires would match Greer's eyes, and the creaminess of the pearls would match her skin.

"A very *good* friend then, and a lucky one!" my excited sales-man says as I add the earrings to my purchase.

He keeps chattering. I don't hear him because I'm too busy trying to justify to myself, in a way I can believe, why I've bought these earrings. I've never bought such a personal or expensive gift for a woman before. Although, Christmas is coming up. Well, it will be in a few months. And she is doing those blue-prints for me. It's the least I can do, really.

Having convinced myself, more or less, there's nothing more than appreciation for her work behind my purchase, I cross the road and sit in the late morning sun with a large coffee, an apricot danish and the weekend newspaper. The warm sun and the village atmosphere soon unravel the tension spending time with my mother inevitably creates. By the time I head back to the cottage in the early afternoon, having stopped at the supermarket for some actual food, I'm feeling much more relaxed.

"I saw some of your work at the gallery in town," I say as I put a cup of fresh tea on the table beside Helen's pottery wheel.

"Yes. The gallery owner is a ninny, but they sell quite well. Especially the large platters and bowls. I think people use them for salads or some such." My mother gulps the tea without looking away from her work. Ah, there's her familiar conde-scension. I thought the gallery owner was quite knowledgeable and personable. Of course Helen would have little time for the relationship beyond its use to her work.

As I watch her rhythmically working the clay, I have one of those odd moments of clarity. There's not much I have to thank either of my parents for, but I realise my mother has inadver-tently taught me to be a good boss. I never want to make anyone feel as small as she manages to make me—and everyone else she comes in contact with—feel. I work hard at giving everyone around me the respect they deserve. So, thanks, Helen. Maybe some of my success can be credited to you, after all.

Courtesy of the stop at the supermarket, dinner will be more generous than last night. For me, at least. I clean up the barbeque, which hasn't been used in what looks like decades, and throw on the enormous steak I picked up. As I watch it sizzle, I think back on what Greer said about spending more time with my mother. Is there a chance we could connect? I doubt it. But I'm here. Nothing ventured, nothing gained.

We eat at the rickety outdoor table, where Helen picks through the salad I threw together, dressing on the side, of course, leaving behind the delicious, ripe avocado. Good. All the more for me.

"Things are going well at work," I start. "We've picked up three big pieces of new business since I started."

"Good. Being busy will keep you out of trouble." Her response says she still sees me as a wayward teenager in need of distraction. I concentrate hard on not grinding my teeth.

I try again. "The house I bought in Manly is a lovely old Federation bungalow. I think you'd like it. Needs a lot of work, though. Greer Carter is doing the designs for me."

"You still see that Carter family?" she asks with her trademark disdain. "I don't understand how they all live in each other's pockets. Very strange." The fact I still see the Carters is what she took from that statement? Unbelievable.

I bite hard on my bottom lip to stop the response that threatens to burst from my throat.

I'm about to make one last attempt at engagement when Helen pushes her plate away and stands up, waving her hand over my plate. "You put a lot of dressing on your salad. It's not good for you." And without another word, she heads into the lounge room and picks up the book she left on the coffee table last night.

I spent my teen years hurt and angry. Lashing out. I refuse to do it now. In the past ten years, I've devoted a lot of time to working on my anger, and I know it gets me nowhere. The temptation to tell her to go to hell is strong, but she is who she is, and I only hurt myself by expecting more from her. It's pointless even trying.

I stand and start stacking the dishes with exaggerated care, so I'm not tempted to pick the lot up and hurl them in frustration.

After an early night, when at least I was able to sleep without a rumbling belly, and the obligatory early morning walk, I put my bag in the car.

"I'm heading out, Helen," I say as she's buttoning up her smock.

"Alright," is all the answer I get, as she holds her cheek out for a kiss. I annoy myself no end when I hesitate, holding on to the fragile hope she'll walk me to my car. Wave me off. Nope.

I drive back to the city, a welter of emotions churning in my belly. I don't know why I even bothered to come. And I vow not to bother again. It should be heartbreaking to realise your relationship with your mother is irretrievable. Weirdly, it's kind of a relief. Maybe I am as cold and heartless as she is.

But then I think about my relationship with Stella and Harry and Will. Greer. I'm not heartless. Just a bit broken.

At least I have a spectacular painting and a bed to show for it. And those earrings for Greer—which mean nothing more than a thank you for her work. Or a Christmas present. Because as much as I wish things could be different, someone as broken as me is not the right person for someone as wonderful as her.

CHAPTER TWELVE

GREER

"Hey stranger." Jessie gives me a fierce hug as I arrive at our regular table in a quirky little café we love near Dee Why Beach for one of our favourite things—brunch. Dee Why is a bit of a hike, but it's worth it for the post-feed beach walk.

"Oh, I've missed you. Sorry I've been MIA the last couple of weeks." I settle into my chair and pick up the menu, which gets an eye roll from Jessie. She knows what I'm going to order. If this is an emotional crisis brunch, it will be the full catastrophe. Scrambled eggs, bacon, hash browns and toast. With two serves of haloumi. If it's a catch-up, it will be the smashed avo and feta on sourdough. Yes, I'm one of those. A lover of smashed avo. Especially if it comes with a healthy drizzle of balsamic. And I don't care if it is a cliché.

The server knows. We eat here a lot. Even he will be able to take my emotional temperature by my order. "What'll it be today, ladies?"

"The full catastrophe for me, please. And hot chocolate. In a bucket."

"Oh. Wow. So, it's like that." Jessie's light blue eyes pop. "I'll take a cheese and tomato omelette, thanks. And a latte. A mug will do. No need for a bucket." Jessie hands him the menus and leans her elbows on the table as he heads off to put in our order.

"Okay. Hit me with it. Where are we at?"

I drop my forehead onto the table. "I don't even know," I moan.

"Well, I'm guessing this crisis eating is about Josh?" I don't miss the slight eye roll as she says this. I think she's already getting sick of the broken record I'm becoming, even though she would never say so. She's the best support team a girl could ask for.

"Yes." My voice is tiny and muffled by the hair falling around my face.

"Right. Last I heard, you had agreed to do the designs for his house. And then there was the accident, and you took care of him for a couple of days. And you've been pretty much radio silent ever since. What's happened?"

I sit up straight and push my hair back behind my shoulders as our drinks arrive.

"Everything and nothing. It's so frustrating. I'm sorry I haven't been around. I started the blueprints for Josh and haven't been able to focus on anything else. The good news, though, is I've finished the first draft. If he likes them, all I need to do is finalise them and submit them to council. And I'm really proud of them. If he goes ahead, it'll be a beautiful house."

"Of course it will. You know your stuff. So, if things are good with the plans, this must be about Josh himself."

"We had another moment, Jess. A real one."

"What? When?" she screeches, and people at the tables next to us look over. "Sorry. Sorry." She waves at them in apology before turning back to me. "When?" she hisses.

"Right before the tree came down. He was about to kiss me. Then—bam. We were both on the floor."

"Nooo. What shitty timing." More eye rolls from Jess.

"I know, right? And afterwards, there was no time to talk about it because I had to get him to the medical centre, then there was the SES and blah, blah, blah."

"And you haven't spoken about it since?"

I fill her in on Josh's stay, our conversation at his apartment, and me dropping his car off to him. "And that was the last time we spoke."

"Wow. Mummy Dearest sounds like a real prize. No wonder Josh isn't interested in relationships."

"I know. I mean, I knew his family were messed up, but this is next level. So, what can I do?"

"That kind of stuff takes time—and therapy, probably—to get over. I think you just have to be ..."

I know what's coming. "Ugh. Here we go with the patience thing again." I throw my hands up dramatically.

"Afraid so. Yep. The good news is, you're doing everything right. You're showing up for him, and even if he doesn't always say so, that will mean a lot to him."

"You're supposed to say go over there in a trench coat and nothing else and jump him," I grizzle. Which makes Jess laugh.

"Anyway, enough about men. Harry told Ethan there are a couple of jobs on the table?" Jessie changes the subject with no subtlety whatsoever. And I let her because right now, there's no resolution to this conversation.

"Yeah. There's one job in particular I'm quite interested in. Applications close at the end of the month. I should hear if I've got an interview within a couple of weeks."

"Oooh, fingers crossed then." Jessie crosses her fingers and eyes at me, which always creeps me out.

"Stop that." She might not have been subtle about the subject change, but it worked.

After brunch, we head for the beach, roll up our jeans and walk headland to headland, ankle-deep in the icy water, deluding ourselves we're walking off the calories we've hoovered up.

As we walk, I tell her all about my plans for the house. The second-storey master suite, the open-plan living, the use of recycled materials and traditional stained-glass windows in the extension at the back to link it to the front of the house. I'm so excited by the design I can hardly wait to show Josh. I hope he loves it as much as I do.

We sit on the sand and watch the surfers, which reminds me of Josh.

"Is it weird that I still have these feelings for him, even after he was away for so long?"

"Maybe you need to dial it back a bit." Jess' silvery blonde brows knit together over her nose, and she wraps an arm around my shoulders. "I know it felt big at the time, but you were a kid. He wasn't much more than a kid himself. I get what you felt was intense, but it wasn't love. It was a crush."

"Maybe. But what about you and Ethan? You've been together since you were sixteen. Was that a crush? Or love?"

"Not the sort of love we have now. More like puppy love, I guess. And we've grown together. You haven't spent time with Josh in ten years. Maybe you need to take some time to get to know the adult Josh. See if you still feel the same. You know, before you tear his clothes off."

"Hey! You've seen him. Who wouldn't want to tear his clothes off?"

"True. He's pretty hot. But there's more to a relationship than that."

"Gah. Why do you have to be so sensible?" I dig my toes deeper into the damp sand, a physical reflection of my metaphorical heel-digging. I know she's trying to help. And I will take on board what Jess said. I also know, in my heart, there's something between Josh and me. I knew it the minute I looked into his eyes at the airport. And it's not about his extreme hotness.

One of the surfers comes wading out of the water, board under his arm, and stops not far from us to peel the top of his wetsuit down, exposing a beautiful round tattoo, which takes up most of his very impressive left pec. Jess gives me wide eyes and a dirty grin.

"Not going in for a swim, ladies?" he asks, moving closer. Like any committed surfer, his chest and abs are taut, his arms strong. And his face isn't a challenge to look at either.

"The water's still a bit cold for me. Maybe in a month or so."

"Is this your regular beach?" He sidles closer to me, saltwater dripping from his board onto the sand at my feet. Even from this distance, I can read the interest in his eyes.

"One of them." I don't want to be rude, but I don't want to encourage him either.

"Maybe I'll see you down here again, then?" Hope is written all over his face. He's opening the door for me to show some interest, but as nice as he seems, as hot as he is, he's not Josh.

"Maybe."

He hovers for a few more minutes, pretending to watch the surf, then turns, and with a wave and a "See you", heads off down the beach towards the car park.

"He was totally hitting on you," Jess says as soon as he's out of earshot.

"I know." Being a little naïve doesn't mean I'm stupid. Or entirely clueless. It's not like I've never dated. I've had boyfriends. Lovely boyfriends who treated me well and, in theory, were perfect for me. Better suited to me than Josh, Jessie always said. I even slept with a couple of them. But it never felt quite right, and I could never work out why. Spending time with Josh again has helped me realise maybe I was subconsciously comparing them to him. Using Josh as some kind of yardstick for every man I met and finding them wanting. One thing I do know. None of them made me feel like I do when Josh looks at me.

Jess sighs and leans her head on my shoulder. "The heart wants what the heart wants, I guess."

We both laugh as I make a gagging noise. "You're wasted as a teacher. You should get a job writing Hallmark cards. Or movies. Or those cute little affirmation artworks—"

Which gets me a push sideways into the damp sand.

"Just be careful. Josh is a player. You know this. And I don't want to watch him hurt you." Jess reaches down and pulls me up off the sand, back to sitting. "Anyway. Tell me more about this house you've designed."

We brush ourselves off and start the walk back to our cars while I talk some more about the plans. "He's visiting his mother in the mountains this weekend. I think he'll be back tomorrow. As soon as he's seen them, I'll show you."

"I can't wait. Maybe soon you'll be able to design a house for Ethan and me."

"That would be ... Wait. What? Are you guys making *plans*?"

"Not yet. But it's not long till he finishes his PhD, and we always said once he was done, we'd talk about the future. So ..."

"Oooh, yay." I stop and give her a smacking kiss on the cheek. "Then you'll be my really truly sister. I can't wait."

"Me either," she sighs.

CHAPTER THIRTEEN

JOSH

I arrive back in Sydney early afternoon, and as I let myself back into the soulless serviced apartment, I sigh. God, I'll be glad to get out of here. It's sterile and cold. Moving in with Will for a month or two will be a great relief. Not to mention fun.

I check my phone, and there are multiple voicemails from Will insisting I come for family dinner, and one from Greer. My heart rate picks up at the sound of her voice.

"Hi Josh, it's Greer. I guess you're out of range up in the mountains. Anyway, if you get a chance, please give me a call. I have something for you I think you might like. Bye."

Oh yeah, she has something I might like, alright. Just the honeyed sound of her voice makes me hard. I can't call her back in this state. I head into the bathroom, turn the shower on full, strip off and take my cock in hand. Jesus, this is getting to be a habit. Lately, more often than not, I start the day jerking off in the shower. If I think of Greer, *when* I think of Greer, it doesn't take long.

Recalling her voice from her message, I feel an uncomfortable combination of guilt and relief as my release begins to bubble, my hand stroking faster, squeezing tight at the base and easing up the length. I picture Greer in the wet t-shirt she was wearing the day of the accident, how it clung to the perfect curves of her breasts, and I can't hold back the moan that bursts from deep in my gut. I focus on the memory of her voice. Her scent. The warmth in her eyes. I explode, the release and warm water washing away the last of my tension. And there's no sign of the guilt I started with. Just a deep sense of need. Which doesn't seem to go away.

Feeling more relaxed, I throw on some fresh jeans and a t-shirt before calling Greer back. The phone rings a few times before she answers.

"Hey, Greer. You rang?"

"Hi. Yes. I wasn't sure when you'd be back. How was your trip?"

"Pretty much what I expected. What's up?" Apart from me. Because seriously? Could I be getting hard again already? This is beyond a joke.

"Would you like a surprise?"

I'd like something. But I can't have it. Ever. "Yes?" I have to stifle a groan.

"I've finished your plans! I was hoping maybe you could call in and have a look at them this afternoon if you're around?"

The thought of spending the afternoon alone with Greer, after what I did in the shower, seems risky.

"Wow. That was quick. I'm going to Harry and Stella's tonight. I could look at them there if you like?" I hadn't been planning to go to dinner, but right now, it seems the lesser of two evils.

"Well, I'd rather not do it with all those people around. I want to have the chance to talk about it properly, and you know what a zoo it can be over there. I was thinking maybe you could call in here and then give me a lift to Mum's. If you like what I've done, we could take them with us."

I'm completely unable to think of a reasonable reason why not. Maybe because there's no blood flow to my brain. In no time at all, I find myself heading to Greer's flat with a combination of anticipation and dread.

Her door is ajar when I reach the landing, so I head down the hall to the lounge room. Greer is bent over the dining table, making notes on the swathes of paper covering the surface. But that's not what I notice. What causes my lungs to seize and steals my tongue is the sight of long, slender legs exposed by short, frayed denim cut-offs, clinging tightly to a perfect arse as she bends over the table. She smiles at me over her shoulder before straightening up.

"You're looking better than the last time I saw you."

"Yeah, the stitches came out on Monday. All better." I lift my arm to show her the small bandage on my arm, still protecting the healing wound.

"Do you want a cuppa before we get started?"

Just to get her out of the room—away from me—for a minute, I agree. Somehow I have to get a hold of myself. And not literally. Not until I'm home at least.

All too soon, she's back, the shoulder of her white peasant blouse dropping alarmingly off her shoulder, her mass of hair pulled into an untidy ponytail, her skin smelling of desire and cinnamon. I wish I could say it was purely physical. Then it would be easier to ignore. And take care of. It's the rest of her. She's smart and talented. Funny and kind. And yeah, sure, I've hooked up with plenty of women you could say the same about. But none of them have been, well, Greer. It's as simple and as complicated as that.

At first, it's torture to sit shoulder to shoulder with her at the table, but as she starts to explain her drawings, I get caught up in her enthusiasm and swept away by the creative and innovative ideas she's come up with.

"This is brilliant. I would never have thought of half this stuff. You're really talented, Greer." I'm honestly blown away.

"You really like them?" The eager nervousness on her face is touching and reminds me how young she is.

"Really, really. I can't think of a single thing I would change."

"Oh, give it time. I'm sure you'll think of plenty." Her eyes roam over the blueprints with pride, fingertips tracing the lines on the laptop screen. The muscles in my belly clench as I watch the movement, and I'm again aware of how close we're sitting. Of the brush of her thigh, the scent of her hair, the warmth of her skin.

Without warning the air is charged with tension. Raising her eyes from the plans, she meets my gaze. Her body seems to soften and melt towards me. My skin feels hot and tight.

"Do you have any ... er ... questions?" Her voice is nervous, low and husky.

We're close now. Close enough for me to feel her breath on my skin.

"No. I ... I think I need some ... time."

"Time. Okay. Yeah. Time is good." Somehow my lips are brushing her cheek, her ear, raising shivers along her skin. The air feels thick and heavy. Her eyes drift closed as my lips move to the throbbing pulse in her throat. "Do you want—?"

"Yes," I start, a heartbeat before my lips settle delicately on hers. Our first kiss at the auction was spontaneous, a joyous meeting of lips. This kiss is different. Our lips are so gentle, so light, they barely touch, but I can feel it with everything I am, smooth and dark and intense, underpinned by a visceral need that takes my breath away.

I don't plan it, yet somehow I find myself lifting her from her chair, sliding her onto my lap, so she's straddling me with her beautiful thighs, our kiss unbroken until she settles the heat of her core over my cock. Jesus, have I ever been this hard? My hormones have taken control of the wheel. My lips move down and across her jaw, her throat, her exposed shoulder. She tips her head back, giving me better access and pushing her breasts forward as my fingers slide her blouse further off her shoulder, exposing one breast. Fuck, she isn't wearing a bra. I can't help myself. I suck her deep pink nipple into my mouth, and she gasps, grinding her core against my hard-on as her hand comes up and sweeps the other shoulder of her blouse down before sliding under my t-shirt.

I growl at the feel of her long fingers sliding along my skin, up my side and around my back, her nails digging into my shoulders as I lift her from my lap and slide her arse onto the table.

"I have to taste you. Now. Just this once." I groan as my fingers make short work of the button and zipper on her shorts. I pull them, along with her knickers, down her long legs in one swift motion, dropping them on the floor before pressing her thighs apart. Greer leans back, bracing her hands on the table behind her, knocking notepads and pencils to the floor.

"God, you smell incredible." I take in her glistening folds. She's bare, apart from a tiny triangle of red curls. A signpost saying 'press here'. Smooth and bare and pink and so very, very wet. Any self-control I might've been able to scrape together vanishes as I bury my nose between her thighs, inhaling deeply.

With a low moan, Greer presses her hips forward and I flatten my tongue along her opening, swiping up to her clit before sucking her in. Within seconds, her hips are bucking. "Oh, yes. Right ... yes," she whimpers as my lips, teeth and tongue work their way up and down her swollen pussy again and again. Her thighs tense beside my head, and I know she's close.

"Come for me, beautiful." I breathe into her folds, one hand holding her hip, the other pinching her nipple. Her back arches, muscles tightening as she cries out, somewhere between a gasp and a moan, and collapses back onto the table, panting and boneless. I'm almost as undone as she is and drop my head to her quivering belly.

Pounding on the door brings us both to our feet.

"Greer—it's me," Will calls.

I freeze, my hands on her shoulders.

"Fuck!"

My gaze travels from Greer's flushed face to the enormous bulge in my jeans.

"Damn. Quick. You go into the bathroom and get, umm, yourself,"—Greer waves her hand in the general direction of my cock—"under control. I'll stall him." In seconds, she's pulled her shorts up her legs and straightened her top. "Calm your farm. I'll be there in a minute," she calls to Will, whipping her hair out of the ponytail and into a messy bun as she walks. I dart into the bathroom before she has time to open the door.

"What took you so long?" I hear Will grumbling as footsteps move down the hall. "I've been trying to get hold of Josh. He hasn't returned my messages. Have you heard from him?" Their conversation is muffled by the door, but I can make out what they're saying.

"Yes, actually. He's here. In the ... in the bathroom. We've been going over the blueprints for his house." Even through the bathroom door, I can hear the stammer in Greer's voice. I can't believe Will hasn't noticed anything out of the ordinary. She had an unmistakable glow about her as she went to let him in. Thank God he's generally oblivious to what's going on around him.

"Really? You're finished already? Can I see?"

"Well, it's up to Josh."

He bangs on the bathroom door. "Hurry up, Josh. Get yourself out here. I want to see your new house. Which you should own in the next couple of days. At a substantial discount, by the way. Negotiated by yours truly, courtesy of that tree. No need to thank me."

"I'll be out in a minute," I call, flushing the toilet to make it look believable.

I lean against the sink in the bathroom and splash cold water on my face before taking a couple of big gulps to calm myself down.

It's a fortunate thing my cock shrivelled fast at the fear of being caught with my face between Greer's legs. Christ that was close. Saved by the pounding on the door. Another minute and I would've been balls deep in a whole load of trouble. I should be relieved. What I am is disappointed. Which is not even a little bit okay.

I check my face in the mirror, and what I see looking back at me is a sordid mess of guilt, unresolved lust and a big chunk of self-loathing. I only hope Greer doesn't hate me as much as I hate myself right now. Although, if she does, that might work in my favour.

The idea of standing next to Will and looking at Greer in what feels like an obvious state of orgasm-induced bliss is horrifying. Luckily, Greer manages to convince him to wait until we get to their parents' place to look at the plans she's come up with, using the excuse that she can explain them to everyone at once.

Greer takes a minute to change her clothes—thank God she puts on jeans instead of those tiny shorts—and we head off with Will driving so Greer and I can 'celebrate' with a drink. Except I can't think of a much better celebration than the one we've already had. Oh. Wait. I can. One. It doesn't involve champagne. And it absolutely can't happen.

When we arrive, the plans are immediately spread out over the massive dining room table, and everyone gathers around as Greer explains what they're looking at. Of course, the whole family gush over them. Because they're brilliant. And because that's the kind of family they are. There is total love and support, which I'm grateful extends to me. And I can't ever do anything to jeopardise my place here.

Stella leaps straight into asking about colours and finishes and tiles, while Harry beams like he'd done the damn things himself.

Champagne is opened. Greer and I are congratulated, and there's lots of excited chatter around the table.

"In other news, Josh will be moving in with me until his house is finished," Will announces as things start to calm down. "I'll send a save the date for the big moving in party. Put it in your diary, people."

After dinner, we all head to the media room to kill zombies, leaving Stella to clean up at her insistence. I feel guilty, but Stella is never happier than when she's taking care of her family. At least there's not much to clean with dinner being a barbeque.

I need to talk to Greer about what happened at her place. When I see her head towards the bathroom, I leap at the opportunity, excuse myself and intercept her, detouring us into her childhood bedroom.

"We need to talk." As soon as the door closes, I realise my mistake. Being in a bedroom with Greer is not a good idea. Especially with the door closed. My skin feels too tight, right along with my jeans. I have to keep thinking with my head, and not the other parts of me.

"About?" As if she doesn't know. She takes a step towards me, and I back up. It's clear from her expression she's enjoying making me uncomfortable.

"About what happened earlier. At your flat. Greer, it can't happen again."

"Are you trying to tell me you didn't enjoy it?" she says with a flirty challenge in her voice.

If my face reflects my feelings, I must look guilty as all hell. And conflicted.

"No. That's not what I'm saying ... "

"Then what are you saying?" She takes another step towards me.

"You're my best friend's little sister. A guy just doesn't go there."

"And yet, you went there. Well, to third base at least." Now she's got me backed up against the wall until we're almost touching.

"Christ, don't. I know what I did. And I'm trying to fix it." I can feel sweat breaking out on my forehead.

"Not sure there's any way to put the genie back in the bottle, Josh." She edges closer, her perfect tits brushing my chest.

"Stop it," I hiss as I step out from between Greer and the wall, backing away. "Like I said at the pub, it's inappropriate and can't happen. Harry would have my head on a spike and my balls shoved down my throat in two seconds flat if he knew."

That gets a laugh. Which was not my intention.

"It's not funny. We have to work together on getting these house plans done. If I pull out now, they'll all wonder why. I need you to promise me there'll be no more flirting. And looking like—that." I wave my hand up and down in front of her. "And no more kissing."

Her eyes, bright with humour and a hint of stubbornness a moment ago, are now serious, the smile slowly slipping down her face until it's a frown. She looks dejected, as though the idea of not being able to finish what she has started and seeing the house through to completion hurts, but she doubles down. Her expression rallies as she crosses her arms in front of her.

"I don't think that's a promise I can keep. And I don't think you'll be able to keep it either." It's a challenge I know I have to win.

"I can and I will. I'm sorry if I gave you the wrong impression. Whatever you thought you felt, well, it was a momentary lapse of judgement. And there won't be another one. Ever." My jaw is so tight my teeth are starting to ache, and I can feel a pulse throbbing in my temple. "I mean it."

Her eyes narrow as her cheeks start to flame.

"Right. Well, I can keep my hands to myself if you can," she tosses at me. "You're not that irresistible, you know." I know she's hurt, but there's anger there too. Hopefully, she'll feed on that.

"Good. So, friends?" I ask, more hopeful than expectant.

"Sure. If that's what you think you want."

"It doesn't matter what I want. This is the way it has to be."
Without another word, I turn and head back to the media room.

Shit. In my typical selfish style, I've made a mess. I've betrayed my oldest friend. And the only people who ever showed me any real affection. And I've hurt the one person in the world I wish I hadn't. Oh, and let's not forget I've bruised my own stupid heart in the process.

Fuck my life.

CHAPTER FOURTEEN

GREER

After the confrontation with Josh in my old bed-room—thank God I had redecorated and taken down all the One Direction and 5SOS posters years ago—I let Will know I'm ready to head off whenever he is and we say our goodbyes.

I'm relieved we came with Will. If we'd come alone, as orig-inally planned, the drive home would've been awkward as hell. Oblivious, Will keeps up a running commentary plan-ning all the shenanigans they'll get up to once Josh moves in with him, so my silence isn't noticed. Although, I do catch Josh looking at me over his shoulder more than once.

If he thinks he's had the last word, he can bloody well think again. *Just friends* my arse. I might not have much experience with men, but I know what I see in Josh's eyes. What I feel in his fingers and his lips when he touches me. And it's not common garden-variety lust. If I thought that was all it was, I might take him at his word. But there's something there, something deep. And I know in my heart he feels it too. I come from a long line of stubbornness, and as much as I wish he would hurry up and recognise the inevitability of us being together, I'm prepared to wait him out.

I spend the next couple of weeks slogging through interviews, psych tests and panel ambushes, looking for the perfect job. My New York internship has set me up pretty well as a 'saleable' commodity, as the recruiters say, and in the end I have three offers to choose from. Like everything, each has pros and cons, and after a long video chat with my New York mentor I settle on the one with the best creative fit, even though it's not the highest paid.

Conlan and Covey specialise in sustainable and energy efficient architecture, which is one of my passions. They're also doing a lot of work in the public and low-cost housing sector, which is a big draw for me. And the managing director, Jonathan Covey, is not only brilliant, but he's also friendly and laid-back, and the office is within walking distance from my place. I'm sold.

Adding icing on the cake, Jonathan is happy for me to supervise the build on Josh's house when I start working for them. I showed him the blueprints during my final interview, and he was impressed, which gave me a lot of confidence. It's with the council now, and all we're waiting on is their approval to get started.

Between interviews and tinkering with the plans, I've done a bit of power shopping. I'll need a better business wardrobe than the couple of suits I've been getting by with, even though Conlan and Covey seem pretty casual. My dad always says, dress for the job you want, not the one you have, and the job I want is Jonathan's—Conlan, Covey and Carter has a certain alliterative ring to it—so I need some sharp suits and power dresses to look the part.

I haven't seen Josh since our awful conversation in my bedroom. I emailed any changes he wanted to my drawings, and he emailed back comments and approvals. Once they went to council, there wasn't much to discuss other than minor details and thoughts about builders and timing.

Today I want Josh to meet Dave, the builder I'd like to use for the job. He worked on my flat and has done a bit of work for Mum and Dad over the years. I trust him implicitly, which is important because I won't have time to micromanage the build once I start work.

We agree to meet at eight, and I'm there before Josh and Dave, with a coffee for each of them and a peppermint tea for me. Even though it's nearly spring, the mornings can still be cold.

Dave runs at me and picks me up in a bear hug as soon as he sees me.

"Little Gee. It's been too long. How the hell are ya?"

"I'm good, Dave. Happy to know you can work on this project for me."

"Aww. I'll never say no to you, darlin'." Dave is a flirt, but it's all harmless. His wife manages him and their kids like a drill sergeant and he loves it. And her.

My heart skips a beat at the sight of Josh strolling towards us, looking edible in his regulation man bun, t-shirt and jeans, his expression uncharacteristically sheepish. And well it should be after the way we left things the last time we saw one another. Sometimes I wish I could shake the reaction he sparks in me. Then I see him again, and nothing else seems to matter.

As I introduce them, Dave keeps his arm around my shoulders, causing Josh to scowl. Good. Let him stew.

We're twenty minutes into our walk-through of the house, Dave and I workshopping ideas, before Josh warms up to Dave. Maybe it was the mention of his wife and kids. Or maybe he just realised Dave's like yet another big brother to me. Whatever it is, I sense a bit of a bromance brewing. I knew they'd get along.

We're about to start talking about the kitchen when Josh's phone rings. He looks perplexed for a second before holding it up to indicate he needs to take the call.

Even though he steps away, I can still hear what he's saying. Hear the worry in his tone.

"Hang on, hang on. Calm down. Start at the beginning."

I don't recognise the frantic voice on the other end of the line.

"Right. Okay. It's okay. Don't say anything. To anyone. Where are you?"

More frantic words from the other end. Josh checks his watch, frowning.

"Right. Hold tight. I'll be there in thirty minutes. Forty-five tops. And don't say anything to anyone until I get there. I mean it. Not a word." Josh's brows are drawn tight together over the bridge of his nose.

"Is everything alright?" I ask, worried by the snippet of the conversation I could hear.

"No. It's not. That was my brother."

"Your little brother? What's wrong?"

"He's been arrested."

CHAPTER FIFTEEN

JOSH

I can't quite believe the words that have come out of my mouth, although I shouldn't be surprised. He is my brother. Apples and trees and all.

In typical Greer style, she leaps into action.

"I'm sorry, Dave. I think we'll have to finish this up some other time. How about I call you?" I vaguely hear Greer say as I leg it out the door. I'm almost at my car when I feel a pull on my elbow.

"Wait up, Josh. You're too worked up to drive. Give me the keys." Greer holds her hand out. I can't think straight. "I'll drive."

I drop the keys in her hand, and we strap in. "Where to?"

"Bondi Police Station."

She doesn't waste time putting the address into the satnav, just takes off, adding the address when we stop at the first set of traffic lights.

"What happened?" she asks, nipping in and out of the Saturday morning traffic like a race car driver. Damn. Her confidence behind the wheel is hella sexy.

"I'm not exactly sure. He was talking a mile a minute. But it involved a car." My stomach rises into my chest, and I close my eyes for a few deep breaths. I won't be able to help him if I panic. "I'm going to call Will. He might know someone who can help us out."

"Good idea," Greer agrees without taking her eyes off the road.

Predictably, the call to Will goes to voicemail. I leave a message and hope by the time we get to the station, he'll have called back. Will doesn't handle criminal stuff, but I'm sure he can recommend someone good.

"How old is he now? Oh. I don't even know his name," Greer says as we speed up the south side of Spit Hill. I have no idea how we got here this quickly.

"He's seventeen. His name's Tyrone." I wince as I say it because she snorts out a laugh.

"Seriously? Tyrone? Did they want him to get bullied?" The laugh I can't hold back feels good, breaking the tension that's been winding tighter inside my chest since my brother called me. This whole thing is throwing me right back into my teenage years. I'm glad Tyrone felt he had someone to call. Even if it was only me.

"Yeah. Well, his mother's an idiot. What can I say? I think he mostly goes by Ty."

"And why wouldn't you?" We travel in silence for a few minutes before she adds, "You know, if he's seventeen, then he's still a minor. That should work in his favour, surely?"

"Christ, I hope so." Greer's calm certainty is helping bring my anxiety back down to a manageable level.

"I didn't know you guys were in touch."

"We weren't. I haven't laid eyes on him since he was ... maybe five or six? When Dad heard I was coming back to Sydney, he sent Ty my number. For emergencies. I guess this qualifies. How fucked up is that?"

Greer says nothing in response. Just pats my hand, which is running up and down my thigh.

I contemplate calling my father, who now lives on the Gold Coast, and decide it's best left until we've at least seen Ty and know what the situation is.

We're whizzing through the Harbour Tunnel, nudging the speed limit, when the phone rings. It's Will, who does know someone who can help and offers to co-ordinate them. I give him what little information I have, and he tells me he'll keep me posted.

Nearly forty minutes after Tyrone's call we pull up outside the police station and head inside. Not bad for a trip from Manly to Bondi on a Saturday morning. Maybe Greer missed her calling as a drag racer.

They take us through the station to an interview room. It smells of sweat and fear. Tyrone is sitting in a plastic chair, looking very much the worse for wear. He gives me a chin tip and a face full of attitude. The little shit. A middle-aged cop with a doughnut belly and thinning hair comes in and fills me in on what Ty's been up to. It's an impressive list. Speeding, drunk driving, drugs in his system, and trying to avoid an RBT before crashing his car into a hedge at the front of a nursing home. None of which seems to have had much effect on his attitude as he gives the cop an insolent sneer. At least he wasn't hurt, other than a bruise on his forehead from the airbag.

"Are you the next of kin? Guardian?"

I shake my head. "No. I'm his older brother." The cop looks like he's about to tell me I can't help, which isn't going to work.

"Mum is overseas. Dad's in Queensland," Ty tells him. I roll my eyes. It all feels far too familiar.

I can see by the weary look in his eyes the cop understands the situation all too well. There's a lot of kids in this area with more money than sense and not enough adult supervision. He's about to launch into why Tyrone can't be released into my custody when there's a knock on the door.

A tiny woman in the world's ugliest suit, carrying a battered briefcase, walks in.

"Susan Kirby." She introduces herself, shaking my hand before turning to the cop. "Lawyer for the accused. I hope you weren't talking to my client without a lawyer present, Sergeant," she adds, in a voice I imagine wouldn't go astray in a military school.

We all instinctively sit up a little straighter in our chairs. Even the cop.

Tyrone is the only one who seems impervious. He gives her a scathing once-over. She might not look impressive at first glance; however, in the two minutes between when she introduces herself, and we all walk out, we're left in no doubt about who the boss is. Including my bolshy younger brother.

We cross the road to a nearby café and settle in. Greer gets us some water, glasses and menus. Susan gets right to business, telling Tyrone how it's going to be.

"This will only work if you do exactly as I say. Which starts with you staying squeaky clean until this is all resolved." Her laser eyes pin Ty to his chair. He's got balls because he gives it one last try.

"What do you mean ..." he starts to argue until her hand flies up in a stop motion.

"Are we clear?" she barks.

He looks ready for another objection, so I give him a swift kick under the table.

"Yes," he mutters.

"Yes, what?" I aim for the type of glare Harry has perfected, and catch a small grin from Greer, so maybe I got close.

"Yes, ma'am," he manages, with a little less attitude.

Susan snaps her briefcase closed and stands, refusing Greer's offer of coffee or breakfast.

Turning to me, she smiles. At least I think it's supposed to be a smile. It's hard to tell. "I would suggest getting in touch with his father as soon as possible. If you're going to handle this, you might think about getting a power of attorney. I'll call and discuss the idea with him and keep you posted. Either way, it will be easier if you're the point person, given he's interstate."

Jesus, this is a runaway train. And I'm not looking forward to my father getting on board.

"I'll be in touch," she tells me with a firm handshake.

"I can't thank you enough, Susan." And I mean it. With the impressive list of misdemeanours Ty has under his belt, juvenile detention isn't outside the realm of possibility. But I'm confident Susan can sort this out. The question is, who's going to sort Ty out? Because it sure as shit won't be his parents.

Once she's gone, the three of us sit looking at one another. It doesn't escape my notice Tyrone is giving Greer the once-over.

"How about I order us some breakfast?" Greer suggests. We let her know what we want, and I hand her my card as she heads to the counter.

Tyrone's eyes follow her across the room.

"She's hot," he comments. Which earns him a light slap upside the head.

"She's off limits. And so are disrespectful comments like that. Unless you want me to hand you back to the cops. Or send you up to Dad."

He shudders. "Fuck. Not Dad. Anyway, he won't care. Probably won't even answer the phone."

"He will when Susan Kirby calls him." And we both grin, thinking about Dad being wrangled by the tiny little pit bull.

As Tyrone starts hoeing into a big breakfast and chats to Greer about where he goes to school and what subjects he's taking, I look him over. He's kitted out from top to toe in expensive designer wear and a pricey haircut. You wouldn't know we're brothers to look at us. He's blond, brown eyed, and despite still being a kid, a bit stockier than me. But I recognise his angry expression as the one that used to look back at me in the mirror every morning.

No sooner has he finished his food than Tyrone stands up, hitching his fancy jeans and smoothing back his hair.

"So, thanks for the bail and the feed, bro. Catch ya."

He starts to walk—maybe strut is a better word—out of the café. He doesn't get far. I stand and put my hand on his chest, stopping his movement.

"Oh, no you don't. I didn't spend my Saturday morning bailing you out of the cop shop just to let you back out on the streets." Out of the corner of my eye, I catch Greer trying to hold back a smirk.

"Fuck off. I don't need you coming around taking over. You're not my father." The déjà vu is almost overwhelming me.

"You're right, kid. I'm not. I'm the stupid bastard who saved your arse this morning. So you can park the attitude and show some manners, thanks."

Greer puts her hand on my arm, and I feel my blood pressure drop back to a safe level. "Maybe you'd like a lift somewhere?" she suggests. "Since your car's been impounded."

"Sure. Okay," he concedes. There's a loaded silence as we head back to the car.

"Right. I'll drop you at school and have a word with the dorm master," I say as we buckle in.

"No. You can't take me back to school." Even in the rear-view mirror, I can see the panic in Tyrone's eyes.

Greer and I exchange a glance that contains a whole conversation.

"Why not?" Greer asks with cool curiosity.

"Because ..." he trails off, clearly buying time to invent a plausible excuse.

"Okay, well, there's always the police station. I hear the beds are uncomfortable, but you'd get three square ..." I start the car.

"I can't go back to school. I don't board over the weekends. I go home," Ty blurts.

I can't believe what I'm hearing. It's almost like *Groundhog Day* and Tyrone is the young me.

"What do you mean you go home over the weekends? Isn't your mother overseas at the moment?"

"Yes. But the school doesn't know that."

Greer sighs, and I have to resist the urge to punch the steering wheel. Looks like I'll be spending the weekend watching over a scrotie teen. You can bet I'll be having a long chat with his dorm master about their lack of duty of care. I don't hold the school responsible, to be honest. I snuck out often enough to know there's not much they can do when a kid is determined to get away. Hopefully, by next weekend, his mother will be back to take care of him. Although, I don't have much faith in that being a success either.

Tyrone's mother, Cristal, lives in an enormous, glossy penthouse apartment. It looks like Versace decorated it himself. Not my style, but it suits her down to the ground. It's clear Ty has been living it up while he's been on his own. Empty bottles, takeaway containers, clothes and wet towels are scattered over the floor and the ugly, overpriced furniture.

As soon as Ty hits the shower, I call our father, expecting to leave a voicemail. He surprises me by answering.

"Josh, nice to hear from you, son." I try and fail to hold back a snort of disbelief. He's such a liar.

I don't waste any time with small talk. After the weekend with my mother, I'm not inclined to give either of my parents the benefit of the doubt.

"I've just spent the morning with Tyrone. He was arrested for drink and drug driving and crashing his car last night." I walk out onto the balcony. Greer doesn't need to hear what I'm sure is about to go down.

"Jesus Christ! Why are you calling me? Can't his mother deal with this?" Dad growls.

"As it happens, no. She's overseas. I think you should come down." The view from this balcony is million-dollar. Shame the apartment is all flash and no substance.

"For fuck's sake, I can't come flying down to Sydney every time that boy gets himself into trouble. Can't you sort it out? Don't you have a friend who's a lawyer? Get him onto it. Let me know how much it costs, and I'll send the money." If it wasn't so tragic, I'd laugh at the predictability of his response.

This is nothing more or less than I was expecting. Still, my stomach bottoms out with disappointment at knowing Dad hasn't changed. And realising Ty has nobody but me, a virtual stranger, in his corner.

"Really, Dad? You can't spare a couple of days to take care of your own son?"

"Not right now, no. I'm leaving on a cruise in two days. You spent enough time in a police station when you were his age. I'm sure you know how to handle it." I flinch as his words hit home. That was low. Even for my father.

"You know what? Don't worry about it. I've already got it covered. And you can keep your fucking money. I'll cover that too." I wish I could slam the phone down in his ear. Damn mobiles.

"Oh, and by the way, he's fine, Dad. Not hurt in the accident. Thanks for asking." I disconnect before I add, "Arsehole."

Greer gives me a questioning look when I head back inside.

"I take it your call didn't go well?"

"It went exactly how I expected," is all I can manage to say as I start searching the apartment like a man possessed. I need to get rid of anything Ty can do damage with. Starting with his wallet, I take his credit and debit cards, then check his room for party drugs. It makes me laugh to realise kids haven't yet come up with better hiding places than the ones we used as teens. I flush them all down the toilet in the powder room before gathering all the alcohol I can find—and there's lots of it—and pouring it down the sink. Next, I grab his phone and check for spare keys to his car and his mother's. I wouldn't put it past him to take off.

"Are you sure all this is necessary?" Greer asks as she watches me put the empty bottles in the recycling bin.

"Absolutely. No alcohol, no drugs, no keys, no phone and no money. That should at least slow him down." I'm speaking from personal experience, and I think she knows it. "Oh, could you check his bedside for condoms ... on second thoughts, don't. I'll do it." Then I realise it's probably better to leave them. The last thing we need to add to this shit soup is an unexpected pregnancy.

"I'm going to have to stay with him for the weekend," I sigh.

"Of course you are. You can't leave him alone."

"You take my car home, Greer. I'll grab an Uber to drop him at school tomorrow night and work out how to get your car back to you. I don't expect you to hang around."

She's already gone above and beyond by being here this long. Especially after how we left things the last time we spoke.

"I'm not leaving you alone with him. You might need help. You can't leave him unsupervised. What if he tries to sneak out while you're in the shower?"

It feels good to laugh. "Now you're getting the idea."

"Besides, you're going to need help cleaning this mess up. I'm happy to stay. Be your deputy."

I'm torn. I know I should tell her to go. It's not fair to expect her to spend her weekend playing babysitter. As usual, the selfish side of me wins over. And I can't deny having her here is making this whole mess a little less unpalatable.

"Thanks, Greer. I owe you big-time." Yet again. The favour balance is really starting to stack up on her side.

"That's what friends do, right?" Our eyes lock, and I know she's referring to what I said about being friends. It hurts it can't be more.

Ty comes out in a clean tracksuit looking a little less rough, but very tired. And young. My heart cracks a little bit. He's a kid. Just a kid. The adults in his life are failing him. And he doesn't have a Harry and Stella to be there to pick up the pieces. I guess the role of responsible adult is falling to me. God help him.

"Time for a chat, mate." I steer him back into his bedroom. I've had enough come-to-Jesus talks from Harry over the years to know how they go. And now I get to pay it forward. Fun times.

CHAPTER SIXTEEN

GREER

By the time Josh comes out of Tyrone's bedroom, I've almost finished clearing away the mess in the lounge room. The dishwasher is running and there's a load of smelly teenage-boy clothes in the washer.

This situation is a nightmare. Part of me wishes I could just go home. This is nobody's idea of a good time. And after our conversation the other night, when he made it clear there would never be anything between us, I feel like it wouldn't be unreasonable. The expression on Josh's face stops me. He looks exhausted. And worried. And more than a little scared.

Right now, he needs a friend. And as much as I want more, being his friend is the least I can do. Because if there's one thing we Carters are good at, it's being there when a friend is in need.

Even though they look nothing alike, I can't get over how much Tyrone reminds me of a young Josh. Maybe a little ruder—I can't remember Josh ever disrespecting my parents the way Tyrone disrespected him—but they have the same wounded animal vibe going on. Which gives me hope for Ty. Josh made it through. He will too.

"How did you go?" I'm not sure I need to ask, based on his drooping shoulders.

"He's having a sleep. Didn't get much last night, apparently."

"I can imagine. Do you want a coffee? There's no milk, but I found some pods in the pantry."

"Yeah. Sounds good, thanks." He glances around at the now tidy room. "Wow. What a transformation. You didn't have to do all that on your own."

"Don't worry, there's plenty still in the kitchen for you to clean up. It'll take a few loads of the dishwasher before this is over. I think he used every cup, plate and glass in the place."

Josh follows me into the kitchen, and I put a pod in the coffee machine while he pulls a cup out of the dishwasher mid cycle.

"Did he open up to you?"

"A bit. Yeah. He didn't even bother trying to call Dad. You know why? Because he never picks up. He knew he was on his own. He's seven-fucking-teen and has a fucking sports car and enough money to buy himself all sorts of drugs, but his father won't pick up the phone. How fucked is that?" Josh's voice is laced with disgust and despair.

"Where's his mum?"

"Some clinic in Thailand, getting another face lift. Or boob job. Or something."

"And she left him here—alone?"

"Hmm. She gave him a note to give the school about boarding on the weekends while she's away. Seems he might have *lost* it." Josh air quotes, signalling Ty chose to keep his living arrangements to himself.

We settle on the sofa, Josh with his coffee and me with a glass of tap water. The fridge is completely empty, other than a tray of ice cubes and a couple of pizzas in the freezer. I see there's more Josh wants to say, so I wait.

"Why the hell did he even have another kid? Didn't he fuck me up enough? He had to go and do it again? It's not Tyrone's fault. He's just looking for attention. And there's not a single person he could call." This whole situation must be triggering all sorts of bad memories for Josh, and it speaks to his character that he's even here.

"That's not true. He had you," I remind him. "And you dropped everything and came. Bailed him out. Found him a lawyer. Took care of him even though he gave you attitude."

"Fuck. It's the least I could do. I haven't even seen him since he was tiny. What sort of a brother am I?"

"Hey, this situation is not on you. It's entirely on his parents. And you're here now, when it counts."

"He said he called me because he couldn't think of anyone else. It was blind luck Dad had given him my number. Or good planning on Dad's part. Anything he can do to kick the can of responsibility down the road until it's someone else's problem. If I hadn't answered, he would've had to wait for social services."

"Well, he didn't, because you came. And you've been great with him."

Josh huffs a humourless laugh. "If he thinks he's getting away with this shit, he's sorely mistaken. Someone needs to get him under control before he fucks his life up completely, and it looks like that someone's going to be me. He's not getting his damn car back, for a start. And he can work off every last cent of the lawyer's cost and anything else this clusterfuck costs."

I don't even try to hold back a laugh. "You sound like Dad."

Josh's face lights up. "Huh. Well, maybe there's hope for Ty yet. Because more than once, Harry was the only thing standing between me and a long stay in juvenile detention."

"And look how you turned out, right?" I'm proud of how Josh turned his life around.

"You're not making your case here, Greer. Argh." He scrubs his hands over his face. "Who am I kidding? I have no idea what I'm doing. What if I screw this up?" There's real worry in his voice. So much for the selfish, self-absorbed guy he claims to be.

"Seems to me you're doing okay so far. And you know what? If you do screw up, you can always call on the brains trust. Dad eats this shit up for breakfast."

All the annoyance and frustration I've felt over the way Josh has pushed me away has melted in the past few hours. The way he dropped everything to help his brother, no questions asked, shows what a deep down good person he is. He's the only one who can't see it because he's so attached to the screw-up narrative his father embedded when he was a kid. Getting him to see himself for who he is now won't be easy.

Tyrone sleeps until late afternoon, and by the time he wanders out of his bedroom, Josh and I have cleaned up the mess and stocked the pantry and fridge. He looks relaxed until he spots the recycling bin full of empty bottles.

"What the fuck?" he shrieks. "Where's all my booze?"

"Down the drain. Where it belongs. You're seventeen, not twenty-seven. There'll be no more alcohol, no more drugs and no more car," Josh responds, calm but firm.

Ty groans and runs to his bedroom. We can hear him tearing his room apart. "No, no, no. Not the drugs. Shit man. Not the drugs."

"Yep. The drugs. All gone, kid."

"You're an arsehole, you know that?"

"I've been told. Now, you and I are going to take all these empties downstairs to the bins. Then how about some pizza for dinner? Or would you prefer Thai?"

"What? What are you even still doing here? Go home, old man."

"Oh, I will. Tomorrow afternoon, after I drop you at school. Until then, you're stuck with me."

"Us," I chip in.

Tyrone gives me one of his so-not-sexy teenage once-overs. "You, I can handle," he says, and it's all I can do not to laugh at his attempt at a Joey Tribbiani-style come-on.

"We're a package deal, I'm afraid." I grin at Josh, who doesn't say anything to contradict the suggestion we're a couple.

"Aww, damn. What a waste. Any time you want to trade up, Greer, you let me know." Ty gives me a wink. I worry about the state of the world if this stuff works on young girls.

"I'll be sure to remember that." I have to turn away so he doesn't see my smile, but Josh catches it in my reflection in the window. The same way I catch him clipping Ty over the ear.

"Respect, kid. Don't forget it."

It takes three trips for them to get all the rubbish out of the apartment and into the bins, by which time both the dishwasher and the washing machine are on their final loads. At least the place is now smelling less like a seedy pub, since I opened a few windows and lit a candle I found on the sideboard.

In the end, we order burgers and chips, and Ty gripes about drinking cola rather than beer. By the time we've finished dinner and a stupid movie about some sort of alien monsters the guys both loved, it's obvious we're all ready for bed.

Ty gives me one of his t-shirts to sleep in, and Josh gives me the bed in the spare room, making himself up a nest on the sofa.

"There's another bed, you know," I remind him, pointing to his stepmother's room. "Although you might need the window all the way open. Even though she's not here, there's an over-powering perfume fog in there."

"Yeah, not on your life. I'm sleeping here, where he has to go past me to get to the front door. And when I say sleeping, I mean lying in wait."

"You don't think that's a bit of overkill?"

"Watch and learn, Greer. Watch and learn."

I feel like I've barely drifted off to sleep when I hear a blood-curdling scream.

CHAPTER SEVENTEEN

JOSH

It takes a little longer than I expected. I guess Ty really is exhausted. My phone is showing just shy of two when I hear the almost imperceptible click of a door opening and closing. Ty creeps towards the hallway, pausing as he passes the sofa to check I'm asleep. My eyes are closed. I keep my breathing deep and even. And Fuck, it's a struggle to keep the grin off my face. I wait until he's almost at the front door.

"Going somewhere?"

The scream my little brother lets fly is piercing.

"What the fuck?" He rounds on me, furious. He's dressed in another head-to-toe designer outfit that makes him look like some kind of up-and-coming rapper.

"What did Ms Kirby say? Squeaky clean, Ty, squeaky clean."

Greer comes running out of the bedroom, her face pink and pillow-creased, her long legs bare, gorgeous red hair a tangle around her face.

"What happened?"

"Ty thought he should check the front door was locked," I tell her, trying and failing to keep a straight face. "And now he's going right back to bed. Aren't you Ty?"

"I thought you were cool. You're no better than the cops," Ty grumbles as he turns towards his bedroom.

"Oh, I wouldn't say that. The cops have got nothing on me, brother. I learnt from the best. Something you might like to remember."

Greer and I watch Ty slink off, slamming his bedroom door behind him.

"An old trick I learnt from Harry," I say in answer to her unasked question.

"See, you do know what you're doing." Greer gives me a kiss on the cheek as she heads back to her bed.

I settle back onto the couch, hopeful we'll all be able to get some sleep now. And maybe even a little bit confident I can do this. After all, I did learn from the best.

I take Ty and Greer out for a late breakfast on Sunday morning, relieved Ty is finally starting to drop the attitude, at least a little.

I'm shattered. Yesterday was exhausting. Not to mention I didn't get much sleep after our middle-of-the-night adventure. Not only because of Ty. Spending the weekend with Greer and not being able to touch her has been the bitterest, sweetest kind of torture. The way she looked last night, in the t-shirt Ty loaned her to sleep in, I thought my dick was going to jump ship, waltz its way over to her and tuck itself inside her warm body all on its own. There wasn't much chance of sleep after that.

I knock back three coffees in quick succession to try and snap myself out of my stupor. Ty manages to hoover up the biggest breakfast I've ever seen, which is good because I think he's been living on alcohol and drugs since his mother took off.

Greer waits with Ty in the foyer at the school while I have a chat with the dorm master, who is horrified by what's gone on. It takes a promise of a large donation from my father to avoid Ty getting expelled, and I agree to some pretty tough detention rules.

All the time I'm talking with the teacher, I have half an ear open for Greer's voice, quietly chatting with Ty, and his responding laughs. Fuck, she's perfect. I don't know any other woman who would've dropped everything to spend the weekend with such an argumentative and troublesome kid. Greer didn't even hesitate. Even when it meant borrowing a t-shirt from Ty to sleep in. She wasn't even phased by his sleazy comment this morning about how he wouldn't be washing it again, ever. Which earned him a swift elbow to the ribs from me. Not that I can blame him.

After dropping Ty off at school, we go back to Manly to pick up Greer's car, so it's early evening before I get home. Dinner is a bowl of cereal before I fall into bed, eager to make up for last night's lack of sleep.

I'm feeling remarkably relaxed, all things considered, by the time I head in to work on Monday morning, prepared for a full-on couple of weeks, knowing we have a tricky pitch to a potential client coming up. I'm so deep in the weeds with this client, two weeks fly by and I barely notice. I manage to make time for Ty, whose mother is still MIA, and not much else.

By the day of the pitch, the whole team is exhausted. They've worked like the clappers to get it ready, and I'm really happy with what we've come up with.

The client is in a bit of a PR mess, and they're looking to change direction, rehabilitate their reputation and expand their business all at the same time. Not an easy ask, but I think we nailed it.

I take the team out for a well-earned lunch to celebrate. Long lunches are part of the deal in advertising, although today's lunch might be a bit of a record-breaker—it's after nine by the time we wind it up. I've made it a policy never to have more than two drinks at work functions. When you're the creative director, you have to keep yourself tidy. Sadly, the same can't be said for the rest of the team, and once I've poured them into Ubers, I find myself on the pavement outside the restaurant reluctant to go home.

It's not long until I move in with Will, and I can't wait to get out of the serviced apartment. It's lonely to be honest. And spending too much time alone gives me time to think about Greer. I know she started her new job this week, and apart from sending her a text to wish her luck, we haven't spoken. I'm finding it hard to ignore the feelings our weekend with Ty dredged up. Avoiding her seems the best option.

Ty is on lockdown at school all weekend, although I did promise to take him for lunch on Sunday. He wasn't happy when I said Greer wouldn't be coming, but too bad so sad. She doesn't need a repeat performance from him.

I notice a club across the road that looks busy. The name seems familiar, and I think maybe Will's brother Ben hangs out there from time to time. My staff have gone home, and I could really do with letting my hair down. Maybe there'll even be someone there to take my mind off she-who-shall-not-be-thought-of.

It's still quite early, and while the club is busy, it's not packed. I head straight for the bar and order a vodka before looking around. I'm not oblivious to the attention I get. But as has been typical of late, I can't seem to work up any interest. Until a flash of red catches my eye. And right there on the dance floor is Greer in a figure-hugging black dress pressed up against a guy in a suit, dancing like she's auditioning for *Dirty Dancing* the stage show.

Before I even stop to think, I'm shouldering my way across the dance floor.

"Josh," Greer gasps, breathless and flushed.

"What the hell are you doing?" I hiss, unable to keep the irritation out of my voice. The guy she's with looks like he doesn't know whether to turn tail and run or protect her. Run would be my advice.

"I'm dancing." Greer sounds confused. As well she should be. I'm making a scene. But I can't seem to help myself.

"No. That wasn't dancing. That was ... That was foreplay."

Greer laughs. "Don't be ridiculous. We were just having fun. Did you notice the song? We were re-enacting *Dirty Dancing*. It was a joke." She turns and stomps off the dance floor towards a table full of people I don't recognise, who are so far unaware of what's going on. The guy from the dance floor trails after her.

"Come on. I'm taking you home. Get your bag." I wish I could say I'm watching out for my best friend's little sister. But that would be a lie. There's no rational thought. My reaction is pure emotion.

"I beg your pardon?" Greer turns on me, hands on hips.

"You heard me. Home. Now." I scoop up the only bag that's unattended. Hopefully it's hers. By now, all eyes at the table are on us.

"Hey, wait a minute ..." Dance Guy starts. It takes one look from me to have him screeching to a halt.

"It's okay, Tony. He's a friend of my brothers." She snatches the bag from my hands before giving him a quick hug. "Thanks for the dance. I'll see you Monday."

My patience is all out. I don't know who this guy is, or why she'll be seeing him Monday, and right now I don't have the critical thinking skills to reason it out. I take her by the elbow to steer her around the dance floor and out of the club.

Greer pulls away with a swift jerk.

"Don't you dare touch me," she growls.

No sooner have we hit the damp night air on the street than she rounds on me.

"What on earth was that about?"

"What was what about? What were you about? Don't you know what happens to women who flirt like that with men in bars?" Even I can hear how douche-y I sound. I fling my arm out when I see an approaching taxi.

"Yes. Actually. I do. They get asked on dates," she shoots back.

I feel like my head might explode. "Just get in." I throw open the taxi door. By now I'm snarling, having noticed her take-me-home-and-fuck-me shoes.

Without another word, she climbs in. I follow and give the driver the address. I don't trust myself to speak, and we sit in fuming silence. The ride is just long enough for my temper to start to settle and for me to realise how badly I fucked up. I've never seen her look so angry. I don't think I've ever seen anyone look so angry. And I can't blame her. The way I behaved was inexcusable. I don't know what came over me. I've never felt such a wave of anger and … jealousy. Jesus, I was jealous.

The taxi has barely come to a stop when Greer throws off the seatbelt and climbs out.

"Thank you ever so much for the lift." Her tone drips sarcasm before she turns on her heel and heads into her building.

Panicked, I jab my credit card at the reader, leap out after her, stop the security door with my foot before it closes behind her, and bolt up the stairs, catching up with her on the landing as she fishes in her bag for her key.

"Hold on a minute. I want to talk to you."

"Well, you're out of luck. I have no desire to talk to you." She lifts her head, and I see her face in the harsh light from the landing, cheeks flushed, eyes chips of fury. "You embarrassed me in front of my new work colleagues. Over nothing. What the hell is wrong with you?" She pushes open the door and turns to slam it in my face, but I'm faster and stronger. I catch it and hold it open.

The glitter of her eyes and the tightness in those full pink lips tell me she's not only angry but also distraught. I'm an arsehole.

Her new work colleagues. Fuck. I have to apologise. I want to apologise. I don't want to see the look of accusation and anger on her face. Directed at me.

"I'm sorry, okay? I'm sorry I embarrassed you. I'm sorry ..."

"You're sorry? What—is that supposed to make it all better?" Her voice is cold and a little shrill.

"I don't know. I saw you rubbing yourself all over that guy and I ..." I choke on the words threatening to come out of my mouth. I didn't like it. I wanted it to be me. Despite everything I've said, I still wish it was me.

"You saw me dancing, Josh. Dancing. With a work colleague. And even if it wasn't a work colleague. And even if I was rubbing all up against him, what business is it of yours?"

I try to hold the words in. I try so hard. But they shoot out of me like the cum that shoots out of me every time I think of her in the shower. Every damn morning.

"Because I wanted it to be me."

Those narrowed eyes pop wide, and the quick rise and fall of her breath stills. Time stops. Her lips move, yet no sound comes out. And the last of my control snaps.

I'm through the door and pinning her against the wall before I even think about it, and my lips come down on hers with all the pent-up desire of the past months. My obsession with her is off the chain, and I don't know if I can get it back on.

She tastes of joy and honesty and something so sweet and out of reach it hurts. And even that's not enough to stop me.

I hear a thud as Greer's bag and keys drop to the floor and she jumps into the whirlpool of sensation with me. Her hands are in my hair, dislodging my bun and pulling hard. Not away from her. Towards her. My hands hit the wall on either side of her head, needing something solid to support me as the floor drops away at my feet.

"This is what I want," I gasp as I drag my lips across her cheek, down her neck, feeling the pulse racing under her skin. My hips press her to the wall, my cock grinding into her flat stomach.

I know it's wrong. Somewhere in my head is a voice of reason, but it's lost in the pounding of blood in my ears, in her gasps as my teeth close over her earlobe, her whimpers as my hands slide up her taut thighs and under her dress, fingers hooking in the flimsy fabric of her knickers.

"Is this what you want?" My voice is a growl against the curve where her neck meets her shoulder, and she shivers.

"Yes." She's almost breathless. "With you. Only with you."

And if there was any hope of me getting control of myself, it's gone. With a few whispered words. Her hands work the buttons on my shirt, pushing it off my shoulders. She pulls me closer. I'm lost.

I slide my hands down, taking her knickers with them until they drop to her ankles. My hand hooks behind her knee and hitches it to my hip, opening her to my fingers. She's wet. Wet and hot and swollen.

I grapple with my wallet, sliding it from my back pocket one handed. Flipping it open I find the condom and drop the wallet where we stand. Her hands are busy with the button and zip on my jeans. She pushes aside my boxer briefs, and her warm fingers grasp my thumping hard-on. I freeze. This is it. In another second, the die will be cast. And I already know I'll never be the same.

"You sure?"

"Shut up," she murmurs as her lips land, hard and desperate, back on mine.

Our lips and tongues do battle while I tear open a condom and slide it over my erection.

In one swift motion I push Greer up the wall, pull her legs around my hips, notch my cock at her entrance and slam inside so hard I see stars.

"Fuck," I gasp, but I don't slow my desperate thrusts or my desperate mouth. The rhythm is relentless and pounding. It's like this is my first time. Like I've never experienced this before. I can't breathe. The only thing keeping me alive is the taste of Greer and her tight heat around my cock. Finally, around my cock.

Greer's climax hits fast, convulsing every muscle. She makes a sound somewhere between a moan and a scream, and seconds later, there's an echo from me as my cock jerks and my whole body shudders to a climax.

We stay pressed together, foreheads touching, our breathing harsh in the otherwise silent hallway.

I can't believe what I've done. I crossed a line I promised myself I would not go near. And only half of me is sorry.

"Ah Jesus, Greer. What have we done? What have I done?"

CHAPTER EIGHTEEN

GREER

My racing heart plummets. Not the words you want to hear right after the best sex of your life, even if we are both still fully clothed. The saving grace is, I know he enjoyed it as much as I did.

"We did what's been brewing since we ran into each other at the airport, Josh." I try to keep my voice steady, despite the threatening tears. Tears of heartbreak. Tears of anger.

"And we shouldn't have. I should've stopped this. We can't ever be ... this."

"I think maybe we already are."

"No. No, we're not. This was a one-off thing." Josh slides me down the wall. Settling me on my feet before he pulls back, slips the condom off, ties it and sets it on the floor. Then he tucks himself back into his jeans and zips up.

I don't know what my face is saying, but he takes one look at it and his pinched expression softens. Pushing my hair gently off my face he kisses, my forehead.

"That was incredible, Greer. Amazing. But you understand why it can't be any more than this. We've talked about it."

"No. You've talked about it. I don't get it at all. I want you. You want me. Simple."

"Well, it's not that simple for me. Will is like a brother. And Harry and Stella are the closest things I've ever had to real parents. I can't do this to them."

"I understand you're worried about what they'll say, but I'm a grown woman. I can make my own decisions."

"It's not just about that. You're incredible. Amazing. You deserve the best. Of everything. And I can't give it to you. I'll never be the type to settle down with two-point-five kids and a white picket fence. Surely you know that."

"Who said anything about settling down? I'm twenty-four years old. It's way too early to be thinking about that." Which is a bit of a lie. I've been thinking about that with Josh for what feels like my whole life. Although, the two point five and fence are negotiable. What is also a lie is what he's telling himself about his value as a partner and a man. The weekend with Ty, and the way he's supported him since, is proof of that.

"Oh, come on. You deserve better than me and you know it."

My heart cracks a little at hearing him talk about himself like that. I push off the wall, straighten my dress and, taking his hand, lead Josh into my bedroom.

"Can we at least talk about this?" I sit down and pat the bed beside me. Talking isn't entirely what I have in mind, but baby steps.

"I don't know what else there is to say, Greer. I don't want to hurt you. Or your family. I'm trying to do the right thing here. You may not think this now, but it's for the best if we nip this in the bud."

"And we forget this ever happened. Is that the plan?" Which is one of the stupidest things I've ever heard.

Josh lets out a deep, pain-filled sigh and wraps a comforting arm around my back as I rest my head on his shoulder. "Well, yes. I guess so. I wish it could be different. I really do."

Minutes go by in silence, Josh's palm rubbing circles on my back, my hand sliding up and down his thigh. It doesn't take long for the atmosphere of comfort to begin changing to something a little more electric.

Before Josh pulls away, I lift my head, cup his cheek and meet his sad gaze.

"Well, if this is all we ever get, how about we at least make the most of it? Maybe work it out of our systems. Get closure. Then we'll both be able to move on. No regrets."

I can see by his expression he's not buying the logic I'm pedalling. I can also see the overwhelming temptation, the wheels of justification turning, the moment he makes his decision. All the roadblocks in his particoloured eyes drop and what's left is a potent mix of vulnerability and desire.

"No regrets. Just tonight." The yearning in his voice is clear.

"Just tonight," I reply, my fingers sliding into the wild mass of his hair.

The skin of his shoulders and back is smooth and firm with muscle as I run my hands across them before sliding up his arms and into the light sprinkling of hair on his chest that disappears to a thin trail down his flat belly.

We're not in a hurry. The sharp desperation of our need has been smoothed by our assault on each other in the hall. Now I want to explore every inch of him. If this really is the last time for us ... No. I won't think about it. I push those thoughts from my mind. Time enough for consequences tomorrow. For now, I concentrate on savouring every moment, every touch, every movement. I revel in the dips and curves of muscle and bone, soaking in the arousal offered by his quivering golden skin.

"Beautiful," Josh murmurs as he slides the fabric of my dress out from under my arse, up my body, and off my shoulders, dropping it on the floor by the bed. My bra quickly joins it before he eases me back on the mattress, hovering over me on his elbows. His eyes track from my head to my toes, followed by his fingers, trailing a delicate line across my collar-bone, onto my shoulder, down the side of my breast and waist to my hip, where his hand settles, warm and firm. I can't suppress the shiver of need. I don't even try.

I stretch to take my shoes off, but his hand stops me. "How about we leave those on for now?" he growls, sending a shiver down my spine.

Josh pulls away to stand as I reach for the button on his jeans and shucks them, along with his boxers, socks and shoes, in one impatient movement before lying down again, his gorgeous length stretched out beside me. We take our time, drinking each other in, until eventually, the need to touch, to feel, is too strong. His lips lower to mine for a mind-melting kiss before moving down my neck, across my chest, sucking an already tight nipple into his hot mouth. I want to imprint the feel of his lips and hands on my body like an invisible tattoo.

My body arches off the bed towards him, my hands reaching for his arse, pulling him closer, trapping his cock between our bellies.

"Not yet, gorgeous." He slides further down my body, his mouth moving across my ribcage, down my stomach until his shoulders are nudging my thighs apart. "Let me taste you again."

My mind slides back to the day Josh went down on me on my dining table, and I'm one hundred percent on board with experiencing it again. It was like nothing I'd ever felt before. He knows what he's doing down there, and what's more, he loves doing it.

I open my thighs, sliding my feet up the bed and dropping my knees to the side, giving him all the access he needs. His tongue slides through my folds as one hand holds me open, and the other slips a finger into my opening, working in and out as his mouth closes over my clit and he sucks. Lightning strikes, and Josh continues to lick and suck and rub as my orgasm fires through me, not stopping till I'm limp and boneless on the bed beneath him.

His lips work their way back up my body, and when we come face to face, I smile at the satisfaction in Josh's eyes.

"Your turn." I push him onto his back, straddle his thighs, and take his burning erection in my hands, smoothing the silky flesh with a rhythm that has his breath catching in his throat. Just as Josh did, I start at his flat brown nipples, working my way down his belly before moving across to his hip and down one thigh. I can feel the tension in his body and give him a dirty grin before swiping my tongue up the length of his cock. Opening my mouth, I fit my lips over the tip of the head, sucking in the bead of pre-cum swelling there before I slide my lips down his length, taking him deep into my mouth.

"Jesus. Oh. Jesus." Josh's hands fist the sheets, and his hips rise off the bed while I use my hands and mouth to drive him towards the cliff. I can feel the power I have over him, and I'm loving it. Loving the realisation I can take him to the same wild places he takes me.

"Stop. Please stop. Now." Josh is close, I can feel it. He slides his hands into the hair at the side of my head and pulls me up for a brutal kiss before he flips me onto my back.

"Condom?" he gasps.

My arm flails around, searching for the drawer handle, opening the bedside table, grabbing the box of condoms I put there the day after I showed Josh the first draft of the plans. He tears it open, strips of condoms flying around the bed, and in seconds he's all suited up. He doesn't thrust right into me. Instead, he slides his cock along the length of my seam, back and forth. It would be dry humping if I wasn't so wet.

"Fuck you feel good." He hisses as he drives us both crazy with his thrusting.

Without slowing the surge of his hips, he drops his thumb on my clit and my body implodes, again. The sounds coming out of me are barely human as Josh lines himself up and slips his magic cock into my still-quaking body.

His thrusts are long and slow and tantalising. My hips come off the bed, unbelievably chasing another release before I wrap my legs around his waist, the spike heels of my shoes digging into his tight arse muscles.

"Not so fast." His breathing is laboured, the concentration on his face telling me he's struggling to maintain control. For what seems like hours, his hands hold my hips still, his hips rolling in a lazy rhythm. It's driving me wild.

"Now. Again. Please," I gasp, unable to construct a whole sentence.

The rhythm picks up, and I push my hips higher as his hands release them, meeting each thrust as the speed builds until the pace is frantic, our tongues and hips in a matching beat.

It's pounding now, and I feel an almost unbearable rush of pleasure as Josh lets out a roar of release. I can feel his cock pulsing as he takes my hands and falls forward to lie gently against me. Heartbeat to heartbeat.

CHAPTER NINETEEN

JOSH

I wake to light streaming in through open curtains, my arm across Greer's waist, holding her pressed tight against my chest, our legs curled together. I hadn't meant to fall asleep. I hadn't meant to be here this morning. I don't generally do sleepovers. Fuck and run is my usual style. Even with the few girls who might've considered themselves my girlfriend, or something close to it. Sleeping, and waking up, has always felt too personal. Too intimate. And here I am doing just that with the one woman in the world I should be staying the hell away from.

I should get up. Get out of here before she wakes. But that would be a dick move. And in all honesty, I can't bring myself to get out of bed. My hand seems to have a mind of its own and is currently stroking Greer's hip and thigh.

I feel it the moment she wakes up, aware of my very loud morning wood pressed against her arse. Her hand slides behind her to stroke me and I know I won't be getting out of this bed any time soon.

The strips of condoms that leapt out of the box last night are still scattered around us, so it only takes me a second to find one and roll it on. Then I'm lifting her knee and slipping inside her from behind, taking her with long, languid strokes. My lips roam across her shoulder, fingers pinching a nipple before sliding south across her belly and onto her clit, slipping through her wet heat, pressing and rubbing as I thrust. This time our orgasms are like gentle waves in a warm sea, lifting us to a glittering peak before dropping away, leaving us spent and satisfied.

"Mmm. Good morning." Greer stretches like a cat, rolling over to face me, the sight of her taking my breath away.

"Do you always look this gorgeous in the mornings?" comes out of my mouth before I think better of it. Her hair is mussed, her cheeks pink, her eyes bright. She's never looked more beautiful, and it breaks my heart to know I'll never see her like this again.

"I don't know. I don't think being woken up by an alarm clock has quite the same effect as an orgasm."

It occurs to me that some time, some day, some other guy will be waking up with her like this. The knife of jealousy cuts me, and it's bitter. I need to get out of here before I say something we'll both regret.

"I should grab a shower and get going. I didn't mean to stay all night."

"You're still sure about what you said last night?" Greer sits up, making no effort to cover herself, and the sight of her bare breasts has my cock stirring again. Treacherous bastard. Greer's suggestion we work this out of our system clearly failed.

"Yes. I'm sure." That's a lie. I'm anything but sure, and I hope she can't see the conflicted emotions on my face. "I need to get moving. I have work to do."

"You are aware it's Saturday, right?"

"Yeah, I know. But we've got so much work on right now; I need to spend a few hours at the office. I'm hoping I can get away in time to crew for Will in the races this afternoon."

Will and I have been sailing together for years. It's another one of the many things I missed when I was overseas. On Saturday afternoons we race at the yacht club whenever life allows.

"Okay. Well, hop in the shower and I'll get you some breakfast." Greer gets out of bed, giving me one last good look at her perfect body before she swings a silk robe over it and heads for the door.

Standing under the pounding hot spray, I wrestle my conscience against the overwhelming sense of satisfaction I feel this morning. I've never had sex like it. Which is a sobering thought. I've had many, many partners and have never believed emotions needed to be involved for it to be good. Turns out maybe I was wrong. Because I've never felt this bone-deep sense of satisfaction before.

I find Greer in the kitchen plating up scrambled eggs on toast.

"When you said breakfast, I thought you meant coffee and cereal."

She laughs as she hands me a plate. "I figured you'd need more than that to rebuild your strength."

She's right. I'm starving and tuck into the golden eggs before taking a swig of the coffee. I nearly choke.

"These eggs are great, but what happened to the coffee?"

She winces. "Is it terrible?"

"It's not good." Which is an understatement.

"Sorry. I don't drink coffee." She lifts her mug of tea as evidence. "Poisonous stuff. I guess I've never learned the knack of making it."

Which makes sense of the two almost untouched mugs of coffee left behind when Sean and Fiona came over while I was recuperating. And now that I think about it, I realise I've never seen her drink coffee. Tea, hot chocolate, herbal concoctions. Never coffee.

"Well, it's good to know you're not perfect. Remind me to make my own next time." The words are out before I even realise what I've said. Her expression lets me know she didn't miss the slip.

I push back my chair and take my plate and cup to the kitchen. "I'm sorry. Look, I'd better go before I say something we'll both regret."

"It's okay, Josh. I get it." Greer shoos me out of the kitchen and I head back to the bedroom to collect my shoes and socks.

"Will you be at Mum and Dad's for dinner tomorrow night?" She opens the front door for me to make my awkward and somewhat cowardly exit. My face must show my conflict because she sighs.

"Look, don't let this make things weird. For either of us. You've made your position very clear. But it's pointless if you pull away from the rest of the family because of me, isn't it? They're expecting you, and they'll be disappointed if you don't turn up."

"Yeah, you're right. I might need a day or two to work through it, that's all. And I do have a lot of work on. Also, I promised Ty I'd take him to lunch tomorrow. How about I see how I go today? If I get enough done, I'll be there."

Her face lights up. "You've spoken to Ty? How is he?"

"As obnoxious as ever. The school has him locked down so tight that he hasn't been able to get up to any more mischief. Thank God."

"I'm glad you're keeping in touch. Tell him hi from me. You know you can always bring him to dinner if you'd like."

"Might be a bit too soon, but I'll keep it in mind."

"Okay, well, maybe I'll see you tomorrow."

I should leave well enough alone, but I can't stand the look of sadness she's trying hard to hide.

"Greer, there's something I want to say before we forget all this ever happened. You're an incredible woman. And last night—and this morning, for that matter—was amazing. I'm not sorry it happened. Not even a little bit."

I brush her lips quickly with mine before turning for the stairs.

"Me either," I hear her whisper before she closes the door behind me.

By lunchtime, I'm desperate to get out of the office and work out my frustrations on Will's boat. The ideas I need are not coming to me, and every time I move, I smell Greer. On my hair. On my skin. Serves me right for using her soap and shampoo, I guess. And the memories those smells evoke erase all other thoughts from my brain until the whole morning is an exercise in futility.

"You look like you had a good morning," Will helpfully interprets my scowl as I arrive at the club.

"Could we cut the chatter and get this boat in the water?"

"Sure." Will holds his hands up in surrender.

We're almost finished setting up when Nick, a friend Will and I went to school with, arrives. I haven't seen him since I got back, so it's nice to catch up. Will's brother Ben is crewing for Nick and is very much the worse for wear—as usual—despite it being well past noon. There's a healthy-ish competition between Nick and Will because they both work at the same law firm.

"Looks like you won't be beating us today," Will says with a smirk as Ben heads off for some hangover food before the race.

"Don't bet on that. Actually—you should bet. Loser buys dinner?" Nick looks confident. Even hungover, Ben is a good sailor. But the bet gives us a bit of extra incentive to win.

We race well, but not quite well enough to beat Nick. I'm disappointed, though not as bummed as Will. And at least now I smell of salt water and sunblock and not Greer.

Being on the harbour has improved my mood and remind-
ed me how much I love sailing. Somehow, sculling down the
Thames doesn't give you the same rush as the wind in the
sails.

Will checks in with me again as we strip down the boat.

"You want to tell me what was wrong with you when you
arrived?"

"Bad morning at work. That's all." Obviously, I can't tell
him what the catalyst for my shit-tastic day was.

"Working on a Saturday will do that to you, I guess."

We settle on the verandah with a post-race beer. Will's
buying, so Nick and I decide to stay, and Ben heads off
on one of his many secretive adventures. There's something
going on with him. I can't put my finger on it, but it doesn't
add up. He bounces in and out of the country all the time
without explanation. He's living in some fancy apartment
loaned to him by a mysterious friend. I hope he's not into
something dangerous. Or illegal. Harry would freak. At least
he has the right connections to get help if he is.

Which brings my thoughts around to the message Ty sent
me earlier. It seems his mother has extended her stay at the
'spa' and won't be home anytime soon. I'm in no way qualified to take care of a seventeen-year-old, but if it's not me, I
don't know who will. Maybe I'll see about getting him into
some sailing lessons to keep him occupied and out of trouble.
And somehow I have to help him find a job, because paying
off the repairs to his car and his legal bill is a non-negotiable.

"Speaking of women ..." Will starts, which we weren't, but
they're never far from his mind, "there's someone I'd like to
introduce you to, Josh. She's an interior designer and artist.
Fun, beautiful, talented. Exactly your type."

"Cut it out, Will. It's thoroughly inappropriate to be pimping out a work colleague. Do you even know if she's single?
Or straight?" Nick appears unusually pissed off by Will's comments. Interesting. He's normally what you'd call inscrutable,

so the show of emotion makes me wonder what might be going on there.

"I'm not pimping her out. I'm simply offering to introduce them. Josh hasn't been seeing anyone since he got back, and maybe Lulu might break his dry spell. And yes. I checked. She's single." Will seems oblivious to the dirty look he's getting from Nick. Despite his overly serious nature, I've always admired Nick. He's got a sharp mind, and you can trust him with anything. I'm not sure what he thinks about me. Probably that I'm a bit of a screw up. Points to him that he's never let on.

"Believe me, mate, dating drama is the last thing I need. Good race today." I try to change the subject, but it goes from bad to worse.

"And speaking of getting laid, I think Greer might've had a gentleman caller." Will prattles on. I'm too scared to take another mouthful of beer in case I choke on it. "I called around to her place this morning to see her. Anyway, there she was in her bathrobe with two sets of breakfast dishes still on the kitchen counter and a definite just-been-had look about her."

Fuck me sideways. I'm glad I didn't take that mouthful of beer. I must've missed him by minutes. My gaze connects with Nick's and I get the feeling he knows what I've been up to. As I said, he has a sharp mind. Funnily enough, I don't fear he will rat me out to Will. Thank Christ.

"Guess I must've just missed him." Will unknowingly echoes my thoughts. "She was cagey about it, though. Wouldn't give me any details. Not even a name. I'm thinking it might be someone from her new job."

It takes me a minute to register that Will has stopped talking and is looking at me expectantly, like I need to respond.

"You know, it's in really poor taste talking about your sister like that, Will. Harry would string you up if he heard you."

Will rolls his eyes. "Cool your jets. Anyone would think she's your sister."

CHAPTER TWENTY

GREER

It's only my second week on the job, but I skulk into work on Monday morning, dressed as unobtrusively as possible in a grey pant suit, thoroughly embarrassed. And furious.

It wasn't until Saturday night when the hormones finally worked their way out of my system that I registered what had happened on Friday night. At the club. In front of the people I've only been working with for a week. At my 'Welcome to the Firm' drinks. How am I supposed to present a professional, businesslike image when I have a Neanderthal dragging me off the dance floor in front of most of the staff? If there's a saving grace, it's that Jonathan wasn't there.

Maybe I should've stood my ground and told Josh to sod off, but at the time, all I wanted to do was get him as far away from my colleagues as possible. As quickly as possible. Defusing volatile situations by getting the hell out is my instinctive response. When faced with fight, flight or freeze, flight wins more often than not. Until I'm forced to fight.

The office is a big, open-plan space, which makes it very hard to hide. I haven't been at my desk for more than five minutes before Tony wanders over.

"Hey, Greer. How are you?" He approaches with caution, and who could blame him?

"Hi, Tony. I'm fine. How are you? How was your weekend?" I don't expect there's any chance we can sweep Friday under the rug, but I'll give it the good old college try.

"I'm okay. I just wanted to check on you. You know, after Friday..." Well, that didn't take long. Looks like I'll have to brazen it out.

"Oh—yeah. Friday. Look, I'm sorry. Josh was so rude. It's ... he's—"

"Jealous? Is he your boyfriend?"

"No. No. Nothing like that. I was going to say protective. He's my oldest brother's best friend, and he's known me since I was a kid. So ..."

"Huh. Well, he didn't look at you like he thinks you're a kid, that's for sure."

And he sure didn't treat me like a kid once we got back to my place. A tremor runs through me as I feel phantom hands on my thighs. Yikes. Focus.

"Anyway, I'm sorry he was rude to you. Are we okay?"

"Sure. Of course. We're good." Tony scuttles away as though he's worried Josh might materialise from behind a glass screen and do him an injury.

Great. Now the whole office will think I'm a nut job. I'm furious with Josh for putting me in this position. Which doesn't sit well with the feelings that come up when I remember what happened as a result of his outburst in the club.

I gather up my work laptop and head towards the conference room for the regular Monday morning Work In Progress meeting, hoping against hope nobody else noticed the Friday night drama. No such luck.

I've already spotted the *Mean Girls*. Three associates who look like they're in their late twenties, are always dressed to within an inch of a Kardashian and have taken an instant dislike to me. It's such a cliché. Pick on the new girl. The one with red hair. Fun. As if I didn't live through all that crap in primary school. Then again in high school. Now, after what feels like a brief respite at university, I'm back swimming with the sharks.

The trouble is our boss, Jonathan, has unintentionally made it worse for me. He's spent weeks talking me up so I sounded like the second coming of Frank Lloyd Wright. In heels. And now I have my work cut out for me trying to fit in.

"So, Greer, who was that delicious-looking man who dragged you off the dance floor on Friday night?" Mean One says, with a sly look towards the boss, who is fortunately deep in conversation with his assistant as he waits for everyone to file in and get settled. Mean One, otherwise known as Zoe, always gets to these meetings early to make sure she snags prime position next to Jonathan.

I can feel my cheeks burning, no doubt clashing delightfully with my hair. If Josh was here, I'd knee him in the balls for putting me in this position.

"Oh, um. Just a friend."

"Is that right? Because he looked like more than a friend." This is from Mean Two, as Mean One and Three snigger behind their perfectly manicured hands.

"No. Just a friend." I aim for a tone of breezy unconcern as I use a tip from Granny, who used to say *tell 'em nothing, take 'em nowhere*, which I finally understand. The less information they have the better.

"What a shame. I guess you'll have to try harder." Mean One jumps in. "Maybe a bit of a makeover would help? I can give you some pointers on where to shop."

If there aren't flames licking up my face and singeing my eyebrows, I'll be surprised. I look down at my short, neat, unpolished nails, my understated, professional outfit and my midrise heels. Maybe I shouldn't have tried to blend in today. Maybe I should've gone hard, as Will would say, and dressed to kill. Over the years, I've learnt there are two ways to deal with bullies. Meet them head on, blow for blow, or avoid confrontation at all costs.

Being the newbie, and with my personal inclination for flight rather than fight, I wanted to avoid confrontation. I was hoping that with a bit of time, I would be able to win these women over. Or at least neutralise their dislike. But The Means have thrown down the gauntlet. I won't make the same mistake again.

Before I have a chance to respond, our boss steps in. "Perhaps Greer has more important things on her mind than the colour of her next manicure, Zoe. Now, can we get down to business?"

I know he was trying to help, but I wish he hadn't. Mean One—I mean Zoe—gives me a death stare before turning to simper at Jonathan, who appears completely impervious.

By the end of the meeting, I have a stack of new work to do, and the compliments Jonathan has thrown me have painted a big red target on my back, if there wasn't one already. Unfortunately for The Means, I don't really care what they think. I'm here to do a job and I intend to do it well. If the rest of the staff don't want to be my friend, I'm okay with it. As long as they respect my talent and my work ethic.

No sooner have I sat down at my desk than my phone rings. We got council approval on the plans late last week. Dave is officially starting demolition today, and I asked him to keep me in the loop. I'm so glad I've got someone I can trust on this, even though Jonathan has given me permission to keep overseeing it to completion. He's aware I turned down offers of a lot more money to work at his firm because of their focus on sustainability and energy efficiency, so I think he's happy to cut me a little slack.

"Hey, Dave. How's it going?" I can hear banging and crashing in the background.

"Good, good, good, Gee. I wanted to let you know we've got the trumpets out and the walls are coming down." Dave is a character. He's always making random references to strange facts in the hope he'll confuse people, which he often does, but I love it.

"I assume you're referring to the Battle of Jericho?" I check.

"Haha. Yep. You got it, sweetheart. When we gonna see you down here?"

"I could maybe swing by late tomorrow afternoon if that would work?"

"Sure. We should be done with all the major external demo by then, thanks to that handy tree. And in more good news, no sign of asbestos, so there should be no holdups."

I hang up from Dave and give a quiet little squeal under my breath. I can't wait to get down there and see the hole in the ground where this house will take shape. For most people, that's all it will look like. For me, that empty space will be full of walls and windows and furniture. I see my plans in my mind's eye, kind of like holograms, or virtual reality without the headsets.

I shoot off a text to Josh suggesting he meet me there at four thirty tomorrow if he can spare the time. He bounces one straight back, agreeing, and I confirm with Dave.

Josh and I haven't spoken since he left my place on Saturday morning, not more than five minutes before Will turned up, except for the text he sent on Saturday evening, checking if I was okay. And letting me know he wouldn't be at dinner on Sunday night. Eye roll. Like I didn't see that one coming. But since he was with Tyrone, I can't really complain. If ever there was a kid in need of some guidance, it's Ty. And Josh is the right guy to give it to him.

I spent all weekend bouncing between anger at his behaviour and post-orgasmic bliss. And fixating on what he said about how we couldn't and shouldn't. Another thing Granny used to say is *coulda, woulda, shoulda*. And maybe he coulda woulda shoulda kept his hands to himself. But he didn't. And if he thinks I'm letting it go and putting what happened on Friday night behind us, well, he's got another thing coming. Because if

Friday night showed me anything, it's that what's between me and Josh is more than garden-variety lust. Which is something you don't walk away from.

CHAPTER TWENTY-ONE

JOSH

I arrive at what's left of my house at four thirty on Tuesday afternoon. Bloody hell. It looks like I paid a small fortune for what amounts to a hole in the ground. But I have complete faith in Greer's vision.

I've been pulling fourteen- and fifteen-hour days pretty much since I arrived, so I don't feel the least bit guilty cutting out of work early.

There's a security fence inside the perimeter of the property. All the tradies seem to have gone home, except Dave, who is such a giant bear of a man that he dwarfs Greer as they sit on the dilapidated old front fence, waiting for me.

After a punishing handshake, Dave hands us a hard hat and leads us through the front of the house to the gaping hole in the back. I can't believe how much they've achieved since they started demolition yesterday.

Greer manages to look both adorable and sexy in tight-fitting jeans, steel cap boots, a high-viz vest and a shiny white construction helmet. My heart rate picks up and my breath catches. I didn't know whether to go in for the hug when I arrived. Greer took the decision out of my hands with a cool cheek kiss that I guess you could describe as politely friendly. To the outside observer, it probably looked like business as usual. But I felt the ice. And I don't blame her.

I can't quite read whether she's hurt or angry. She's within her rights to be both. Despite the slight chill in her manner, she's acting as though it never happened. But it did. And I can't stop thinking about it. Or feeling it. Over and over again. Like the tune of a song I can't shake.

I'm both pissed and relieved that she seems to be putting it behind us. Just like I suggested.

Dave and Greer chatter on like the old friends they clearly are, talking some sort of building shorthand I have no hope of understanding. It's noting more than a bunch of holes and piles of dirt until Greer starts pacing around, spraying hot-pink lines and shapes on the ground with a can of paint, and I can start to see how it will look.

There are two old trees in the backyard. An enormous jacaranda and an equally giant gum. The tree coming down on the roof really opened up the back yard and it looks much bigger than I remember.

"What do you think, Josh?" Greer asks. I'm miles away. Thinking about the day the tree took Greer and me out. What might've happened if it hadn't. And what's happened since.

"What do I think about what?" I shake off my contemplative thoughts and try and focus on her words. She gives a huff of irritation.

"Dave was saying his nephew has just qualified as a landscaper and is looking for his first solo job. He'd give you a good rate. And it would be good to get anything structural done before we get too far along with the house because access to the back yard will be tricky. What do you think?"

"Great idea. Let's get him on board."

"Righto. I'll get him down tomorrow, and he can draw something up for you." Dave pulls out his phone and knocks out a text, presumably to the nephew.

"Do you have any idea what you might want?" He raises expectant brows at me.

"You know, Greer's the one to talk to about those things. I'll be happy with a bit of a deck for barbeques and a super low-maintenance garden." I have no idea about gardens. This will be the first time I've lived in a house since I was a kid. Even then it was mostly boarding schools. Then apartments in New York and London. A house means a home, which is what I'm looking for. "Oh, and a bit of grass. For a dog."

Greer's eyes light up. "Ooh. Get him to give me a call, Dave. I have some ideas." I'll bet she does. It crosses my mind that this house, when it's finished, will be more Greer's than mine. Which causes a pain somewhere in the vicinity of my heart. Or maybe it was the chilli crab I had for lunch. Yep. Definitely. The chilli crab.

"Okay. Will do. Anyway, I'd better hit the road, Jack. Gotta pick the kids up from soccer practice. Talk tomorrow, Gee. Don't forget to lock the gate." And with that, Dave is out the gate, returning Greer's wave as he goes. Leaving me alone with Greer. She doesn't waste any time.

"Is there something you might like to say to me?" she asks, her tone telling me the answer had better be yes, and I'd better get it right or be prepared for her to tear me a new one.

I've spent plenty of time thinking about this over the past few days, so I'm prepared. Even though I apologised on Friday night, it bears repeating, given the magnitude of my stuff up.

"I'm sorry. I'm sorry I embarrassed you in front of your work colleagues. And I'm sorry I can't be what you want."

Greer looks momentarily surprised by my grasp of the situation. And maybe a little disappointed at the thwarted opportunity to tear into me.

"Right. Well. Thank you. You embarrassed me, Josh. It wasn't okay. And just so you know, if you ever treat me like you did in the club again, you'll wish it was Harry who got hold of you and not me."

She turns to lock the gate, fiddling with the heavy chain and padlock. I wish I could tell her what I'm not sorry for. I'm not sorry for what happened in her apartment. Any of it. Because it was the best night of my life. But voicing those feelings is not going to help anyone.

Both our phones ping with a text as we're walking back to our cars. It's Will, suggesting a celebration dinner.

We eye each other warily.

"Well, we have to eat," Greer says, popping the boot of her car and throwing the high-vis vest into a small basket

I'm about to decline when my stomach rumbles. Damn chilli crab.

"Yeah, I guess we do."

Will and Ben meet us for dinner at Will's favourite pub in Neutral Bay and we celebrate the breaking of ground with a bottle of champagne.

Greer turns to me once we're all settled. She warmed up a little after my apology. Thank God.

"How was your lunch with Ty on Sunday?"

Will and Ben turn questioning looks my way, so I fill them in on what's happened with my brother.

"Anyway, his mother has apparently met her 'soulmate' in Thailand and is now heading off to Europe for some 'much-needed down time'. Down from what, I'm not sure since the woman hasn't worked a day in her life. So it looks like Ty will be my responsibility for a while."

"Poor kid," Greer says with a sigh. "But maybe it's a good thing. She's not exactly mother of the year. And if anyone can get him under control, it's you."

"You should bring him round to dinner on Sunday night," Will adds. "Since you and Ben have outgrown your wild ways, Harry could do with a project."

We all laugh, although Ben's smile looks forced. I'm aware he felt let down by Harry more than once when we were growing up, and there's still some tension there.

"Hey Gee, how are you getting on with those bitches at work? Things any better?" Ben asks, changing the subject. He may be a bit of a wanderer without the required 'successful career' of all the other Carter siblings, but Benedict has the most emotional intelligence of anyone I've ever met. I guess it has something to do with his struggles at school. I know he has some sort of dyslexia, which wasn't picked up until quite late. Maybe he's had to learn to read people in a way he can't always read words.

"What's this? And how does Ben know about something I don't?" Will jumps in. Ever the protective oldest brother.

"Calm your farm. Gee and I had lunch on Thursday last week. While you were busy being a high-flying corporate lawyer." Ben pats Will on the arm.

"It's nothing. Just a couple of women at the office think channelling Regina and Gretchen is a good way to get ahead." Greer waves a hand and tries to look unconcerned, but I'm not buying it.

"Regina and Gretchen?" I have no idea who they are.

"From *Mean Girls*. They were the mean ones," Ben supplies, giving me some context. "How were they at drinks on Friday night?" he asks Greer. And an alarm bell goes off in my head.

"Friday night?" I ask under my breath, hoping nobody else will hear. It's unfortunate Ben has ears like a fox.

"Some of the people from the office took Greer out as a bit of a welcome thing. Did they turn up?"

Greer glances at me before answering him. "Oh yeah. They wouldn't miss the opportunity to see and be seen. They were there."

Fucking hell. Of course they were there when I caused my stupid, jealous scene. Which they undoubtedly saw. My bad behaviour is the gift that keeps on giving. I wish I could haul off and kick my own arse. But I can't say anything in front of Ben and Will because that would lead to explanations, which would lead them to information they don't need to have.

"And?" Ben probes.

Greer shifts in her seat and starts to fold and refold the paper napkin in front of her.

"Put it this way. We're never going to be holding each other's hair out of the way while we puke. But it's nothing I can't handle."

Ben and I exchange a look that calls bullshit.

"Do you need me to come in and sort them out?" Will is bristling.

"Holy hell, no! I don't need anyone to come in and *sort them out*. It's nothing. They'll settle down when they realise I don't give a flying fat rat's arse what they think of me." Greer gives Ben a glare, obviously irritated he's raised the issue in front of Will. And maybe me.

I won't go wading in there to sort anyone out, but there must be something I can do to help.

After dinner, we all go our separate ways, but when I get home, I can't settle. I pace the tiny, soulless apartment, going over and over what Greer said. And the thought that I made things worse for her, in an already problematic situation grates at my conscience. I remember Will telling me she was bullied while we were at school. Back then, I had enough of my own problems and didn't pay much attention to the details. I know I won't get any sleep until I get to the bottom of it, so I grab my phone and shoot off a text to Greer.

Me: Hey—I wanted to check in about the mean girl situation.

Greer: No need for you to worry. I've got it covered.

Her curt reply sends the message I'm not yet out of the doghouse. But there are things I need to say. I'm about to text back when it occurs to me it's probably not a good idea to have a written record. You never know who might come across it by accident. She picks up on the first ring.

"I was worried I might've made things worse for you, with what happened on Friday night."

I hear rustling. Christ. She's in bed. Now I'm thinking about her big, comfortable bed. Like fuck. I'm thinking about her lush, warm curves. Naked curves.

She sighs, and even through the phone, I can feel her annoyance with me giving way.

"They have a big, long list of things they think they can torment me with. Don't worry about it. If it wasn't that, it would be something else."

My blood pressure spikes with irritation at these women. "So, they did bring it up? And don't lie to me. You know you're a terrible liar."

"Yeah. Okay. They brought it up. On the positive side, they thought you were hot. Offered to give me some pointers on how I could up my game and snare you." Greer's husky laugh raises the hairs on my arms.

"I'm sorry, Flo. You know I would never do anything to hurt you or make you uncomfortable. At least on purpose. Don't you?" It's not until the words are out of my mouth that I realise I've used my special nickname for her.

"I know. It wasn't your fault. Well, not entirely."

"It kinda was. If I hadn't come charging in like a crazed superhero, they wouldn't be tormenting you. And I couldn't be sorrier."

"Ha. Like I said, they have a long list."

"Why were you bullied at school?"

"You've seen me, right?"

"You were bullied because you're beautiful?" That gets a laugh out of her.

"Because I was skinny. I don't know if you noticed, but I was a bit of a late bloomer. And because of my hair."

"Because it's red? I thought Ed Sheeran and Ron Weasley had put a stop to all that."

"If only. It's okay to be a ginger if you're famous. Otherwise, it's a weapon in the wrong hands."

I guess the boys escaped too much bullying because Will and Ben are more strawberry blond than real red, and Ethan is a dark reddish brown. Greer, on the other hand, has bright, vibrant waves that seem to glow with an internal life force.

"You know they're jealous, right? Because, as a man, I can say with honesty, both objectively and subjectively, you—and your hair—are the most beautiful things I have ever seen."

Fuck. Where did that come from? I need to not be saying that sort of stuff. The silence on the end of the phone tells me she heard me loud and clear. I need to get back onto solid ground.

"I know you say you've got this, but if you need me to play Robin to your Batman, all you have to do is send up the signal. Okay?"

"Okay. Thanks, Josh."

"Least I can do in the circumstances. Anyway, I'll let you get to sleep. 'Night, Flo."

"Goodnight, Josh."

I hang up and hit the shower. Cold.

CHAPTER TWENTY-TWO

GREER

The combination of excitement about the progress on Josh's house, the support of my brothers, and the conversation with Josh last night have put me in a positive frame of mind. I arrive at work the next morning in my favourite don't-mess-with-me suit and don't-even-think-about-it shoes, only to find a spectacular arrangement of red and orange roses on my desk in a beautiful glass bowl. I don't need to look at the card to know who sent them. Just as well because all it says is:

'My favourite colours'

For someone who has said we can only ever be friends, he sure is making all the right moves to take whatever we are—or are not, according to Josh— to a whole other level.

The roses have what I assume was the intended effect. Mean One through Three all stop by at one point during the morning to make spiteful remarks. I can smell the jealousy oozing out of their tightened and minimised pores.

I snap a pic and send it to Josh with a thank you, as well as to Jessie because she's on Team Greer all the way.

One consequence of the flowers is that Tony continues to give me a wide berth. Which is a good thing. He seems like a great guy, but there's no hope of us ever being more than friends and colleagues. Because Josh is the one I want, and there's no point giving anyone else the impression I'm available.

Late in the afternoon, I once again head down to Manly. This time to meet Dave's nephew, Matt, who turns out to be as much of a hoot as Dave, and we brainstorm some great ideas. It's not a huge yard, and Josh wants it kept simple, but when I suggest including a raised shipping-container pool with a glass panel insert I saw in a design magazine, Matt's eyes light up. Dave says we're like a couple of kids planning to get up to no good. By the time I leave, we have a brilliant outline plan which Matt is going to work up in more detail. I can't wait to show Josh our vision. He's going to freak.

On Thursday, I arrive at work to a white baker's box on my desk. This time it's a luscious red velvet cake. He's going with a theme. And who am I to complain. Cake, right?

Friday brings an intricate arrangement of every red lolly I can imagine—frogs, jellybeans, red liquorice, Smarties, Jaffas. All done up in a basket, wrapped in cellophane and tied with a red bow.

This time I decide to call Josh. I wait until the three Means are all out of the office. Probably sneaking in a mani-pedi on company time.

"Enough already." I laugh. "Are you trying to get me fat?"

"No. You know what I'm trying to do. Is it working?"

"Well, if you mean are they green with jealousy, then yes."

"Have they stopped with the snide remarks and bullying?"

"Actually, yes. They had a few things to say when the flowers arrived, but giving them a big slice of the cake seemed to shut them up. After the obligatory complaints about gluten and sugar, of course."

"Good. Let's hope it keeps them quiet. Let me know if it starts up again. I have a few more red ideas up my sleeve." I'll bet he does.

I was right about the pool. Josh freaked. In a good way.

I meet Josh, who has Tyrone in tow, and Matt at the house on Saturday morning to go over what we've come up with. Matt must've worked nonstop to get the drawings finished. He's so keen, and I think Dave is pushing him to get things moving. In part to make a good impression but also to avoid holding up progress on the house.

"Are you freaking kidding me? A pool made out of a shipping container?" Josh and Ty exchange wide grins. Even though they don't look at all alike, their grins are identical.

"Fuck, yes," Ty shouts, earning him a light swat from Josh.

"Language. And what's this on the side?" He peers at the drawings Matt and I have spread out on the trestle table in the back-yard. "Is that a glass panel?"

"Yep. And here at the back is the water feature, which will give you the sound of running water. Very Zen. And super low maintenance." Matt beams, and so he should be proud. His plans have maximised the space and created zones for eating and relaxing, and even include an old-fashioned Hills Hoist where it won't be in the way. They're interesting and quirky without being fussy. And a perfect fit for the house I've designed.

"And this is the total cost? All up? Materials, labour, every-thing?"

"It is. I've given you a bit of a break on the price because this will be my first solo job, and I want to use it on my website and socials, if that's okay? Also, Greer said she might be able to sling a bit of work my way from her new firm, so we're all scratching each other's backs."

"Man, I love it. How about I comp a decent photographer for the photos for you? And whatever you've written for the website, I'll take a look at it for you." Josh can't keep the smile off his face.

I love it when a plan comes together. Not only will Josh have a fantastic back yard, I've also found a great landscaper, and Matt will get a stunning website. Win, win, win.

"Any chance you might need some free labour on the weekends and maybe school holidays, Matt?" Josh asks as he watches Ty attempt to swing from the Hills Hoist and nearly take the whole thing down. "I have a teenager who has a bit of a debt to work off."

"Sure. Dave wants me to get this underway quickly. I'll be working the next couple of weekends at least. It'll just be labouring, but I could always do with a hand."

Predictably, Ty has something to say about slave labour, but Josh holds firm and he and Matt come up with a workable schedule. At the hourly rate they agree, it's going to take Ty a good long time to work off his debt, which seems to be Josh's cunning plan. Keep him too busy to get into any more trouble. Which speaks to the kind of man Josh has become. It would've been so easy to throw money at the problem like his father did. Pay the bail and walk away. But he hasn't. He keeps stepping up.

We spend a couple of hours checking out the progress Dave has made, which is not much more than trenches, footings and the odd wall frame at this point, tinkering with Matt's drawings and starting to look at details like flooring, tiles and bathroom fittings. It doesn't escape my notice that not only do Josh and I generally agree, but if there's any doubt, he defers to me. My personality will be stamped all over this house.

· ❤ · ❤ · ❤ · ❤ · ❤ ·

By the time I meet up with Jessie later for a drink and a movie, my euphoria hasn't settled. I fill her in on what's happening with the house, and the landscaping, showing her pictures of the progress and the plans. And maybe I rattle on a bit about how great it will be for parties and kids.

"Hmmm." She looks serious.

"What? What do you mean by *hmmm*?"

"Oh, I love it. It's gorgeous. But do you think maybe *you're* loving it a little too much?"

"What do you mean? I designed it. I'm supposed to love it."

"Of course. And I don't mean to boo on your yay, but it's not your house, Gee. You won't be living there." And it hits me. I am investing. Too much. I'm seeing myself cooking in the gorgeous kitchen, dancing on the deck, sunning by the pool. And not just me. Josh and me. It's like a wet fish to the side of the head.

"Shit bugger bum. You're right." It's all I can do not to burst into tears right there in the cinema. Despite the dark, Jessie can sense how upset I am.

"Oh, Gee. Don't cry. It's natural you'd be excited. It's your first solo project."

"Yeah. It's not just that, though. It's because it's Josh. I keep seeing myself ... with him. You know?" I ferret around in my bag for tissue to sniffle into.

"Yeah, I know. And I know I told you to give him time for his brain to catch up with his dick, but maybe it's time to think about taking a bit of a step back. Protect yourself."

"I don't know if I can, Jess. There's such a mismatch between his words and his actions." Of course, I told Jessie we slept together. And what happened after. No surprise, she was unimpressed. I know she's worried for me. I'm starting to be worried for me.

"You're right. There is. But he's told you in no uncertain terms there's no hope of a romantic relationship. I think you need to start taking him at his word."

She's right. But I don't feel ready to wave the white flag quite yet.

CHAPTER TWENTY-THREE

JOSH

G reer is so excited about the landscaping concepts she and Matt came up with that I can't resist her insistence I come to dinner on Sunday night, even though I'm still trying my hardest to limit contact. It's the only way I can think of to stay sane. Maybe what they used to say about too much jerking off is true—it does send you insane.

I've spent the day with Ty, helping him with some English homework, and dropped him back at school before I head over to the Carters' place. Ty gave me grief over having to work with Matt, but there was no real heat in it. Despite his complaining, I think he's secretly happy someone is giving a crap about what happens to him.

I can hear splashing and laughing as I make my way down the side path, a welcome sound after the early heat we've had this week. The pool comes into view, and the air gets even hotter when Greer rises from the water and stands poised on the sandstone edging, like something out of a 007 movie. Water cascades from her hair, rivulets flowing down her body. The tiny swatch of fabric she's wearing can hardly be called a bikini and gives me a real-time replay of what I was lucky enough to experience once and can never have again.

Any man with a pulse would want to lick every drop of water from her skin. I bite down hard on my bottom lip and try to concentrate on keeping the blood, which is now on a fast simmer, from draining straight out of my head and into the board shorts I wore, knowing we'd probably be swimming.

"Hi Josh," she calls as she saunters towards me. "Are you up for a swim?"

Cursing her choice of words—up is not a word I want to hear right now—I clear my throat. "Sure, why not?"

Stripping off my shirt, I slide out of my thongs and dive into the pool as quickly as possible, hoping nobody has noticed the situation brewing in my board shorts.

"Hey, how about a game of Marco Polo, for old time's sake?" Will suggests. We played it all the time when we were in high school, generally as an excuse to feel up whatever girls happened to be around.

"Aren't we a bit old for that now?" Chasing Greer round the pool seems like a very bad idea.

"Scared you'll get your arse handed to you, old man?" asks Ethan, who has made it to family dinner this week, and is floating around the shallows with Jess, who gives me the stink eye. Great. She knows. Which doesn't surprise me. She and Greer are tight.

I can't let Ethan's challenge go, I'm afraid, so I make a bad decision. "Bring it, kid." Ethan is only a couple of years younger than me and, more often than not, acts older, but I've always teased him about being a kid.

"You're it Greer," calls Will, bombing into the centre of the pool in preparation for battle.

It's a frantic round. Greer is like a mermaid underwater, and it's only strength that saves Will, Ethan and me more than once. Finally, Ethan gets caught, and the game turns rough as he uses strength and speed to try and exhaust us. Nothing can save me when Greer's legs brush my thighs. I'm completely distracted, and Ethan goes in for the kill.

"Marco ..." I call and close my eyes, listening intently to the sounds of water lapping.

"Polo," come the laughing replies from around the pool. It seems like I'm lunging after them for ages as they duck and dive. Finally, I sense movement in the water to my left. With a quick dive, I clamp my hands around a slender thigh.

Even before I open my eyes, I know it's Greer twisting in my grasp. I won't forget the feel of her skin in a hurry. By which I mean ever. Her red hair is floating about her face and shoulders, huge silver bubbles rising from her mouth, her blues eyes laughing at me, even underwater.

Why do I forget to breathe every time I look at her? I really have to get this raging case of lust—and whatever else this is—under control. Fast.

Releasing her leg as if she stung me, I kick to the surface. The way my blood is bubbling, I'm surprised there isn't steam rising off the water.

"That's it for me, I think." I swim to the side and boost myself out.

Greer floats to the surface, and I can feel her eyes on me as I towel off.

"Chicken," she calls quietly. And as our eyes meet across the water, I know she's not referring to the game.

"Yeah, spoilsport," mutters Will, hoisting himself onto a raft and closing his eyes.

Greer presents the landscape drawings before dinner, and predictably there's lots of oohing and aahing. Which is well deserved. When we finally sit down to dinner, conversation turns to work.

"Hey, Josh, tell the fam about the awards you're up for," Will the Bigmouth says during a rare lull in the conversation.

Of course Stella is right onto it. "An award. What is it? Why didn't you tell us?"

"It's nothing really. Just a company thing." I try and wrestle the potato bake away from Will, who has taken more than one man should be able to consume. I don't know where he puts it. He's like a bean-pole.

Will snorts. That's the last time I tell him anything.

"Yeah. *Just a company thing* and you're up for how many awards—three, four?—after only being there four months." It's kind of nice how excited Will is for me, even if it is making me cringe.

"Are you going to make us drag it out of you?" Harry asks.

"Yes, he is. You know what he's like." Ethan jumps into the conversation. All eyes are on me.

"It's a thing the agency does. Every office across the region gets together, and they give out awards for things like Best Campaign, Most Successful Agency and such. This year it's in Sydney."

I'll go along. Reluctantly. I'm not looking forward to it. I have a conflicted relationship with these sorts of nights. They always remind me of the many end-of-year awards ceremonies neither of my parents ever bothered to attend. I can't count how many certificates I have for First in English, Excellence in Creative Writing or Best School Magazine article. All delivered with nobody watching other than Harry and Stella in the later years of high school.

"Best Creative Director, I think. Most Successful New Business Team. And maybe Best Campaign Creative. It's no big deal." I'm aware downplaying it is a trauma response, but I can't seem to help it.

"And how many offices are involved?" Harry asks.

"Eight, I think. Mostly in Asia, two from Australia, one from New Zealand."

"Wow. That's fantastic. You should be so proud. Especially after only having been there such a short time." Harry holds his glass up in an informal toast.

With the whole family watching me, I feel uncharacteristically shy.

"When is it?" Stella reaches across the table and pats my hand, looking as excited as she would be for one of her kids.

I wish I could lie and say I couldn't remember, but I don't think they'd buy it.

"Last Saturday in October."

"And who are you taking as your date?" Will demands.

"No date. Going solo."

They all look at me like I've told them I'm joining Scientology. This family would no more send one of its own out to something like that alone than, well, than join Scientology. Will turns to Greer.

"You busy, Gee? Looks like Josh needs a plus one."

I can't quite catch my breath.

"Greer probably has something on that night already. Don't you, Greer?" says Jessie, with an arctic tone in her voice. Yep. She's definitely not my biggest fan. That's fine. I don't like me much these days either. In fact, my level of annoyance at myself is off the charts.

Greer checks her phone calendar. "As it happens, I'm free." Her expression tells me she knows exactly what she's doing. "What time, Josh?"

I've been snookered. If I say no, they'll all wonder why. And if I say yes, well, we all know where this might go. At least Greer and I do. And, apparently, Jess.

"Honestly, Greer, you don't have to. It's no big deal. Happy to go solo." I make one final attempt at getting out of this, knowing it's doomed to fail.

"Nonsense," Harry chips in. "You need someone there to cheer you on and celebrate the win with you. Take plenty of photos, Gee, won't you?"

Unwittingly, they've managed to give the fox the key to the henhouse.

CHAPTER TWENTY-FOUR

GREER

Josh talked this awards event down at dinner. However, the fact it's being held in the Grand Ballroom at the Park Hyatt, and the invitation says black tie, suggests tonight is no small deal. Meaning I had to shoot out and buy a suitable dress. And shoes. And don't forget the bag. It was lucky I had three weeks to find the right ones. Because between work and managing Josh's build, I've been frantic.

The agency has put all the department heads up in rooms for the night, but Josh has made it clear he's organised a car service to get me home at the end of the night. Right. Sure.

I can tell by the look on his face when he picks me up that I've hit the mark with the dress. It's more revealing than anything I would normally wear. I don't plan on leaving anything to chance tonight. And I don't plan on going home in a car all by myself.

The dress is a lush satin in a dark, rich blue and makes my eyes and hair pop. It clings to every curve down to the floor, and the split up the front shows my leg all the way up every time I take a step. My boobs look sensational cupped in the fitted bodice, which has the thinnest most delicate diamante straps over the shoulders. And the back dips in a low vee, exposing my skin all the way to my waist. I love it.

Josh looks out of this world in a fits-like-a-glove tux that is obviously not off the rack, contrasting perfectly with his messy man bun and three- or four-day growth.

"You look ... spectacular," Josh whispers in a tone you might use to describe a work of art. My heart warms, and my pulse picks up.

I drop a tiny curtsey. "Thank you. And you look very handsome in your tux. I don't think I've ever seen you in a suit." I run my hand down the satiny lapel of his jacket.

"Well, don't blink because this is probably the one and only time it'll happen," he says, effectively defusing the electricity in the air as he takes my arm and leads me down the stairs to the waiting car.

"Who is taking care of Tyrone this weekend if you're here?" I ask as we settle into the back seat.

"He's staying at school this weekend, except for work. Matt picked him up from the ferry this morning and dropped him back after. He grumbled a bit at first, out of habit more than anything else I think. Matt said he's been working really hard, and it sounds like they got on like a house on fire. No dramas. So far, at least."

"That's great. I can see how they'd get on. I'm glad you can relax tonight and not worry about him." Matt has a laid-back and jokey vibe Ty would appreciate.

"Me too."

The ballroom is buzzing when we arrive, packed with hundreds of people all dressed to the nines. Josh is greeted with lots of back slaps and warmth. I'm glad I met a couple of his team members at my flat, so there's at least a couple of familiar faces. Crowds of people I don't know can be challenging for me, but Josh couldn't be more attentive, never leaving my side, and making sure to introduce me to everyone we see. The feel of his hand on the small of my back, his fingers occasionally slipping under the satin of my dress, is comforting and arousing at the same time, and by the time we sit down for dinner, I feel every nerve ending singing.

Dinner is delicious, and the wine is flowing, although I notice Josh alternates a glass of water for every glass of wine he drinks. As soon as the plates are cleared away, the regional managing director, a handsome older guy with silver hair and a much younger wife, gets up onto the small stage.

"And now it's time for the real reason we're here."

Someone from the back calls out, "I'm here for the free alcohol," and everyone laughs.

After a brief speech about how each agency in the region has performed during the year, which included reference to how great it was to get Josh on board as the Sydney creative director, the awards begin. There are more of them than I expected. Innovation in Media, Fastest Business Growth, Best Account Director, the list goes on. Each agency cheers loudly when they win, although the couple of tables from the Sydney office do seem the most raucous. Finally, they get to the creative awards.

"And Best TV Creative goes to ... Parachute, Sydney."

The table erupts around us, everyone laughing and hugging. Josh looks shocked and thrilled, and just like he did at the auction, he turns to me. Framing my face in his hands he kisses me, brief but deep. Then he's being dragged up onto the stage by his team. While they're getting to the stage and jockeying for position, an ad I vaguely remember for a new distillery and restaurant plays on screen. It's beautiful and evocative, and I'm so proud to know Josh had something to do with it.

As the ad rolls to a stop, Josh steps up to the microphone and lifts the beautiful glass trophy high in the air before handing it to one of his team. They pass it round, beaming. Finally, the cheering from the Sydney tables dies down, and Josh leans down to the microphone. I have my phone on video, ready to capture the moment for the family.

"Thank you." He laughs. "This award is very much a team effort. Everyone who worked on the campaign went above and beyond. And I'm incredibly humbled and grateful to be part of such a dedicated and creative team. Thank you." And they're all hugging and laughing and back-slapping all the way back to the table.

My hands are sore from clapping.

"Josh. I'm so proud of you." I'm on my feet, hugging him, and I can barely hold back the tears in my eyes.

"It really was a team effort. I just happen to be the guy with my name on the door," he says, dropping into his chair and taking a big swig of water.

"Hey, boss, don't sell yourself short. We could never have done it without you." One of the guys in the team claps him on the shoulder as he passes on his way to his own chair.

No sooner has everyone subsided back into their seats than they're announcing the next award, Best Creative Director, which is apparently voted by clients and staff. Josh ducks his head with a shy smile when his name is called as one of the three nominees, and the Sydney tables erupt with catcalls and whistles. I slide my hand over his on his lap, squeezing his fingers in anticipation.

Before they even get to the end of his name, I'm on my feet shouting and clapping with the rest of the table, and now crying for real. This time, Josh finds himself on stage all alone.

"Wow. Lightning really does strike twice." He grins as the spotlight hits him. "A creative director is only as good as his team. And I'm lucky enough to have what I consider the best team of writers and art directors working in the business right now. This is for all of you guys. Thanks for all the hard work and support." And with that he's heading back to the table.

It's obvious what a great boss he is in the way he talks about his team and the camaraderie when they're together. I don't think he gives himself enough credit for his management of these guys. Throughout the evening, a couple of them have mentioned what a difference having Josh on board has meant to them and how much they're learning from him. And it strikes me that he still doesn't understand the positive impact he has on others. From his brother to his staff. It's baffling how such a confident guy can be so clueless about his effect on people.

I pull him in close, forehead to forehead, when he sits down. "You are amazing," I whisper as his thumbs come up to wipe my tears away. "I'm so glad I was here to see this."

"Thank you. I'm glad you were here too." And before either of us thinks better of it, he's kissing me again. Short and sweet and tender.

There are a few more awards before the big one—the advertising agency equivalent of Best Motion Picture, I guess—Agency of the Year. And it doesn't surprise me at all when I hear "Parachute, Sydney."

Once again, Josh is getting up on stage, this time with the other department heads and the MD, whose speech is nothing more than an ear-piercing *Woo-hoo*.

Dessert is served as we all admire the three trophies in the middle of the table. I spare a minute to send the videos and pictures I've taken to the family group chat, which predictably goes off like a frog in a sock. I mute my phone and put it away so I can enjoy the rest of the night because the band has finally started up.

By now, everyone is well-lubricated, and whilst Josh and I aren't drunk, we are pretty relaxed.

The managing director comes over and asks me to dance and I laugh at the disgruntled look on Josh's face.

"How long have you and Josh been together?" he asks as we sway to a slow dance.

I know I should tell him we're not, but in my heart of hearts, I believe we are, in a strange and unconventional kind of way at least. In the end, I give him a non-answer.

"Oh, we've known each other since we were kids."

"Well, he's a very lucky man."

"Thank you. I'm the lucky one, though. And your agency is very lucky to have him. Make sure you look after him," I counter with a grin.

When the song ends, he drops me back at the table, where Josh is chatting with Fiona, although I didn't miss that he kept an eye on the dance floor while I was out there.

"This one's a keeper, Josh. If your talent doesn't get you to the top, her attitude will."

Josh quirks an eyebrow at me before excusing himself from Fiona and leading me back onto the floor.

"What was that about?"

"Oh, nothing. We were just chatting about you." I try for an innocent look, which makes Josh laugh.

"Yeah. Right."

The beat picks up, and before long, we're surrounded on the dance floor, which turns into a mass group dance and has us spinning away from each other. It seems like hours before the music slows down again and Josh is in front of me, taking me in his arms.

If this was a regency romance, people would be clutching their pearls and fanning themselves at how close he's holding me. I might need a fan myself. Because as much as Josh protests we can never be anything more than friends, what's pressed against my belly, the emotions I see in his eyes, the possessiveness of his touch, all tell me otherwise.

CHAPTER TWENTY-FIVE

JOSH

I didn't want Greer to come to this awards night. But fuck, I'm glad she did. It's unbelievable how much having someone in your corner makes the wins so much sweeter. And she gets on with my team like they've known each other for years. Not to mention whatever she said to impress my boss.

Even Will hasn't been there for me the way Greer is. The way she keeps on showing up for me, no matter how hard I try and push her away? It's seductive and terrifying at the same time. And tonight, I don't know if I have the strength to resist.

Which makes it all the more painful to know it's going nowhere. Except while I'm dancing with her, it doesn't feel like it's going nowhere. It feels like the most natural thing in the world to have her in my arms and to know there's a king-sized bed upstairs waiting for us to test it for comfort. Or strength.

I know she can feel my hard-on pressing against her stomach. I can see the pulse beating at the side of her neck. She presses closer. And I'm desperate enough, enchanted enough, to let her. And to tell her at least a little of how I'm feeling.

"Thanks for coming tonight, Greer. It meant a lot to me." I lean back and look into her eyes, trying to convey my sincerity. "I don't think I realised how much until now."

"I'm really glad I was here. And not only to see you win. To see you with your team. The way you are with them. You know they idolise you, don't you?" Her lips brush my ear, causing a shiver to run down my spine.

"That's the booze and the adrenaline talking." Everyone is pretty drunk, and deservedly so. We took out three top awards tonight in the creative department alone. Not a bad haul if I do say so myself.

"It's not, you know. And you don't have to be so modest. You're very impressive."

"You'd rather I brag?" I tease. Right now, the awards, what my staff think about me, or my boss's opinions, are not what I'd like to brag about.

"Is it bragging if it's true?" she asks, and I don't miss the invitation in her tone.

"What's true is that right now I want nothing more than to take you upstairs and prove to you how impressive I am." I throw her words back at her. I know I should bite my tongue off rather than say things like that, but I can't help myself. My emotions are all right on the surface. I wish I could say more. Tell her how she makes me feel. The way she makes me feel seen. And worthy. The way she makes me want to be more than I am. But it wouldn't be fair to either of us.

"Oh, I can feel how *impressive* you are." Her smile is wicked as her hand strays down my back to my arse, pressing me closer still. Her pupils have swallowed almost all the blue in her eyes, and the pink in her cheeks owes nothing to the dancing.

"That's just the tip of the iceberg." And I mean it. Because as hard as my cock is, my fingers and mouth are itching to prove themselves just as impressive.

"What are we waiting for, then?" She pulls out of my arms, trailing her fingers down from my shoulder to take my hand in hers and leading me off the dance floor. With her spare hand, she swipes up her tiny purse, tucks it under her arm and hands me the Best Creative Director award.

We're out the door and into the lift without a word to anyone. No sooner do the doors close than she's palming my cock through my trousers, her eyes fixed on mine.

"Fuuuck," I groan. It's not beyond the realms of possibility that I could come right here, right now. Especially when she lowers the zip and slips her hand inside. I drop my head back against the wall, but it's all over too soon. The lift dings, and we're on my floor. I'm right at the end of the corridor, though the long walk with an open zip and hard-on does nothing to calm my raging arousal. Fortunately, Greer doesn't touch me again until the door to my room is whooshing closed behind us; otherwise, I don't think we'd make it inside at all.

We leave the lights off. There's enough ambient light coming into the room from the harbour lights outside.

Her hand is inside my trousers again as I back her up against the wall. Her other hand reaches behind for the zipper on her dress.

"Leave it. I want to fuck you in this incredible dress first." And I'm leading her into the room, over to the window with a spectacular view of Sydney Harbour. Spinning her around, I place her hands in front of her on the glass and press down on her back so she's bent over with the window for support. I want to fuck her from behind, and this way, I can see her reflection in the glass too. Best of both worlds.

Before she has time to react, I'm on my knees behind her, flipping the long skirt of her dress up over her back and admiring the bare, creamy cheeks of her arse, bisected by a sheer black lace thong. I slide the lace off her legs and lift one foot, then the other, tossing the thong aside, before nudging her feet apart and running my hands up her calves to stroke the back of her knees, the inside of her thighs. Those luscious lips are already engorged and wet, glistening in the low light, and I can smell her arousal. I bury my nose in that beautiful cleft, taking a deep breath before parting her lips with gentle fingers, holding her open for my eyes and my nose and my mouth.

Greer shudders and gasps at the first touch of my tongue, flat against her opening as I lap up some of that wetness before I slide my thumb across her swollen clit.

"Oh, God, Josh," she moans, pushing back against my face. "That feels ... argh."

I interpret her groan as approval. While holding her still with my mouth and thumb I pull my wallet out with the other hand, grab a condom and drop it on the floor beside my knees, ready for when I need it. And then my fingers are sliding up her leg, slipping inside her dripping entrance, curving up to hit that magic spot.

My cock has worked its way out of my open trousers and is already leaking pre-cum, creating a spreading wet patch on my boxer briefs.

It only takes another couple of seconds and I feel Greer's already taut thighs tighten and quiver. Her opening grips my fingers, and unintelligible sounds fall from her mouth.

I'm on my feet, cock out, sheathed and notching against her entrance before the quaking of her orgasm starts to recede. And then I'm inside her, feeling the aftershocks of her release fluttering against my shaft.

I pause, taking in the reflection of her face in the window. Hair wild, cheeks pink, eyes glassy. I've never seen anything more beautiful. I start a slow rhythm as our eyes meet in the glass, unlocking a surreal connection much more powerful than our physical one.

"I need to fuck you hard, Greer. Okay with you?" I gasp as my thrusts build pace and force.

"God, yes," is all she can manage. And then I'm pounding hard, holding her hips steady with one hand, plucking at her clit with the other. Watching the emotions thundering across her face in the window glass as her orgasm approaches.

A strangled sound, somewhere between a grunt and a snort, bursts from her lips and she's coming again, clamping on my cock like a vise. I'm so sensitive that the extra pressure is too much and I follow her over the edge, pumping through my orgasm. Feeling like I'm draining my life force into the condom.

We're both still fully clothed. Our reflected gazes meet. And we start to laugh.

"That's what I call a celebration," Greer gasps, trying to catch her breath between laughs.

"That's what *I* call round one," I reply. It may have taken the edge off, but there's plenty more where that came from, and tonight she's going to get it all. I can't tell her how I feel, but I can make her feel better than she ever has before.

CHAPTER TWENTY-SIX

GREER

After shedding our clothes, Josh leads me into the shower and we spend some time wasting water before falling into the cloudlike king-size bed for round three. Which turns into round four before we fall asleep in a tangled heap like a pair of kittens.

I'm dead to the world the next morning when Josh wakes me with room service breakfast. I'm sore all over, not that I'm complaining, and Josh gives me a massage, which turns into a happy ending for both of us. I could seriously get used to this.

"Looks like I'm doing the walk of shame today. I sure hope I don't run into your boss on my way out," I say as I pick my hideously expensive dress up from the crumpled heap on the floor where we left it.

Josh knew he was staying here last night, and he got ready for the dinner in the room, so he has an overnight bag with a change of clothes. I'm not so lucky.

"No, I'll sort something out. Wait here." Josh throws on a t-shirt and jeans and heads out the door.

Wrapped in a robe, I lie back on the chaos of the bed and think about the incredible night we had. About the sex, which was out of this world. And about the awards night. The way Josh is with his staff. The respect he has from them and his boss. He's come a long way from the boy who got Will into trouble on the regular. If only I could get him to see himself as I see him. To see the possibilities of us.

Josh is back in no time with a bag from the expensive designer shop across the road from the hotel. He's picked me up a cute, strappy little sundress and a pair of canvas espadrilles. The cut of the dress means I don't need to worry about a bra, and while I don't make a habit of wearing last night's knickers, I can't bring myself to regret the necessity.

I'm glad about the dress because we do see Josh's boss as we're checking out. He's looking pretty ragged, and his wife is nowhere to be seen.

"Have a good night, you two?" he asks, noting the award stowed under Josh's arm. I have no idea where the other two got to, but I'm sure someone has them safe.

"Great night. Might need a nanna nap this afternoon, I think," I suggest, even though I'm feeling fine if I'm honest.

"You won't be the only one."

We all laugh and go our separate ways. Josh is about to call an Uber when I suggest we take advantage of the beautiful day and go for a walk along the Circular Quay waterfront.

He leaves the award and his overnight bag, now also stuffed with my dress and shoes, with the concierge, and we wander towards the harbour.

The sky is cloudless, so we buy some sunhats and sunblock, which Josh rubs into the skin of my shoulders and arms exposed by my new favourite sundress. There's enough breeze to take the bite out of the late spring sun as we walk along, dodging tourists and enjoying the sparkling water of the harbour.

I don't know what last night meant to Josh. We explored our profound physical connection but haven't talked at all about what might come next. For me, it's more proof our being together is inevitable.

I don't want to ruin the beautiful day and the morning-after glow I've got going on by bringing it up, so we chat about the awards, his plans for restructuring the agency, and how I'm settling in at my new job, bullies and all.

Eventually, we move on to the house and how things are going there. I couldn't be happier with the progress Dave and Matt have made, and it seems Josh is also impressed with them. And with me, my ideas and the way I'm managing the build so far.

As we wander, Ty blows up Josh's phone with pictures of him with Matt and his team digging holes and horsing around, which makes us laugh. It's good to see Ty dropping the angry young man persona and acting more like a happy teen. And good to see Josh beam with pride when he sees the pictures. We snap a selfie with the harbour and Opera House in the background and send it to him. When Ty returns a string of emojis, including eggplants, peaches and fire, Josh scowls, although there's no real heat in it. It's clear Josh has fallen in love with his brother. And vice versa.

Before we know it, it's early afternoon, and my tummy is starting to rumble. Rather than sit in a café, we grab a couple of wraps and some fresh-squeezed juice and sit on the grass in the park under the Harbour Bridge. The shade is a nice respite from the sun, and the echo of the traffic on the bridge above provides a relaxing white-noise effect that's soothing after the clamour of the tourists.

It's time to bring up what's going on.

"We seem to have crossed the line. Again," I say, lying back and closing my eyes. Josh lies down beside me.

"Yeah. Seems like it." He lets out a sad-sounding sigh.

"I know you think my family would be upset if they knew, but you might be wrong about that."

It takes him so long to answer I turn to face him, propping myself up on my elbow, thinking he might've drifted off to sleep. He turns too so we're mirror images of each other.

"It's more than that, Greer. I've done some pretty shady shit in my day. Honestly, if you knew half of what I've done, you wouldn't want anything to do with me."

"If you mean about getting Will into trouble, I know about the stuff you got up to."

He laughs without a hint of humour. "Not all of it, you don't."

What Josh doesn't realise is that when he and Will were teenagers, I was often around to hear things I probably shouldn't have. And once I started hearing things, I made it my business to listen when I thought things might be going sideways.

"Let's see. I know about the time you took him to the sex shop."

He grins despite himself. "Everyone knows about that."

"I know about the girl you thought you got pregnant."

His expression drops faster than a hot pie at the football. "What?"

"I know she told you she was pregnant. I know you told her you'd stand by her decision, whatever it was, and I know in the end it was a false alarm."

"Shit. How did you find out about all that?"

"Mum and Dad were so worked up about lecturing Will that they didn't notice me sitting in the corner. I can be very still and quiet when I want to be."

"Well, that's not even the half of it—" he's goes to continue, but I cut him off.

"And I know that more than once you took the blame for things that were Will's idea because you didn't want him getting into trouble and ruining his chances at a law career. Like when it was his idea to hot wire the headmaster's car and go for a joy ride. Or the time—"

It's Josh's turn to interrupt me. "Yeah, okay. I get it. You know more than you should. And even if some of it was Will's idea, I was still there, a willing participant, not an innocent bystander. Taking the fall was the least I could do for Will and your parents. The point is, even if you could overlook it, why would your parents let a guy like me anywhere near their princess?"

"Right. Why *would* they want to see me with a man who stood by their son through thick and thin? Who stepped up when his brother needed him. Who has a brilliant career ahead of him?"

Josh snorts. "You're missing the point. I'm not long-term relationship material. You only have to look at my parents to see that."

I know he thinks he's making a valid point, but in my opinion, it's misguided.

"I agree; your parents didn't give you much to work with. But you're not them. As you've proved over and over again. So you know what? Stop selling yourself short." I'm starting to get frustrated, and I can feel burning behind my eyes. The last thing I want to do is dissolve into tears.

Josh sits up, balancing his forearms on his bent knees. He's quiet again, teeth gnawing on his bottom lip.

"Greer, I don't want long-term. I never have. But if there was anyone I could imagine wanting to spend the rest of my life with, it would be you." He glances sideways at me, eyes awash with guilt. "But it's not on the cards for me. And I won't be changing my mind, so don't be waiting around on me."

My heart leaps, then crashes back to earth. He may have said he didn't want me to wait on him. What I heard was, I'm the one. The problem for him is, maybe I've waited long enough.

CHAPTER TWENTY-SEVEN

JOSH

Walking into the office on Monday morning is a bit like walking through a guard of honour. No sooner have I stepped out of the lift than there are people surrounding me, lining up to slap my back, congratulate me and plan celebrations. I had no idea this was such a big deal, and I welcome the distraction from my convoluted thoughts.

On the one hand, I'm feeling blissed out from my time with Greer. From the sex, which has been in short supply since I arrived back in Sydney, but also from spending time together. The walk around the harbour, sitting on the grass and eating lunch. It was fantastic. Until it wasn't. Until I opened my big mouth and told her how I felt. Pretty sure that's going to come back and bite me on the arse.

Which brings me to the other point. I'm beginning to understand the phrase 'suffocating guilt'. It's an unfamiliar feeling. Now I feel guilt around every significant person in my life. Guilt that I'm lying—even if it is only by omission—to Will. Guilt that I'm betraying the trust of Harry and Stella. Guilt that I'm somehow not doing enough for my brother. But most of all, guilt that I can't be what Greer wants me to be. Needs me to be.

Which is the worst of all. Because wrapped up in that guilt is regret and a bone-deep melancholy. Huh. There's another phrase I now understand. 'This is hurting me more than it's hurting you'. Because it is. Well, at least as much. Because what I've finally got through my thick skull is that a life with Greer would probably make me happy. And in a life full of sad shit, that's just about the saddest thing to ever happen to me.

I wish I could talk to someone about this. Unfortunately, all the 'someones' I have are related to Greer.

When I finally make it to my office, I gather up my notes and laptop and head to the conference room for our Monday morning Work in Progress meeting. Which turns into more of a Celebration in Progress, with pastries and champagne. Hey, this is advertising. Day drinking is still a thing. Although, even in advertising nine am on a Monday is a bit extreme.

After the meeting, I have a smaller team briefing in my office to make sure we're all up to speed on what's going on. If we're going to replicate our success at next year's awards—and if I have anything to do with it, we are—we can't afford to drop the ball. By the time my office is clearing out, it's nearly eleven, and I'm looking forward to an hour of peace before my boss and I take a client to lunch. No rest for the wicked.

I get back from my client lunch to find our department co-ordinator has added a late meeting to my schedule, with no client details, so I have no idea what it's about. I groan. Five o'clock meetings are never a good sign.

I'm sitting in the conference room waiting for my mystery meeting when I hear a booming voice I wasn't expecting.

"Josh, my man," shouts an enormous man in an electric blue suit and Daffy Duck tie.

"Dude." I'm up and out of my chair, grabbing him by the side of the head and bumping foreheads with my old friend Rob. "What the hell are you doing here?"

"Job interview, man. They're looking for a creative director in your Singapore office. The MD is in Sydney for a few days and suggested we meet here. Two birds, man."

Rob is an art director, and we were a team at my London agency. He's incredibly talented, and a great guy. If we had a job for him here, I would employ him in a heartbeat.

"How long are you staying?"

He laughs. "Just three nights, unfortunately. But imagine the trouble we can get into in seventy-two hours. I got the interview over with this morning, so I'm all yours. Jetlag and all."

Rob has never been to Sydney before, so I do the right thing and take him to the Opera Bar, where we can sit and drink in the beauty of Sydney Harbour at night, along with our craft beers. I give Will a call, and he turns up with Ethan and Jessie in tow. Predictably, it's not long before Greer appears too, invited by Jessie, and looking mouth-watering in a sixties-inspired burnt orange and hot pink shift dress and sky-high heels.

I don't fail to notice the way Rob's eyes nearly pop out of his head as he spots her or the way he makes enough room for her to squeeze in tight next to him at the table. He wastes no time flirting up a storm while I can barely even look at her, let alone speak to her. Because when her gaze connects with mine, it's like a lightning strike to my heart. I have to look away before I do something stupid, like launch myself across the table and ravish her in full view of everyone at the bar, not to mention her brothers.

By the time we leave the bar, or more accurately, by the time we're asked to leave the bar well after official closing time, everyone is well oiled. I'm happy Rob's had a good time, but not so happy he's gotten on so well with Greer.

I've never been the jealous type before. Greer has changed all that. Tonight my blood was running pure green. Rob's a good-looking, charming and charismatic guy. I wouldn't blame Greer for being interested. And there's not a damn thing I can—or should—do about it.

Most of the crew head home, except for Rob and me, who settle in at the bar in his hotel to finish off the night.

"Want to tell me what that was all about?" he asks as the server deposits a bottle of scotch and two glasses on the table.

"What was what all about?"

Rob laughs, handing me a nearly half-full tumbler.

"You know what. Those filthy looks you were shooting my way all night. And the way you avoided talking to Greer. In fact, you barely even looked at her. And she's a fine sight. Spill."

Looks like Rob's neither as drunk nor as clueless as I supposed. And maybe that's a good thing. Because right now, I really need a sympathetic ear and a solid moral compass.

I sigh. "I'm up shit creek, man. Not a paddle in sight."

"Yeah, I spotted that much. So, let me guess. You've got the hots for Greer—and who could blame you, she's smokin'. But she's your best friend's little sister. That about sum it up?"

"It scratches the surface, yeah. Thing is, she feels the same. And I haven't quite been able to keep my hands to myself."

"Oh. Right. Well, I definitely picked up on the vibe she was interested. And how much have you had your hands on her?"

"All the way. More than once. But it can't happen, man."

"Because of the brothers?"

"Yeah. But also because she's a long-term kind of girl. And that's not for me, you know?"

"I heard that loud and clear when you broke off with, what was her name? Rebecca? In London." He tops off my glass, which is mysteriously empty, even though I don't remember drinking it. "She was as close as I've ever known you to get to an actual girlfriend."

"And look how well that ended." I stare off out the window and think about my relationship—maybe *situationship* is a more accurate descriptor—with Rebecca, which ended badly to say the least, a little over two years ago. Looking back, it was probably what started me thinking about leaving London and coming home.

We'd been seeing each other for a couple of months when she wanted to have the where-is-this-going talk. I'm ashamed to say I panicked. I never meant for things to get as far as they did. We kind of drifted into it. And for me, even though she was a great woman and far too good for me, we were going nowhere. I had no desire to pin myself down to an exclusive arrangement. She didn't take it well.

As she gathered up the few things she had left lying around my flat, tears running down her face, I watched on. Feeling bad for her, yet not a skerrick of regret for the ending of the relationship. Before she slammed the door for the last time she turned.

"You know what? You have so much potential. But you're emotionally constipated, she shouted, hitting me with a full-throttle glare. "You're thirty years old and one day you're going to have to grow up and have a proper adult life. I'm not wasting any more of my time on a man-child. I deserve better." And then she was gone.

I hate knowing I hurt her. She did deserve better.

Rob swirls the scotch in his glass. "Yeah, it was a shitshow and no mistake."

"Which proves my point. I'm not boyfriend material for anyone. Much less husband material. Especially not a woman like

Greer. And if I broke her heart, my best friend in the world would never forgive me."

He takes a moment to respond, sipping his scotch and watching me with serious eyes.

"You sure forever is not for you?"

"Absolutely. I lived through the way my father broke my mother. I can't do that to another human being. And I'm too much like him to risk it. Forever is not in my DNA."

"Man, I saw the way you looked at each other. I wish I could tell you differently. But you've given me two good reasons to keep your distance. Because if you don't, everyone is going to get hurt. Including you."

And that's the bottom line.

This conversation has not made me feel any better. All it did was confirm what I already knew. There's no way Greer and I can ever be ... anything. And Greer? She deserves everything.

Why is it the only woman I've ever felt something real for is the only woman on the planet I can't have? Up until recently, a life on my own didn't seem so bad. Now I know what it feels like to have someone wholly on your side, supporting and believing in you, I can see how shallow and empty my life has been.

Two years down the track, Rebecca's words are coming back to haunt me. She was right. She was a nice girl. Smart. Funny. Pretty. But I felt nothing more than mild affection for her. I wish I could say the same now. Because what I'm feeling for Greer is something I've never felt before. I can't see an end to it. And it's threatening to overwhelm me.

CHAPTER TWENTY-EIGHT

GREER

On Tuesday morning, I arrive at work with a sore head. It was a late night out with Josh and his friend Rob. I had a lot of fun. Rob is a terrible flirt and it was nice to feel his charm turned on me, even if we both knew it was nothing more than a bit of a laugh. Josh barely spoke to me all night, which stung a little. But occasionally, I would catch him looking at me in a way that went straight to my knickers, which almost made up for it.

The mixed messages I'm getting from Josh are giving me whiplash. On the weekend it was all hot—so, so hot—and heavy. By Monday, we were back to arm's length.

Jessie calls midmorning while I'm trying to dial down my hangover with a second dose of Berocca.

"What the hell was that last night?" she starts, without even a hello.

I don't bother to play dumb. I don't have the energy.

"Hello to you too. Shouldn't you be in class enriching the minds of the leaders of the future?"

"The little heathens are at sport right now. Thank God. My head is pounding."

"Mine too. Please don't get all up in my face about Josh. I don't have the strength today," I moan, taking a tentative sip of the fizzy orange liquid. I don't need it making another appearance here in the office kitchen.

Jess sighs.

"Alright. All I will say is you need to take him at his word, Greer. He's told you how it's gonna be. Start believing it. Before you get hurt any more than you already are." And without another word, she hangs up.

I know she's pissed at me. And part of me thinks she's right. But she hasn't seen the sides of Josh I have.

Luckily, I'm flat out busy at work these days. I hardly have time to think about Josh and his insistence we're going nowhere. Well, not more than once or twice an hour at least.

Between getting up to speed on all the projects I've been handed, dealing with the snide remarks of Mean One to Three, and keeping an eye on things with Dave and Matt, I hardly have time to scratch myself.

Josh and I communicate about the house via text and email, which is weirdly comforting and painful at the same time. On the positive side, things are steaming ahead with the build. Matt seems to have inherited Dave's ability to pull off miracles, and I couldn't be happier with the progress.

I know Josh is moving in with Will on Saturday. They're having a welcome party. I consider not going, but the last thing I need right now is an interrogation on my whereabouts from a high-powered lawyer. Even if he is my oldest brother.

Late Friday night, I get the call I've been expecting for months. Maybe years.

"Gee, we're getting married," Jessie squeals down the phone line at me. I can hear Ethan laughing in the background.

"Tone it down, Jess, you'll pierce her eardrums."

I can hardly talk through my tears as I congratulate them, and Jessie and I start to talk about wedding details. Like all that hasn't been nutted out ages ago. Jess sends me a picture of the ring, which Ethan chose himself and I have to laugh. It's gorgeous and very practical. Bezel set and quite flat. So Jessie can wear it at school without worrying about it catching on anything. Typical Ethan.

"Okay, first things first. What about an engagement party?"

I agree to meet with Jessie and both our mothers tomorrow to start the planning and then hang up so they can call anyone else they need to tell.

I'm thrilled for Jess. I'm thrilled for me. Because, at last, I'll officially have the sister I've always wanted.

That said, I'd be lying if I didn't admit my heart feels tender to the touch. I'm trying to stay positive about Josh and believe he'll eventually come around to my way of thinking, but every day that goes by chips at my conviction.

The trouble is, I can't seem to let go. And since I've had a taste of what things can be like with Josh, physically at least, I don't think I could ever go back to something less ...well, less. It would be like switching to vegan cheese when you've had the best, creamiest, yummiest French brie.

Josh is right when he says I'm the white picket fence type. I totally am. And the babies. I want the babies. Although not for a few years yet. Which leaves me needing to rethink my position. Do I take him at his word or follow my instincts, which tell me not to give up hope? Not yet. Because I won't settle for second best. Maybe in the future I'll feel different. Right now, though, I can't imagine being with anyone else.

But Jessie is my best friend, and she deserves the best of me. So, I put those feelings in a box and close the lid, preparing to be the best sister and maid of honour a girl could ask for. And one day soon, I hope, the best auntie any kids could want.

CHAPTER TWENTY-NINE

JOSH

By the time I move into Will's apartment, not only is Dave well into construction, the shipping-container pool already sits pride of place in the back-yard, partially installed. These guys move like lightning.

Almost everything I own is still in storage—including the bed and painting I bought in the Blue Mountains—so it's just me, my clothes, and a few books to move, which I get done in one trip.

Will lives at Neutral Bay in a flashy new apartment with views of the harbour. I'm looking forward to spending more time with my best friend. And we'll be kicking it off in style with a party on my first night. The only cloud in my sunny sky is that Greer will be at the party.

We haven't seen each other since our night out with Rob when he confirmed my worst fears. Well, that's not entirely true. I've seen her. In my imagination. Every night. Whenever I close my eyes. Whenever I smell cinnamon. The list goes on. The texts and emails we've been exchanging about the house have been friendly with a side of caution. It will be tough to see her tonight and not fall on her, drag her to my room, and beg her to never leave.

By ten o'clock, the music is pumping and the apartment is packed with old friends as well as the new ones I've made at the office. I decided to invite my whole department, plus a couple of the account handlers I get on well with, and everyone seems to be having a great time. But no sign of Greer. Which is a good thing. It is. Except every time the front door opens, I look up to check who it is. And every time it's not her, my heart drops. Which is ridiculous.

Will wraps an arm around my neck and shoves a fresh beer into my hand.

"What's up, Josh? Why so glum?"

"I'm not glum. Maybe a bit tired after moving today." Which is a ridiculous thing to say. The move took one trip in my car.

"Yeah, nah. We'll be having none of that." He swipes the beer out of my hand and propels me towards the makeshift bar against the wall. "What you need is a bit of ..." He scans the dozens of bottles on the table until his eyes light up. "This," he says as he triumphantly lifts a bottle of Crystal Skull before splashing it into two shot glasses.

"Bottoms up." He's knocked back his shot before I even get mine to my lips.

He's right. I need to get my head back in the game. So, I follow Will's lead. Twice.

And that's when she walks through the door with Ethan's new fiancé. And the vodka goes down the wrong way. Because my throat closes up.

She's in red again. Redheads shouldn't wear red. It shouldn't work. But she does. And it does. And tonight it's like every light in the room swivels and shines only on her.

"Choke on your tongue, Josh?"

Greer's smile is almost predatory. Being the prey is an unusual position for me. After a couple of heavy thumps on the back from Will, I manage to get myself under control.

"Shot went down the wrong way," I gasp-croak.

"Mmmhmm."

Yeah. Mmmhmm alright. Her dress ought to be illegal. Like the black dress she was wearing at the club that night, it's not skimpy or short. Somehow, even with a hem almost at her knees and a neckline skimming the pulse at the base of her throat, I've never seen anything so sexy.

Will shoves the forgotten beer back in my hand, and I take a long pull on it, buying time. Because I'm doing the Pavlov's Dogs thing. And it's not just the drooling.

Will disappears without a word, and I finally manage to remember my manners.

"Would you like a drink?"

"Sure. Have you got any pinot grigio?"

I fish an unopened bottle from the ice bucket on the table and pour Greer a generous glass as Will returns, dragging a tall blonde by the hand. I know he's been worried about my lack of female companionship, and if he knew the reasons, he'd probably throw me over the balcony. He's already tried to set me up with a couple of women tonight, and I've managed to lose both of them.

"Josh, this is Lexi. Lexi, Josh. Lexi is an influencer. And she wants to dance. Come on Gee, let's give these two some space." And Will spirits Greer away, out onto the balcony. Leaving me alone. With Lexi. The influencer.

An hour later, I'm beginning to think limpet mine might be a better description than influencer. Nothing I do to shake her seems to work. Meanwhile, Greer is laughing and dancing and chatting with a long line of guys who clearly haven't heard of personal space. Including one of the account handlers from my office who she met at the awards night. At least none of the creative team have gone near her other than for a quick chat. I'd hate to have to fire someone.

It occurs to me I might be overreacting. A little. Maybe a lot. But several shots and a couple of beers in and any tenuous hold

I had on my thoughts is long gone. I can only hope they remain thoughts and don't become words.

"I'm going to the bathroom. Want to join me?" Lexi asks, running her hand down my chest to rest on my belt, her intention obvious.

"Nah. You go ahead." Maybe once she's in the bathroom, I can find somewhere to hide. Luckily, I spot Sean and Fiona and the rest of the crew gathered at one end of the balcony, where the lights are nice and dim.

"Hey guys. Having a good time?" I sidle around the group till I'm in the darkest corner, hoping I'm hidden.

"Yeah. Great party. What a view, man," says Brad, one of the art directors, gazing out over the harbour.

"What's the go with the blonde?" Sean gets straight to the point. He's really taken a liking to Greer and seems to be keeping an eye on me. Not sure how to feel about that.

"Nothing's the go with the blonde." My words come out defensive.

"Right. Gotcha." Fiona's voice is soaked in a nice combination of disapproval and disappointment. Apparently, the Greer effect hasn't only worked on the guys.

The sound of Greer's laugh has us all turning at the same time. Fuck, she's beautiful. Even her belly laugh is sexy. I can't take my eyes off her. Which is a problem for a whole lot of reasons. Not least because I don't see Lexi approaching until it's too late, and she's sliding both arms around my waist and pressing her sticky, glossed-up lips against my ear. Which is when Greer turns. Even in the dim light, I can see the surprise and hurt ripple over her face.

"So, Josh, I was thinking maybe we could get out of here? Go back to your place?" Lexi is rubbing her almost bare body against me. Not sure what part of 'moving in party' she didn't get.

"I live here. Remember?" I've told her this more than once. To say she has the brain of a goldfish would be insulting to goldfish. There was a time in my life when it wouldn't have mattered to me. And it isn't lost on me when, exactly, it started to change.

"Oh. Okay. Well, we could go to mine then." She beams like this is the best idea ever.

"Yeah, thanks, but no thanks." Predictably, she pouts her unnaturally full lips. I'm aware I'm being borderline rude, but all I can think about is the look on Greer's face. I push Lexi away and look around for Greer. There's no sign of her.

In a move guaranteed to double his Christmas bonus, Sean takes Lexi's arm and leads her over the balcony railing. "I hear you're an influencer ..." he starts as I make my escape.

"Where's Greer?" I ask when I finally find Will in the crowd.

I must look a little frantic, and maybe Will isn't as drunk as I thought because he gives me a look I can't quite interpret, but I decide to ignore it. I have bigger problems than puzzling out my friend's moods.

"Ahh, dunno. She might have gone home? I think she said something about a headache. But she seemed alright. Maybe she's gone to hook up with that guy she was with the other week?"

I know for a fact that isn't the case because *that* guy is still standing right here. Feeling more like a piece of shit than he ever has in his life. Which is saying something.

CHAPTER THIRTY

GREER

It's time to raise the white flag.

Jessie is the best not-quite sister a girl could have. I didn't even have to say anything. She took one look at my face and got me out of there. Thank God Ethan's away at a conference.

It's about a half-hour walk from Will's place to mine. We could've grabbed an Uber, but I needed to move, and Jessie let me storm along without a word, waiting for me to be ready to talk.

It took till we were in my living room in our pyjamas before I let fly. And by let fly, I mean break down in great heaving sobs alternated with angry ranting.

Like magic, a box of tissues, a block of chocolate and a bottle of red wine appear on the coffee table in front of me, and Jessie cuddles me until the bawling slows to a drizzle.

"How could he? Right in front of me." It's a good thing Jessie speaks fluent Greer because I'm pretty sure the average person wouldn't have been able to make out what I said, between the blocked nose and the hiccupping sobs.

"What did he do? I hardly saw him all night."

"He was .... He was flirting. With a girl."

"What a rat bastard. Who?"

"I don't know. I don't know her. Will said her name was Lexi."

"Was it just flirting? Or did they hook up?"

"I don't know. I couldn't stay and watch. She was all over him. He's probably having hot animal sex with her right now." I take a messy slurp of wine and snap off a whole row of chocolate squares.

"I've said it before. I'll say it again, Gee. It's past time you called it with him." Not only is Jessie Team Greer, but she knows when it's time for some tough love.

"I know. You're right." I'm about to stuff another chunk of chocolate in my mouth when my handbag lets out a loud chirp. Jessie and I lock eyes.

"Don't look." She holds up her hand, palm out. But I can't help myself. I'm like an addict. I lunge for my bag. Hoping it's him, while knowing it won't be.

I'm wrong. It's him.

Josh: Nothing happened. I promise. Please let me explain.

At least he noticed I left the party. I should ignore it, but I can't.

Me: Whatever. It's none of my business what you do

Josh: I would never do that to you

Me: Do what?

Like I don't know what.

Josh: Hook up with someone right in front of you. After everything, you know

Me: You don't owe me anything. You can do what you want

Josh: I wish I could. But I can't

Me: Can't what?

Josh: Do what I want. Or who I want

Me: What does that even mean?

Josh: You know what it means. It's not that I don't want you. But I can't

Jessie, who is reading over my shoulder, snorts.

"I'm calling bullshit here, Gee. Don't let him keep stringing you along like this."

"He thinks he's doing the right thing."

"How is it right to tell you no, then have sex with you, multiple times, then tell you no again? And now tell you he wants to, but he can't?"

"It's complicated."

That gets another snort. "It's really not. All he has to do is tell your parents, and Will, he has feelings for you. Pretty simple." My phone beeps again.

Josh: Greer?

Me: I don't know what you want me to say Josh.

Josh: Tell me you believe me. I would never hurt you like that

Me: I believe you about Lexi. It's the rest I'm not buying.

Jessie grabs my phone, jumps up off the couch and starts typing.

(Jessie): I'm tired. I'm turning my phone off. I don't want to talk about it any more

Jessie puts my phone on aeroplane mode and drops it onto the kitchen bench.

"Gee, he needs to grow up, grow a pair and work out what he wants. And until he does, he doesn't deserve a nanosecond more of your time."

I let out a long sigh. I know she's right. But I think I'm right too. For him, it is complicated. And for me, having to work with him over the next couple of months, it's going to be really painful.

"You're right. I don't want to think about it anymore. Let's watch *The Notebook* and finish this wine. I think I have ice-cream in the fridge."

It's late by the time we've finished all the chocolate, ice-cream, wine and the movie. Jessie is asleep on the sofa, so I tuck a rug around her and head to bed for hours of tossing and turning. I finally konk out just as the sky is beginning to get light.

CHAPTER THIRTY-ONE

JOSH

I wake up the morning after the party to the mother of all hangovers.

After my text exchange with Greer, I took myself to bed with a full bottle of Belvedere, which now sits empty on the bedside table. It takes me a good fifteen minutes to drag myself up and out of bed for a long hot shower and three paracetamol.

I need to get my shit together because my liver can't take much more of this.

The living room is littered with bodies, bottles and glasses. I'm tempted to turn around and go back to bed. But the thought of Greer hurting keeps me moving towards the coffee machine. Two cups and a plate of Vegemite toast later and I'm feeling like I might actually make it to her place without collapsing with alcohol poisoning. Thankfully, there's no sign of Will, so I don't need to explain why I'm up and about at this hour. Or why Lexi went home alone last night. Or why I disappeared and left them all to it at barely midnight.

There's no way I'd be under the legal limit to drive, so I decide to walk to Greer's. It's a little further than I thought.

Thankfully, the fresh air and mild morning help move me further along the hangover continuum. By the time I arrive, I'm operating at maybe sixty percent capacity. Not ideal, but it will have to do.

I consider stopping for flowers or chocolates. Nah. That feels like it's sending the wrong message. Not that I know or understand what message it is I want to send. I'm aware I've been giving off all kinds of mixed signals. The problem is, mixed is what I'm feeling. If she were anyone else, I'd consider giving things a go with her, despite the fact I have little to no experience with relationships.

I can't do that with Greer because the stakes are too high. Failure is not an option. And failure seems inevitable given my track record and the DNA passed down through not one but two parents who are both unable to commit to anyone. Failing Greer would also mean failing Will. And Harry and Stella. And that's not something I can do.

Regardless, I need her to know what really happened last night.

No matter what, I would never disrespect her with another woman. Quite apart from anything else, right now, for me, there *is* no other woman. A life of celibacy is not something I've ever considered, but joining a monastery is starting to look quite appealing. Which brings its own set of problems, but my needs are the absolute least of my worries right now.

I don't know why I didn't anticipate Jessie answering the door. Based on the look on her face, she knows what's gone on. All of it. I'm happy Greer has someone in her corner she can confide in. I wish I did. Talking to Rob was great, but he's back to being half a world away. At least until he starts the job in Singapore.

Jess lets me into the flat with very little grace and the dirtiest of looks. If I wasn't so heartsick, it would be comical. With silky blonde hair and light blue eyes, Jess has an almost angelic, fairy-like vibe. She can't quite carry off threatening.

"Do you want me to stay?" Jessie asks Greer, who is still in her pyjamas and manages to make puffy red eyes and dark circles look beautiful. And fuck me if knowing I put them there doesn't make me feel like more of a shithead than I already do.

"No. I'll be okay."

"Right. Well, how about I hit up the café down the road for a latte and some danishes and be back in say, fifteen minutes?" Jessie may be talking to Greer, but it's me she's giving the side eye.

"That sounds great. Thanks, Jess."

I try to send a mind message that she doesn't need to worry, but I'm not sure if it's received. Either way, I get one last glare before she closes the door quietly behind her.

Greer lets out a long sigh. "Why are you here, Josh?"

"I wanted to explain. About last night."

She curls up in the corner of the couch where not so long ago, we sat watching trashy movies and eating stir-fry. There's a long silence. "The floor's all yours." Those elegant brows arch as she pulls a blue velvet cushion onto her lap like a shield.

Fuck. I don't know where to start.

"Nothing happened with Lexi. I would never disrespect you by hooking up with someone right in your face."

"Oh, well. That's good to know. Only when I'm not around then?"

"No. No, that's not what I meant. Shit." Time to get the honesty box out for real. "Look, I meant what I said. Before. Nothing else can ever happen between us. That doesn't mean I don't wish it was different. I'll never be relationship material. If you were anyone else, I'd give it a go, but I can't risk hurting you. Because what hurts you hurts Will and Harry and Stella, and I don't know what I'd do if I lost them. Not to mention they'd probably string me up by my balls if they knew what we've already done."

"So you've said. Repeatedly." Her face reminds me of the bust of Nefertiti. Cool. Composed. Inscrutable. Despite the puffy eyes.

"Lexi was a clinger, and I couldn't shake her. Believe me, I tried. I swear I had—have—absolutely no interest in her, and I gave her zero encouragement."

She's silent for a long time, and I wish like hell I could think of something else to say that didn't involve *I want you so badly it hurts to breathe*. Because while it might be true, it's also not helpful.

"And what happens when you do hook up with someone? Or I do?" Greer asks. Ouch. That was a nine iron to the balls.

"I won't like it. But I guess it's inevitable." She's a catch. No. Scratch that. She's more than a catch. She's the kind of woman every man aspires to and only a few deserving souls ever find. She's not going to be single for long if she doesn't want to be. And I'm going to have to suck it up and deal. Somehow.

Her hand smooths rhythmically over the velvet of the cushion and she gnaws on her plush bottom lip for what feels like an eternity. I'm nearly hopping out of my skin by the time she answers.

"You know what, Josh? I've heard it all before. This is what you said after we hooked up the first time. And the second. And the awards night. And you'll probably say it again next time. Because there will be a next time. There's something between us that's bigger than that. More than that. You can try and put a lid on it, but sooner or later, it's going to burst out the sides."

She's understandably angry at me. Hell, I'm angry at me. This back and forth between my head and my heart is giving me the screaming shits. And I'm scared she might be right about us. Maybe it is inevitable. Unstoppable.

"It can't. It won't." I wish there was less hope and more conviction behind my words.

She's about to answer when the door opens, and Jessie pushes through with a tray holding three takeaway cups and a brown paper bag, butter stains already showing through. It's not until Jessie glares at me that I realise how close we're sitting on the couch and how my hand is a hairs-breadth from Greer's bare leg.

Greer leaps up and heads to the kitchen for plates, leaving Jessie and me to give each other the stink eye.

"Don't worry. I haven't told Ethan what's going on. And I won't. For now. Unless you keep messing her around. She deserves better."

"I know. She deserves way better than I could ever give her."

"Well, then. We agree on something. Unfortunately, she doesn't think so. Now here, take your coffee." She thrusts the tray towards me. "Long black, no sugar, yeah?"

It surprises me that Jessie knows how I take my coffee, but I guess it shouldn't. It's the sort of thing Greer remembers, and they've been tight since they met way back in early high school. I'm even more surprised she bought me a pastry. I hope it's not poisoned.

By the time I finish what's now my third coffee of the day and wolf down one of the best cinnamon scrolls I've ever eaten, the mood in the room seems to have settled, along with my headache and rolling stomach.

"Do you want to head down to the house today? Check out the progress?" Greer asks. She's all business now. Her tone is cool, and I can't blame her. "It'll give you a chance to catch up with Ty too."

A quick look at Jessie tells me we won't be going alone, and before I know it, the three of us are in Jessie's SUV, swinging past Will's to pick him up too.

Things are moving fast at the house. The backyard is now less like a hole in the ground and more like the bones of a garden. Matt and his team are working hard in the tiny front yard when we arrive, and Ty is working right along with them, shovelling bark into a wheelbarrow. He appears to be having the time of his life.

Predictably enough, Will and Ty hit it off when I introduce them.

"So, this is the famous younger brother, following in big brother's messy footsteps, hey?"

"Following? Nah. I've got him well and truly beat," Ty responds. Another shovel full of bark flies through the air and misses the barrow, only to land on my shoes. Accidentally.

"You've got a lot to learn, kid. You and I need to have a little chat sometime," Will suggests, shaking the stray bark off his shoes.

It's lucky Matt is the slave driver Ty claims, and tells him to stop chatting and start working, heading off what could've been an embarrassing conversation. We leave them to it and troop into the house.

The external walls and roof are now up, so we can do a walk-through of the ground floor and even get upstairs via a ladder and scaffolding arrangement. Part of Greer's design was to incorporate traditional stained-glass windows, from the same period the house was built, in the new section, and there are about half-a-dozen leaning against the wall in the new section of the house, all in various states of disrepair.

"I went to a recycled building materials yard and picked up a few windows I thought you might like. They look pretty ratty right now, but a good sand back and a coat of paint and they'll look fantastic. What do you think?"

Some are round and some square, but there's a theme running through them in terms of design and colour. And she's right. They do look ratty. But I have complete faith in Greer's vision.

Before I can answer her, there's a shout from the back-yard.

"What the actual fuck? The pool is already in? This is so cool." Will is beyond excited and with good reason. The pool is amazing. I leave Jessie and Greer inside discussing paint colours and benchtops and head out the back to chat with Will about how the back-yard will look.

"This place is going to be amazing. I couldn't see it when you first brought me here, but this is epic."

"Yeah, Greer's done an incredible job. And the way she manages the tradies is mind-blowing. I can't wait for it to be finished." I pull up one of the folding chairs the tradies have left behind and sit down in the sun, close my eyes and lean my head back.

"What happened last night, man?" Will drags another chair over and sits too.

"What do you mean?"

"With Lexi. I thought you'd be keen. Then you blew her off and the next thing I knew, you'd disappeared. Everything okay with you?"

Loaded question. "Yeah, all good. I don't know. I guess I wasn't feeling it."

"You haven't been feeling it since you got back. Any particular reason?" Will tips his sunglasses down and fixes his blue and red gaze on my face. His hangover is easily as bad as mine. Maybe worse.

"Nah. Just busy. You know. Settling in. And the hooking up thing. I don't know. It's getting a bit … old, I guess."

"Whoa. I finally get my favourite wing man back and you're bailing?"

"Not bailing. I'll still be your wing-man. But I think it's time for me to take things a bit more seriously. I don't want to stuff up this job. It's full-on. And then there's the house …"

"Sure, sure. I get it. You know you can always talk to me. About anything." I've never heard Will so earnest, and my throat tightens at how he always has my back. If he knew what I'd done, what I think about doing over and over again, he wouldn't be so supportive.

"I know, man. And I appreciate it. If I had a problem, you'd be the first person I came to."

Well, except for the fact that I do have a problem, and he is absolutely the last person I can go to about it.

CHAPTER THIRTY-TWO

GREER

Taking Jessie and Will with us to check on the progress of the house, not to mention seeing Matt and Ty, made it easier to be in Josh's company. After his stupid speech in my apartment, I was so angry with him I wanted to smack him upside the head. But that wouldn't get us anywhere. And I'm ashamed to say I have trouble staying mad at him, despite his appalling behaviour, which pisses me off even more.

I let it go for now, but Josh is deluded if he thinks he's heard the end of this. I am my father's daughter, after all. Dad may appear jolly and friendly and oh-so harmless, but if you cross him, he has a very sharp bite.

After our tour of the house, we head to Mum and Dad's for Sunday night dinner, and because Ty was there, we take him with us. Josh looks shy and hopeful as he introduces his brother to my parents as if their approval means the world to him.

Dad takes to Ty right away, and I can almost see Ty opening up under the attention. It reminds me so much of Josh at the same age. At last, I'm starting to understand where Josh is coming from. The depth of his fears. The affection and respect between Josh and my parents is plain for anyone to see. Josh has been trying to tell me all this time he can't lose them. And despite the fact I don't believe that would happen, I can see how even the spectre of it would be too much for Josh to risk.

Since we all have hangovers of either the alcoholic or emotional kind—except for Jessie, who is too smart and stable for that shit—we head home as soon as dinner is over.

Josh makes a few friendly overtures on the drive home, but I give him nothing to work with. Just because I'm beginning to understand where he's coming from, doesn't mean I have to like it.

"I guess your talk with Josh didn't go so well?" Jess asks as soon as we're alone in the car.

"He gave me all the usual excuses. 'I wish it could be different, Greer'. 'If you were anyone else, Greer'. You know. The equivalent of it's not you it's me."

"And you accepted that?"

"I don't know. Maybe you're right, and I need to back off." Even I'm not sure if I mean this or not.

"At last," Jess says while managing to look sceptical at the same time.

"I don't know. I need some space at the very least."

Jessie laughs as we pull up outside my flat. "Well, giving him the silent treatment tonight sure seemed to unsettle him."

She's right. It did. "Hmmm. Maybe that's what he needs. Less sugar and a little more salt. Or ice." My face must give away my determination because she cringes.

"I can't believe I'm saying this, but I'm beginning to feel a little sorry for him."

"Yep. I think that's the solution. Make like Elsa and freeze his arse."

I'm resolved. Starting Monday, Josh is a client. Nothing more. Nothing less.

· ♥ · ♥ · ♥ · ♥ · ♥ ·

The Mean Girls' situation at work has settled down at last. I avoid them and they avoid me. Although, I do hear them bitching about me from time to time, and there's the occasional petty incident—like the *accidental* breaking of my favourite mug. Nobody else seems to have a problem with me and my boss tells me I'm doing a great job, so I don't even give it oxygen. I'm getting lots of cool projects to work on, and between the office and the house, I don't have much spare time.

Dave and his crew have worked overtime to get the house finished, and the weather has, for once, cooperated, making it an incredibly quick build. Even Dave is amazed at the progress they've made. We're now at the point where decisions can't be made by email. I have to meet Josh there for walk-throughs. And it hurts. My feelings are like a splinter, stuck deep in the tender flesh of my palm. A constant dull throb of discomfort. Seeing him is like trying to dig it out. Sharp and bloody and ultimately futile. I stick to channelling Elsa, no matter how hard it is to ignore the looks he gives me. An uncomfortable mix of longing and guilt with a splash of determination.

Josh defers to me on almost every decision. From door handles to benchtops to light fittings. On the one hand, I love having the creative freedom to create the house I envisaged. On the other, with each choice, this house is feeling more and more like mine.

The house is now well past the lockup stage and the backyard only needs plants and the fabulous wide-plank hardwood on the deck. The pool looks sensational positioned near enough to the jacaranda for beauty, yet far enough away that it's out of the shade and won't get too many of those tiny little leaves in the filter. Matt has done a brilliant job. Although, I could've done without all the low-key flirting. On the other hand, I can see how much it grinds Josh's gears when he sees Matt giving me the once-over. I'm not above enjoying his discomfort.

Matt has offered Ty ongoing work in the school holidays and whenever there's weekend work, and despite the moaning about slave labour and early starts, it's clear Ty loves both the work and being around Matt and his team. Josh lets him keep a tiny portion of the money he earns, and the rest goes towards his legal bills and the repairs on the car. There's still no sign of his mother, so he spends most weekends with Josh at Will's and often comes to family dinner, much to Mum and Dad's delight.

Today we're checking out the placement of the kitchen carcass. I want to make sure there feels like enough room between the bench and the kitchen island. Josh doesn't think he needs to come. And really, he probably doesn't. But how is he going to realise we're worth fighting for if he never gets the opportunity to see me and my Elsa impersonation?

Before I leave the office, I have to get to a meeting about a new community housing project the firm won recently. Jonathan has asked us all to come up with some out-of-the-box ideas. Whoever has the best ideas gets to work directly with him as his second-in-command on the job. And I think I might have the winning ideas. Because the unintended consequence of my cold war with Josh is I've had more time on my hands. Time I've spent working on this project.

We all file into the conference room and as per usual, Zoe slides into place beside Jonathan, along with her entourage.

No sooner has everyone found a seat than Zoe is bouncing in her chair.

"Can I go first, Jonathan? I can't wait to show you all my ideas."

"Sure, Zoe. It's great to see so much enthusiasm." Jonathan gives her the floor.

Zoe isn't what I would call innovative or imaginative, so I have a hard time believing she'll have anything interesting to say.

As she stands, she gives me a look that's equal parts malice, triumph and arrogance. A cold dread settles in my belly, and before a single word has come out of her mouth, I know what she's going to say.

I have no idea how, but she stole my ideas. Word for word. Line for line. Colour for colour. All of them. Not only has she put herself at the front of the pack, but she's left me with absolutely nothing. Not a damn thing.

I'm beyond furious, and I need to say something. But I'm frozen. This is high school all over again, and the memories of endless bullying and gaslighting have me paralysed. Which makes me as angry at myself as I am at Zoe.

My heart pounds. A cold sweat runs down my back. My mind screams, *say something, say something*, while the little girl who had her essay stolen and copied in year eight cowers, remembering how Mrs Baines hauled me over the coals. Going on and on about the sins of plagiarism. Calling my parents in. Putting me on detention. Even when it became clear I was the victim, she still blamed me for not being more careful to protect my work. That year was the one and only time I ever failed a subject.

I'm so overwhelmed I'm not even aware of what's going on until she sits down. Jonathan is full of praise, while Zoe's gaze is glued to me, daring me to say something. To accuse her. I can't manage to get a single word out. It takes every ounce of my energy to pull myself out of the tar pit of memories I've fallen into. I'm not even conscious of the others presenting their ideas. I'm focused on making like a duck. Calm on the surface, while underneath, my mind is working feverishly to come up with one or two new ideas. I won't have anything on paper, but having no ideas at all is not an option.

When it gets to me, I can feel the eyes of the Mean Girls boring into me while they smirk. Waiting for me to fail. I stand and head to the front of the room where the whiteboard sits unused because everyone else had detailed and professional PowerPoint presentations.

I've resurrected an idea that didn't make the cut in my original presentation. It's not brilliant, but I'm sure it's not the worst idea that's been presented, even if it is the least professional.

"Well, thank you, everyone. You've given me lots to think about. I'll let you know in the next day or two who will be working on this project with me." Jonathan stands, and since I'm already at the front of the room, I attempt to get out the door first.

"Greer? Could I have a word before you leave?" Jonathan stops me in my tracks. I hear a muffled snigger from Zoe as she sashays out the door, laptop crushed to her augmented breasts.

Jonathan hitches his hip on the edge of the conference room table and crosses his arms.

"What happened there, Greer?"

I can't answer. My face is burning, and my throat has closed up. If I speak, I'll cry. And I won't give Zoe the satisfaction. I need time to work out the best way to handle this.

"You and I both know what we saw here today was not your best work. Are you spreading yourself too thin? I know I said you could work on the house for your friend, but that was on the proviso it didn't impact your work here."

"It's not that. I ... I guess I struggled to connect with the project." Which is not true. I live for projects like this. But there's no way on God's green earth I'm telling him Zoe stole my work with her and her posse standing on the other side of the office avidly watching my every move through the glass walls. I need a plan first. And to calm down.

Jonathan doesn't look convinced. "Right. Well, I have to say I'm disappointed. I expected better from you. Don't let it happen again."

And without another word, he stands and walks out of the conference room, leaving me in his wake. Fuming. Shaking. Boiling.

I don't give myself time to think. I grab my laptop and bag and leave the office without passing Go or collecting $200.

You might think I'd have time to calm down on the drive from North Sydney to Manly. You'd be wrong.

I pull up out the front of the house ten minutes late, which adds to my fury. I hate being late. Dave is already getting in his truck and gives me a wave before driving off. Great. It's Josh and me. Alone.

"Whoa. Who pissed in your Cornflakes?" Josh asks after one look at my face.

"Not now, Josh," I mutter from between clenched teeth. "Let's look at this kitchen and get out of here."

CHAPTER THIRTY-THREE

JOSH

I haven't been looking forward to this afternoon. Because ever since the party—and the shitful, hung-over conversation the next morning—Greer has been treating me like the enemy. I can't blame her. I deserve every bit of it. But Christ it hurts.

And when she fronts up at Manly with a face like thunder, I want to turn tail and run. She stomps past me into the house, down the hall and through the open-plan family room to the space where the kitchen is beginning to take shape.

I've already been through it with Dave, since Greer was late, and I love it all. But in her current mood, I have no doubt Greer will find plenty to object to.

Over the past few of weeks, I've learned a lot. She's brilliant. She's a perfectionist. And she's a hard taskmaster with the tradies in the nicest possible way. When she puts her mind to it, she can also hold a grudge like an Olympic champion. As is evidenced by the curt one-line texts she sends me these days. And yet she still gives 100% to making this house shine.

Last but not least, I've learnt that any idea of forgetting about Greer and moving on with my life while still being in her orbit is futile. Which is why the phone call I received completely out of the blue yesterday seems like a lifeline I might have to grab.

I stand back and say nothing as Greer paces around, whizzing her tape measure back and forth and muttering to herself.

Finally, she stops pacing and skewers me with her eyes. "Are you happy with this?"

I don't know what the right answer is. I'm happy, but in her current mood, I don't know if she's still unhappy about whatever pissed her off earlier or with the kitchen. Or me. Or all three. And I don't want to make things worse by saying the wrong thing.

"Yes?" It comes out as a question. Silence. "Are you happy?"

She lets out a deep sigh. "Yeah. I guess so. There's plenty of room. Plenty of power points. Plenty of bench space. They're going to have to move those lights two centimetres to the left. They're not centred over the island. Otherwise, it's all good." She picks her bag and laptop up and starts to make for the door. "I'll email Dave tonight."

"Greer," I call as she's about to disappear down the hall. She stops and turns her head but doesn't move any closer.

"Yes?"

"Are you okay?" This feels like the definition of poking the bear, but I can't stand to see her so distressed. And my instincts prove right because she bursts into tears.

I'm across the room and taking her in my arms before I give it a thought, and finally, the pain that's been a constant companion the past few weeks, the tightness in my chest, it all falls away when I touch her.

I let her cry herself out before wiping her cheeks with the hem of my t-shirt.

"Want to talk about it?"

"It's just work," she snuffles.

"Ah. Is it the Mean Girls again?"

She nods against my chest.

Acting purely on instinct, I lead her into the front room where we shared a pizza picnic the day the tree came down on us. There's a pile of tarps in the corner left by the plasterers. I drag them over and help her sit in our spot. I can tell by the look she throws me she remembers what a perfect afternoon that was, despite the pain.

"Do you want to tell me about it?"

She looks unsure for a minute before she decides. "Yes." And she tells me about her afternoon meeting.

My blood pumps faster and faster as the story goes on. I'm furious with her boss for suggesting she's not pulling her weight. I know first-hand how hard she works. But most of my fury is reserved for the piece of shit who stole her work. Intellectual property is no laughing matter, and what she did crosses every line there is.

"You know what? Those aren't her ideas. That's theft. And tomorrow, you're going to go in there and tell your boss what happened and clear this whole mess up."

"I am," she says, but there's little conviction in her voice. I can't bear the beaten look on her face.

"You are. And your boss will support you. Because he sounds pretty switched on. I'll bet he already smells a rat."

"You think so?"

"I know so."

"I wanted to slap her so hard, though, you know? And I'm so angry at myself for not speaking up."

"Cut yourself some slack. You were in shock. But I know you'll work it out. And karma will get her in the end, Flo."

It's weeks since I've called her that. Weeks since we've talked like real friends. Weeks since I've felt like I can take a full breath. I've missed her so much. Missed the closeness. The honesty. The support. More than I ever thought possible. Which proves what I'm thinking of doing is the right thing.

We sit in silence, Greer's head resting on my shoulder, my lips in her hair. I don't know when it happens. One minute I'm comforting her, and the next, I'm stroking her hip and her nipples are hard points under her silk shirt. Images of her spread out on her bed flash through my mind and reality slips away. All the reasons this is a bad idea vanish as my blood pumps south. I can't think about anything but how good she tastes. The feel of her lips on my cock, of sliding into her tight, wet heat. She looks up, and her eyes are glowing. As though she's thinking about it too. And suddenly it's more than thinking.

All the heat that's been smothered by iciness the past few weeks comes bubbling up like a geyser, scalding us both.

My mouth comes down on hers in a ferocious kiss. Lips, tongues, teeth. Maybe if I kiss her hard enough, fuck her hard enough, I can force out this feeling, this longing. Of course, the reverse happens. The intensity feeds on itself. Her hands are pushing at my shirt. My hands are shoving at her skirt. In seconds, we're both naked, her hand on my cock as I slide one hand into her folds while the other cups her breast, brushing her nipple with my thumb. I'm so hard. She's so wet. And we've barely even touched.

I need to fuck her. Spinning her around, I push her onto her hands and knees. Christ, what a view. Her perfect creamy arse and glistening pink pussy. Pressing her shoulders towards the floor and holding her hip, I slam into her. Hard.

No sooner am I deep inside her than I pull out and she whimpers.

"Condom," I say as I fumble one out of my wallet, open it up and slide it on as fast as I can.

Then I'm back inside her. Pumping hard. Fast. Again and again. Her moans and gasps spur me on. I need to fuck her out of my system. I need to brand her as mine for all time. I need … her.

Bending over her back, I pull the delicate skin where her neck meets her shoulder into my mouth, sucking hard, never breaking rhythm. And then she's coming. Her already tight walls squeeze my cock until I can't hold on any longer and I'm filling the condom with jet after jet of burning release before we collapse on the hard floor, glistening with sweat.

"Oh my God. I think I saw heaven." She sighs.

"Your knees. Are you hurt?" We're on a hardwood floor with nothing more than a couple of drop sheets for protection. Her knees will be bruised for sure, but I can't quite bring myself to be sorry.

"I'm fine." And stretching her arm out, Greer threads her fingers through mine and brings our hands to her lips.

"We have to stop doing this." I roll off her and onto my side so I can see her face before I pull the condom off, tie it and drop it on the floor.

"You keep saying that. But your body doesn't seem to have got the message." Her hand wraps around my cock, which is still more than half-mast. In no time I'm fully hard again, throbbing at the feel of her fingers gliding up and down the still-sticky length. With a gentle push, she has me on my back, straddling my hips and rubbing her pussy along the length of my cock.

"Christ, Greer. What you do to me."

"Wouldn't it be a shame to waste such a lovely hard-on?" she whispers, as she trails her lips across my chest and belly until she's taking just the tip of my cock in her mouth, sucking hard.

"Fuck. Oh, fuck." I let out a strangled gasp as she alternates between licking my length and sucking the head, one hand squeezing the base while the other plays with my balls.

"That feels so good. Don't stop. Please don't stop." My hips find a rhythm, lifting off the floor, thrusting into her warm mouth.

"You taste like both of us. It's delicious," she murmurs with a hum that vibrates her throat.

"Fuck. I'm going to come, Greer. I can't stop."

She sucks me right through another orgasm, my cum filling her mouth faster than she can gulp it down.

She licks her swollen pink lips and flops down on the floor beside me.

"You're very good at that." I don't want to think about where she might've learnt it.

"You're good inspiration."

"This absolutely has to be the last time, Greer."

"Saying it doesn't make it so." She slides her hand down her body until her fingers hover over her mound, a look of challenge in her eyes.

"You wouldn't dare," I gasp out, more turned on than I've ever been in my life.

"Watch me." Her fingers have barely grazed the top of her slit when my hand snakes out and snatches hers away, replacing it with mine.

"To be fair, I do owe you an orgasm ..." And then my lips are too busy, licking her juice from her lips and thighs and sucking her clit into my mouth, to say any more.

CHAPTER THIRTY-FOUR

GREER

J osh is so good with his tongue. And I'm still sensitive from the first mind-altering orgasm. It only takes me a minute to come all over his face.

I feel much better now. All the angst of the past couple of weeks, and the anger of my afternoon meeting, have been washed away in a tidal wave of orgasms.

Being the overthinker I am, it doesn't take me long to start wondering what—if anything—comes next. Because we've been here before. I try to distract myself.

"You know, at this rate, you might be able to move in here in a week or two. The occupancy inspectors are all booked in, and I'm pretty sure you'll get immediate approval, thanks to Dave," I say once my heart rate is within a safe range.

Josh goes still beside me.

"Yeah. About that ..."

My spidey senses are tingling. Not for nothing have I lived through the shenanigans of three brothers. I can tell when someone has been cornered into dropping information they don't want to give up.

I sit up and give Josh a look designed to melt his frontal cortex. It doesn't have quite the impact I'd like, given I'm still completely naked.

"What does *about that* mean?"

Josh looks everywhere but at me. He sits up and rests his forearms on his raised knees. The silence stretches on and I'm about to cave and say something when he clears his throat.

"I had a call this week. From one of the biggest agencies in the region. They're looking for an executive creative director. And they want me."

I open my mouth to say that's great when I realise there must be more to it. My mouth snaps shut. Waiting for the bomb to drop.

"And?"

"And their head office is in Melbourne." Josh winces on that last word.

I try to hold it in until I can think clearly. Try to think 'what would a wise person do here?' before I respond. But I can't.

"What the actual fuck, Josh? Are you kidding me?" My pitch is so high dogs start barking in the neighbouring suburbs.

"No, I'm not kidding. Hear me out." His hands go up. And well they might. I feel like I've been kicked in the belly by a prize bull.

I've spent the last nearly four months working my guts out to give him a beautiful home to live in, and before he even moves in, he's off again. Not to mention what we've just done.

I leap to my feet. Well, more like struggle. Either way, I'm on my feet. I don't know what to address first. The fact that he's walking away from a home he said he wanted. Or that he's taking a job with another firm when he said he wanted to start his own agency. Or that he fucked me, again, knowing full well he'd be leaving. And don't even get me started on abandoning his brother. I do the only thing I can under the circumstances. I start pulling my clothes on as fast as I can.

"Greer ..."

I ignore him.

"Greer. Stop." Josh tries to take me by the shoulders, but I pull away, almost overbalancing as I yank up my now wrinkled and grubby skirt.

"Please, Greer. Let me explain."

"No. I don't want to hear another word out of your mouth. I just can't."

Before I've even buttoned my shirt, he races to the door, slams it shut and leans on it. His nakedness would be comical in any other circumstance.

"I need you to listen. I didn't go looking for this. They came to me. And it's an executive role. I'd be in charge of the creative directors in all the offices in the Asia-Pacific region. Shares in the company. It's a huge step up."

Some of the wind goes out of my sails. It does sound like a big opportunity. But there's more to life than winning in business. Surely Josh has seen enough of his father's arse-holery to know that.

"What happened to wanting to put down roots? To starting your own agency? You were the one who said those things. Does that all go up in smoke as soon as someone waves something shiny and new in front of you?"

"No. Of course not. But I can't ignore an opportunity like this. And it would make things easier ..."

"What things easier?"

"Us. This. These things." His hand waves between us and his eyes pinch tight.

It takes me a moment to be able to pin down a single word in my surging thoughts.

"Us? You're going to move to Melbourne to get away from *us*? You're blaming *me*?"

"Yes. No. Not blaming. I don't know. But it would be easier if I didn't have to see you all the time. Wouldn't it be easier for you not to have to see me every time you turned around?"

"You know what? Fuck you. Because that's all on you, Josh. Don't try pinning it on me."

"I know. I know it's all on me. But it can't be any other way and it fucking hurts like hell every time I see you. So yes, I'd rather be far, far away and save my sanity. And let you get on with your life too."

"Don't you dare. Don't you dare make out like you're doing this for my sake. I'm here. Ready to have the tough conversations. To put the effort in. It's you who's scared. You're a coward, Josh. And I deserve better."

His face falls as if I've slapped him. He's still pressed against the door, but I'm stronger than I look, and with a good shove, I'm out in the hallway, picking up my bag and racing to my car before he even has a chance to come after me, since he's still naked.

I don't remember the drive home. Somehow, I find myself in my flat, too angry to even cry. I'm furious with Josh. I'm furious with myself too. Because there's no denying I've been spinning fairy tales in my head that eventually Josh would figure his shit out, and like in a romance novel, we'd live happily ever after in the house I built for myself as much as—more than—for him. As if wanting it badly enough would make it happen.

Well, it all ends now. I will not waste another second of my time on a man who can't be honest with himself, let alone me. Josh and me? We're done.

I down several glasses of merlot, then sit at my computer and email Dave. His wife works with him and is a great project manager. I pass all the remaining tasks over to them—including moving those damn kitchen lights—and tell Dave to bill Josh whatever it takes to get it done.

Then I send Josh an email, telling him I can no longer manage his renovations due to work commitments. I know once the family finds out, they'll have questions. Honestly, I don't even care anymore.

Finishing the bottle of wine, I eat a bag of salt and vinegar chips for dinner and put myself into my cold and miserable bed. Ignoring the multiple calls and texts from Josh.

I get to work early the next morning. No point lying in bed fretting. I might as well be at work trying to repair my tattered reputation. I have a career to save, and it appears a career is all I have going for me right now.

I'm pissed at Josh all over again for hijacking the time I could've spent crafting my approach to Jonathan about what happened yesterday. Because if Zoe thinks I'm going to let her get away with it, she's sadly mistaken. I have all my notes and planning on my computer, some of which are ideas of my own that I was doodling with before this project was even pitched. First thing this morning, I'll be seeing Jonathan and laying it all out.

The only other people in the office when I arrive are Jonathan and Craig, the IT guy. They're deep in conversation in Jonathan's office. I grab my laptop, which holds evidence of all my workings, and make my way towards his office, passing Craig on his way out.

"I was hoping to have a chat with you about yesterday's meeting," I start, perching myself on the edge of a visitor's chair.

"I was hoping you might," Jonathan answers. I can barely hear him over the pounding of my heart.

"The thing is ..." My voice wobbles. I clear my throat and start again. "The ideas Zoe presented yesterday? They were mine."

Mic drop. This is taking every last drop of my courage. But I won't back down.

He spends a few seconds searching my face, his expression serious.

Finally, he lets out a sigh-snort, which I take to mean frustration, though I'm not sure where it's directed.

"I know."

I can't tell what he's thinking or who he's angry at. Past experience tells me it's not always the perpetrator who gets blamed in these situations. Oh, dear God. I'm a whistle blower. And we all know what happens to them.

"You know?"

"Yes. It's come to my attention that we have a problem."

Great. What fresh hell is about to be unleashed?

I manage to croak out an "Oh?" around the stomach that's lodged itself in my throat. I don't think I can take another hit right now.

"There's been a security breach."

"Security?" I squeak, feeling guilty, even though I know I've done nothing wrong. Because maybe Zoe and her gang have struck again.

"Craig accidentally left a copy of everyone's logins on the printer last week. And neglected to tell me."

His eyes never waver from my face. If he's waiting for me to say something, we'll be here a while. I know I should be able to work this out, but my mind is frozen. I have no idea where this is going.

"And it appears someone in the office used it to access files they had no business accessing. Namely yours. Unfortunately, or maybe fortunately, this person was foolish enough to access those files from their own computer. And at a time when you were at an offsite meeting with me."

And now I know where this is going. A tiny chunk of the ice around my heart shears off. Who knows? Maybe one day it will start beating again.

He seems to be waiting for something from me.

"I see."

"The person in question will be dealt with today. I won't tolerate theft or deception of any sort."

"I understand." I want to jump up and shout yes but somehow manage to restrain myself. I'm not a hundred percent sure what he means by *dealt with*, although I have hopes.

"What I can't quite fathom is why you let her get away with it yesterday. It was clearly not her work. It had your stamp all over it."

"You knew?"

"Of course. Why do you think I gave you the opportunity to tell me privately after the meeting?"

"Oh. Well. I was rattled. I wasn't sure how to handle it. And Zoe and her ga ... I mean, the others, were watching from the other side of the office. It didn't seem like the right time."

"I see. Anyway. I would suggest you make changing your login a priority this morning." Jonathan smiles for the first time since I entered his office. "I'm proud of you for standing up for yourself, even if it was a little tardy. Piece of advice? You'll probably come across this kind of behaviour in your career from time to time. Don't let it bring you down."

His eyes go back to his laptop screen, signalling the meeting is over. When I get to the door, he speaks again. "Oh, and by the way. You'll be working with me on the community housing project."

I melt into my chair when I reach my desk. I was fully prepared to explain the whole thing this morning, but I'm so glad I didn't have to. My emotions are on a hair-trigger right now. Thank God Jonathan could see through the dishonesty and had faith in me. Faith in my work.

A tearful Zoe is escorted out of the office by security at nine-oh-five with a box of personal possessions under her arm. She pauses as she passes my desk and gives me a death stare. And I give it right back. I wish I had it in me to feel relieved that she's gone. All I feel is numb. And I can't see that changing any time soon.

CHAPTER THIRTY-FIVE

JOSH

It's hard to believe I could've fucked things up with Greer any worse than I did a few weeks ago, and yet I have. I reread her email for the hundredth time. It's businesslike. Polite even. But the message is clear. She wants nothing more to do with the house. Or me. It opens up a gaping wound in my chest. I can't say I blame her.

Meanwhile, Dave's wife, Megan, has been carpet bombing me with emails about paint colours and floor stains and carpet deliveries and final lighting choices as though I have any interest in, or understanding of, what she's talking about.

And work is no better. It only takes a couple of hours the day after my fight with Greer for the team to work out that I'm not in top form. In fact, I'm not in any form at all. And by the end of the day, the director of client services—who is a real tool and hates my guts—is asking if I need a mental health day. Fucker. Yes. Yes, I do need a mental health day. Or a heart health day. Or ten. Or maybe the rest of my days. All of them. Because I don't know if I can recover from this complete cluster fuck of my own making.

The chairman of the agency attempting to poach me is in Sydney on business and arranges to meet me for a drink after work at a member's only club in the city. *Pretentious git,* I think as I climb out of the Uber. Only he isn't. He's actually a really cool guy, and we have a lot in common. The job is amazing. Huge salary. Lots of travel. Fantastic high-profile clients in business sectors I've worked in before. And he's handing it to me on a silver platter. No other candidates. Mine for the taking.

I should be jumping at this opportunity. Knocking this guy over in a rush to sign the contract. Yet I don't.

"Look, I'll be frank. Sydney is my hometown, and I only moved back here not long ago after a long time away. It's a big decision to move again. There's a lot to weigh up."

"We're aware. Do you have a partner you need to discuss this with?" he asks, leaning back in the insanely soft leather chair and sipping his top-shelf scotch.

"No. I don't. But I've recently bought a house ..."

"Okay. I understand. You need a bit of time to think it through. I'm sure you'll find, once you've given it some thought, it's too good an opportunity to pass up. How about I leave it with you for a few days?"

"That would be great."

"We're not talking to anyone else. We've been watching you for a while now. Before you even came back to Sydney. Parachute beat us to the punch. You're the one we want. That said, if you're going to say no, we need to start putting out feelers, so if you could get back to us sooner rather than later, we'd appreciate it, Josh."

We shoot the shit through one more drink, then part ways, agreeing to talk again within the week.

·♥·♥·♥·♥·♥·

I arrive home at Will's place not long after he does and find him pouring himself a large whisky. He holds the bottle up questioningly.

"Yeah. Thanks. A drink is exactly what I need." Another one. Or ten. Until the pain in my chest goes away. Maybe I'm having a heart attack. A prolonged one. Days and days of a heart attack. Which is also causing me to become a drama llama.

I dressed to impress for the interview, and the tie and business shoes are pinching in more ways than one. I toe off my shoes, rip off my tie, and shrug out of my suit jacket as I fall into one of the cushy chairs facing the view.

"You look like shit," Will says as he hands me the drink. I wish I could talk to him about Greer, but that's not possible. What I can talk to him about, though, is the job offer.

"Thanks. I feel like shit. That's been run over by a fully loaded garbage truck. Then rained on. Nice of you to notice."

Will snorts. "Right. Well, tell Uncle William all about it, then."

"I've been offered a job."

"Well, congratulations." Then he looks at my face. "Or not?"

"Exactly. It's an amazing job. Executive Creative Director of the Asia-Pacific Region. Huge package. Half-a-dozen creative directors working under me. Lots of travel. High profile clients."

"But?"

"It's in Melbourne."

Will's face falls a little. "Well, that's not so bad. I mean, Melbourne's no Sydney, obviously, but it's only an hour away by plane. Not like London or New York."

"Yeah. But I came home for a reason, Wee. I bought the house for a reason. It's time to settle down. Grow some roots."

"You mean like get married roots?" He looks vaguely horrified.

I sigh. If only. Wait. What? That's the first time I've ever thought longingly about marriage. No prizes for guessing why.

Better put that in the pro's column for taking this job. Then again, maybe it also belongs in the con's column. I don't even know anymore.

"No. Not marriage." I can't admit to my thoughts because then I'd have to tell him who I might or might not wish I could marry. And there is nobody else. "But settling in the one place, having a life outside work, spending time with friends, you know? And then there's Ty. If I bail now, who's going to watch out for him? Not Dad or Cristal, that's for sure."

"Uh-huh."

"And I was thinking, soon I might set up my own agency. Be my own boss. Do things my way."

"And now there's this opportunity, and it's too good to ignore?"

"Yeah. Maybe. But is it?"

"Well, I guess it depends on what you really want. Only you can decide that. If being away from home was getting old, it doesn't seem like moving to Melbourne and taking a job with lots of travel is going to make you happy."

He's right. It probably won't. On the other hand, not having to see Greer every day has a certain self-flagellating appeal.

"Thanks, man. I've got a lot to think about, I guess."

"Are you sure there's nothing else?" Will's gaze is uncharacteristically sharp. He's been doing that a lot lately. If I didn't know better, I might think he suspected something. But Will is nothing if not straightforward. If he had something to say, he'd say it.

"Nah. That's it. Apart from bullshit in the office."

"Okay, well, always here for you, brother. By the way, don't forget Saturday night."

"Saturday night?" I have no idea what he's talking about.

"Ethan and Jessie's engagement party?" he reminds me. "No exceptions, no excuses. Straight from Mum's lips."

Great. I'd completely forgotten. And when Mama C says no exceptions or excuses, she means it. I have to be there. With Greer. Fuck my life.

If I thought this craptastic week couldn't get any worse, I was wrong. Because the morning after my chat with Will, I get a call from my father. He's in town for a couple of days, and wants me to have lunch with him and his new fiancé. A woman he met on the cruise that was more important than helping Ty. Her name is Honey. Which gives me a pretty good visual. I think this will make wife number four. Or is it five? I've lost count.

I arrive at the swanky restaurant with views of the harbour a good ten minutes late. Because I don't want to be here. My father is sitting at a table by the window with a woman, who has her back to me. Even from this distance, I can see she's not his usual type. Her hair is salt and pepper grey, and she's dressed smartly. This is a new low. How young can she be if he's had to bring her mother with them?

"Dad," I say, not extending my hand as he rises from his chair.

"Josh. I'm glad you could join us. This is Honey, my fiancé." And he puts his hand lovingly on the shoulder of the woman at the table.

"*This* is Honey?" I can't keep the incredulity out of my voice.

"Silly name, I know. My parents were hippies." Honey rolls her eyes.

I take a seat, and Honey offers me a glass of wine from the bottle already on the table.

"Jim tells me you're a creative director. I'd love to hear about it."

This woman is not what I was expecting. She's easily within ten years of my father's age. She's smart, articulate, unpretentious, and takes no shit when my father starts blustering.

By the time lunch is nearly over, I discover I like her a lot.

"Isn't she wonderful?" Dad says, gazing after her lovingly as she makes her way across the restaurant to the ladies' room. That look alone is a new development.

"She is, yes," I answer with surprise. "Not your usual type, though." I still don't quite know what to make of this. Of her. With him.

"No. She's not. But Josh, after my last divorce, I knew something had to change." If I didn't have thirty-two years' experience with him, the earnest expression on my father's still-handsome face might convince me. "I went to counselling. I can't tell you how much of a difference it's made to my mindset. And then I met Honey. It's amazing what meeting the right woman can do for your outlook."

Of course, Dad being Dad, the counselling hasn't changed him enough to turn him into a proper father for Tyrone. Yet. Maybe Honey will be a good influence there. The thing is, I no longer care. Neither Ty nor I need him. We're getting along fine without his interference.

But meeting Honey and hearing the way Dad talks about her makes me think. If he can change his ways at the ripe old age of sixty-something, maybe there's hope for me? For Greer and me? Nope. I can't think like that. Can I?

Will and I climb out of the Uber on Saturday night to find the party in full swing. Super. Just what I need in my current frame of mind. At least it will be easy to avoid Greer in this crowd. Because avoiding her is exactly what I should do. What I have to do. Which is why the first thing I do is scan the crowd for even a glimpse of her. I feel like a puppy, desperate for attention. A treat. A smile. A word. Even a look. If she would just fucking look at me. But she doesn't.

I still haven't made a decision about the Melbourne job, and I don't even know how to go about making it. The pros and cons list didn't work. Neither did the toss of a coin because whatever came up, I immediately started talking myself into the opposite. I've promised to give them an answer by Monday. No pressure.

Will, Ethan, Ben and I all went to school together and there are a lot of people here I haven't seen for years. It's almost as if Mama C has a sixth sense and is trying to convince me to stay. Which she wouldn't do if she knew what had gone on between her baby girl and me.

Speaking of Greer, she doesn't even look my way. Which might be a good thing because if she did, I wouldn't be surprised if I fell to my knees and begged her to forgive my stupidity right here in front of everyone. And that's not fair. She's right. I am a coward. If I'm not prepared to fight for her, I don't deserve her.

I grab a drink and spend time catching up with old friends before the music is suddenly turned off. We all look in the direction of the house, where Harry and Stella stand with Ethan and Jessie and an older couple, who I assume are her parents. Time for the announcement.

"A little quiet, everyone," booms Harry. "We have an announcement to make."

Everyone cheers and whistles.

"It's been such a long time coming; we might all be forgiven for having given up hope. But Ethan has finally proposed to Jessie, and she has agreed, reluctantly, I imagine, to take him on. Jessie has been like a daughter to us for many years, and Stella and I are thrilled it will finally be made official. Please raise your glasses. To Jessie and Ethan."

There's more cheering and whistling, and Jessie's father attempts to make a speech but can't be heard over the uproar.

While everyone else has their eyes glued to the happy couple, I only have eyes for Greer. And even though she plastered on a wide smile throughout the whole speech and was the first to hug and kiss both Jessie and Ethan, I can see the sadness behind her eyes. Watching the way Jessie whispers to Greer, it's clear Jessie's up to date on what's gone on between Greer and me because, over the heads of everyone, she shoots me a glare sharp enough to cut steel.

I did that to Greer. Double fuck my life.

CHAPTER THIRTY-SIX

GREER

"Are you sure you're okay?" Jessie asks as I hug her for the hundredth time tonight.

"Of course. I'm thrilled for you and Ethan. And I can't wait to get started on helping you organise the wedding. Oh, and the hens' night." Jessie knows me well and can tell right now I'm faking it until I (hopefully) make it. And she knows enough not to press me.

I'm thrilled for them. I am. But right now, it's taking all my effort not to charge up to Josh and kick him in the balls.

"Now get going and do the rounds with your new fiancé and leave me to find another drink somewhere." I push Jessie towards Ethan, and they disappear into the crowd.

I'm about to turn and head towards the bar when a fresh glass of champagne appears over my shoulder.

"Could this be what the beautiful woman is looking for?" a deep voice asks, and I spin to see Ethan's friend Guy dangling the glass in his long, elegant fingers.

"Why, thank you, kind sir. It is indeed what I was looking for." I take the glass and down half of it in one gulp, earning a grin from Guy.

I've known Guy about as long as I've known Josh, although I haven't seen him for a few years. He's gorgeous in a *GQ* kind of way. He's also charming, smart, witty and successful. And an even bigger man whore than either Josh or Will, or so I hear. It occurs to me that a bit of harmless flirting from a good-looking man might be what my bruised and battered heart needs.

"Do you know what else I need? A dance." I gulp the rest of my champagne, put the glass on a nearby table and look at him expectantly.

"Your wish is my command, princess." Guy bows low, takes my hand, and leads me to the crowded dance floor on one side of the garden.

The champagne and dancing go a little way to cheering me up, and my fake-it-'til you-make-it plan seems to be convincing others, if not me.

Guy is a flirt, and it's not long before he's moving closer.

"You know, Greer, I'll bet you look gorgeous first thing in the morning. All rumpled and sexy." His lips brush my ear during a slower number.

I hold back a snort. "Do lines like that ever work for you?"

"Oh, it's no line, baby. I've been picturing it all night. I'd like to find out firsthand if I'm right." He slides closer still, moving sinuously against me as one hand trails up and down my back.

I'm about to tell him no when his body suddenly jerks away from me. Well, this is unpleasantly familiar.

"What the fuck are you playing at, man?" Josh shoves between us and everyone around gasps, moving back to give us space. They're making a scene.

"What's your problem? Greer and I were just dancing." Guy tries to step around him, but Josh is having none of it.

"Well, go and find some other girl to dance with. Greer doesn't need your type hitting on her."

"My type? What's that supposed to mean?"

"You know exactly what it means. Take your hit-it-and-quit-it approach somewhere else. She deserves better." Josh looms over Guy, who is shorter and lighter than him, but Guy doesn't back down.

"Fuck off. What business is it of yours?"

It's taken me a moment, but I finally snap out of my stupor.

"What the hell is wrong with you?" I round on Josh, moving to stand between him and Guy.

"Nothing is wrong with me. I'm saving you from being hit on by this fuckboy."

There's a loud gasp from the crowd, including Guy, who now looks like he might punch Josh, despite the size difference.

Josh tries to move me to the side, but I slap his hand away. My heart is pounding. My tongue is about to run away with me, and I'm powerless to stop it.

"You know what? Fuck you, Josh. You don't want me, but you don't want anyone else to have me either? Well, you can't have it both ways. Get out of my business once and for all and leave me the hell alone."

"You can't be serious? This guy? He's the worst."

"No, Josh, you're the worst. You gave up the right to have an opinion on what I do and who I do it with when you told me we were nothing. At least Guy is honest. I know what I'm getting with him. Straight up."

Josh lurches backwards like I've given him a roundhouse to the chest.

I don't realise how loud I've become until I feel Jessie's hand on my arm. I look around at the sea of faces—which include my three brothers and my parents—and I wish I could say I regret the words I've hurled at Josh. But I don't. Because it's how I feel. And if I've outed us in the process, I can't bring myself to care.

I don't even realise Guy is still standing there until he speaks up again.

"You need to take a good long look at yourself, mate," he spits at Josh. "Sorry for the scene, people. Thanks for having me, Mr and Mrs Carter. I think I'd best be on my way." Guy turns and disappears through the stunned-into-silence crowd.

I'm aware of all this in my peripheral vision because Josh and I haven't taken our eyes off one another. I'm watching his face morph from fury to embarrassment to regret.

"Greer ..." he starts. But I'm not interested in anything he has to say. I throw my hand up in a stop motion.

"Save it for someone who cares. Because I no longer do." And I leave them all standing there. Except for Jessie, who follows me inside and up to my childhood bedroom.

We sit silently, side by side, on my bed for long minutes. I want to cry. I want to rant. I'm scared if I move or make a noise I won't be able to control myself. Ever again.

"Wow," Jessie eventually lets out, almost as a sigh.

And I can't hold it in. I start to laugh. I was right. I can't stop. I knew something was coming, but I wasn't expecting laughter. Jessie joins in, and in no time, there are tears streaming down our cheeks.

It might seem weird that my first reaction is to laugh, but honestly, the whole situation is so ridiculous I can't do anything else.

Once I've calmed down, I insist Jessie goes back to the party. I feel terrible that I ruined the engagement party she's waited so long to have. Or rather, Josh ruined it.

I watch out the window as Jess appears in the backyard and goes into a huddle with my mother. Who immediately disappears. Three, two, one ...

"Greer? Can I come in?"

I nearly laugh again. As if I could stop her. "Sure." I prop myself up on the bed, ready for one of Mum's patented talks. Dad might be the one who wrangles the boys, and God knows they gave him a full-time job of it, but Mum has always been the one to wrangle me. A much easier job. Until tonight, maybe.

"Well, that was a bit of excitement," she says. Understatement.

"I'm sorry, Mum. For ruining the party."

"Oh, don't worry about it. A few more bottles of champagne and it will all be forgotten. Your father's down there now making sure everyone gets topped up." Mum chuckles and gets up to look out the window as if making sure everyone has a full glass.

"Darling. I wanted to check you're okay." The compassion in her voice is almost my undoing, but I manage to keep it together.

"I'm fine, Mum. At least, I will be. Once I calm down."

"I take it you and Josh have been, um ...?"

I don't know whether she can't bring herself to say what she thinks we've been doing or whether she's fishing for me to tell her exactly what's going on. But it's a moot point since whatever the hell it was is no longer happening. Not ever again.

"Yes. And now we're not."

"I see. It seems like perhaps there are some unresolved ... feelings?"

"No. No feelings left, Mum. It's over and done. And the stunt he pulled tonight proved it."

"Oh, I rather think the stunt he pulled proved how strong his feelings are, don't you?"

"Mum," I warn.

"Alright. I won't interfere. But don't let anger guide your decisions, sweetheart. And always remember, some people take longer to work out their feelings than others. Josh hasn't had good role models for that in his life, so bear that in mind. And perhaps he felt like he had much more to lose if it all went wrong than you did. Anyway, if you're okay, I'd better get back to our guests." And with a quick kiss to my forehead, she leaves, closing the door behind her.

· ♥ · ♥ · ♥ · ♥ · ♥ ·

I look out the window again. There's no sign of either Josh or Will. I could stay but would prefer to avoid the risk of interrogation by Dad or my brothers, so I sneak out the front door and walk up to the main road to hail a taxi. The exercise will help me think. Even though my phone is blowing up in my handbag, I don't look till I'm in the back of the taxi. A dozen missed calls and messages from Dad, Ben and Ethan. Interestingly, nothing from Will or—thank God—Josh.

CHAPTER THIRTY-SEVEN

JOSH

I'm frozen to the spot as I watch Greer retreat, Jessie scurrying after her. I feel completely eviscerated. Like every organ is now on the outside of my body, and all that's left inside is empty, aching space.

I'm vaguely aware of Harry telling Ethan to restart the music, which someone must have stopped during the fracas, and encouraging everyone to get back onto the dance floor. Will takes my arm and leads me away.

I know I have to apologise. I have to explain. I have to tell Greer how truly sorry I am. There are so many people I've let down tonight I don't even know where to start.

I wish I could say I don't know what came over me. But I do. It was jealousy, pure and simple. Seeing that sleaze Guy pressing up against her, watching Greer laugh at whatever inane chat-up lines he was using, imagining what might come next. It made my blood boil.

I can't believe I've gone and repeated the mistake I made at the night-club not so long ago. Only worse. Because this time, all the people I was trying to hide my feelings from were there to see it all unfold in glorious technicolour.

Without realising where Will is leading me, I find myself on the bench at the end of the garden, overlooking the harbour. Where we used to come to drink in secret because it was half hidden by a low hedge. I seem to remember we occasionally brought girls down here too.

Will hands me a bottle of Grey Goose after taking a swig himself, and we sit, passing the bottle back and forth for what seems like hours. I can hear the party carrying on further up the garden. Down here it's silent and dark.

I start to speak a couple of times, but honestly, I have no idea what to say or where to start. Will doesn't rush me. Just waits it out.

Finally, I manage to get out the only thing I can think of. "I'm sorry."

"For what?" Will asks. I expect him to be angry with me, but his voice is gentle, and when I risk a glance at his face, it's full of compassion. "For causing a scene at a party? For shit-talking an old friend? Or for falling in love with my sister?"

That last one pulls me up sharp. I can no longer deny it, even to Will. Even though this might mean the end of the most important friendship in my life.

"The first two. And for hurting your sister. I could never be sorry for falling in love with her. That would be the same as being sorry for breathing."

"Good answer." Will holds his hand up for a high five, which I manage to connect with, despite the vodka.

"I'm sorry you found out like this."

"Oh, I didn't find out like this. I've known for weeks. Months maybe."

"What? How did you know?"

"That you're in love with her? Duh. Have you looked in a mirror lately? It's written all over your face. And hers. I might appear clueless, but you don't go to law school for a million years without learning a thing or two about reading people."

"You knew? Since when?" I'm shocked by Will's admission.

"I've had my suspicions for a while. There was the kiss at the auction. Then I thought maybe something had gone on the day Greer showed you the plans for the house. And the day at the sailing club, you looked so guilty. But I think when we played Marco Polo, the way you leapt out of the pool when you touched her, confirmed it." He takes another slug of vodka.

All those clues I thought he'd missed. Because I sure did. He picked up on every one of them.

"Well, that can't be right. I wasn't in love with her then."

"Sure. You tell yourself that." He hands the bottle back to me for another hit. My mind is starting to get a bit soupy with all this alcohol.

"I mean, I was attracted to her. Yeah. Who wouldn't be? But love." And then it dawns on me. He's not angry. "Wait. You knew? You knew how I felt and you didn't tell me to back off? Do Harry and Stella know? I mean, did they know before tonight?"

He barks out a loud laugh. "Of course, they knew. We all knew. We've had a book going on how long it would take for you to fess up. I lost a pineapple tonight. Dad will be pissed. He's down a couple of peppermints."

"If you knew, what was all that stuff at the sailing club about Greer hooking up with someone?"

"I was trying to flush you out, you dope. As I said, I lost money on this."

"Why are you not angry? I broke your trust. I violated the bro code. I *lied* to you."

"Yeah, I think you were lying to yourself, actually. And I am angry. But not why you think."

"What do you mean?"

"I'm angry you didn't trust me enough to tell me. I'm angry you *thought* you had to lie to me. I'm angry you don't think you're good enough for my sister. Most of all, I'm angry you hurt her—and yourself—with your dumb-arse behaviour."

"This is not what I was expecting."

"I'm aware. Now, you accused Guy of wanting a hit-and-run. Are you going to do the same? Or are you going to man up and do the right thing?"

"I wish it was that simple."

"It is that fucking simple. You love her. She loves you. Happy ever after."

"She's made it clear she doesn't want a bar of me."

"Well, I guess you're going to need one of those rom-com grand gesture things then, huh?" He nudges me with his shoulder as if prodding me into action.

"I'm not good enough for her. I should leave her alone."

"Oh, for fuck's sake." He's finally starting to get exasperated with me. "Hold on. Is that what all this going to Melbourne shit is about? You're running away?"

I nod and take a slug of the vodka, spilling some down my shirt in the process.

"You're more of an idiot than I thought. Firstly, I can't think of anyone I'd rather see my sister with, up to and including Harry Fucking Styles, and you know what a crush she had on him back in the day. Secondly, it appears you're the one she wants, and she's a smart woman. So, are you going to do what you have to do and deserve her? Or am I going to have to kick your sorry arse?"

I'm not so drunk that the idea I might actually be able to have a future with Greer doesn't sparkle like some kind of unicorn-esque fantasy. But I'm still having trouble trusting in it.

"What about Harry and Stella?"

"Are you kidding me? They've been going out of their minds waiting for you to make your move. You heard what they said about Jessie tonight? That goes double for you."

"I have no idea how to make a relationship work, man."

"Lucky for you, I expect Greer does. And really, nobody knows going in. You have to work it out as you go along."

It's hard to believe, given how I'm feeling, but I manage a laugh. "How the fuck would you know?"

"I've watched Ethan and Jessie. And Mum and Dad. Not to mention the complete cluster fuck that is Nick Pierce, but that's another story."

"You're really okay with this?" I look him dead in the eye, needing to know there's no doubt in his mind.

"Not as it stands, no. But if you wake the fuck up, get your act together, and work this out, then yes, I am more than okay with this. In fact, I'd be over the moon to have you as a brother-in-law."

And with that, Will claps me on the shoulder, and downs what little remains of the vodka.

"Might be best to wait till you're sober to talk to Greer, though."

For some reason, that cracks us both up.

CHAPTER THIRTY-EIGHT

GREER

As soon as I get home, I hit the button for the family group text and send a message to let everyone know I'm home safe and will talk to them tomorrow, which elicits another avalanche of messages. I turn my phone off, have a long hot shower and fall into bed for yet another relaxing night of tossing and turning until sunrise.

No sooner have I turned my phone on when I finally drag myself out of bed than my mother is calling.

"How are you this morning, darling? Did you get any sleep?"

I open up the French doors to the balcony for some fresh air and settle on the sofa. This is probably going to be a long one.

"I'm good, Mum. I didn't get much sleep, but I'll be okay."

"Do you want to talk about it?"

That gets a laugh out of me. "Do I have a choice?"

"Not really, no." Mum must be outside because I hear birds and the occasional bark from her elderly chocolate labrador, Bert. He used to love to chase the birds. These days, he manages the occasional yap to keep them on their toes.

"Have you spoken to Josh?" I ask, despite the fact I'd promised myself I wouldn't ask about him.

"No, but I understand Will has. He was very tight-lipped about it, though. I can't give you any details beyond that he's okay."

"I really don't care whether he's okay or not, Mum."

Mum laughs. "Darling, I've watched you idolise that boy from the moment you met him, so don't even try that shit with me."

Wow. She must be distraught. Mum rarely swears. Usually only when Will or Ben have done something truly awful.

I sigh. "Fine. I care. But I have to work on not caring. Because as much as I wanted things to work out, they're not going to."

"Do you remember that movie—*The Best Exotic Marigold Hotel*?" I have no idea where she's heading with this.

"Yes?"

"Remember what the boy—Sunny was it?—said? It will all be alright in the end, and if it's not alright, then it's not the end. I have faith things will work themselves out as they're supposed to."

"Hmm." I had the same faith once upon a time. Not anymore. "Josh said we couldn't be together because he was bound to screw it up. And then he'd lose you and Dad and Will. And I get that. Maybe I didn't want to hear it before, but I do understand where he's coming from. I want you to promise me, whatever happens, you won't hold any of this against him."

"I can't promise it won't be difficult, Greer. But Josh will always be part of our family. Whatever happens."

The last thing I want is for her to feel any animosity towards Josh. She's the closest thing he's ever had to a loving mother, and I can't take that away from him, regardless of where we stand.

"Thanks, Mum. I'm going to take a shower. I'll talk to you later."

I don't want to burden Jessie with all my crap. This should be a shiny, happy time for her right now. But I can't sit around this flat on my own, wallowing. Once I'm out of the shower, feeling slightly more human, I decide the best bet is to call Ben.

Funnily enough, for the family screw up, Ben is probably the most in touch with his feelings of any of my brothers, and I often go to him when my emotional turmoil needs a calm and steady hand.

"I know the perfect thing. Be ready in half an hour. Comfy clothes." And he hangs up without another word. Which is how, an hour later, I find myself walking into an axe-throwing parlour. Ben is bloody brilliant. This is exactly what I need.

"You're a genius," I tell Ben as they hand me a danger waiver to sign.

"Never forget it. Best anger management therapy ever." He's grinning from ear to ear.

The girl on reception shows us to our cage, all the while flirting with Ben, who, friends tell me, is hot in a way that transcends the physical—although he's physically hot too, I hear. Apparently, it's something about the look in his eyes. Whatever it is, I've never known a girl not to flirt with him. If he ever kept their numbers, his little black book would be more like a large black filing cabinet.

The space smells of woodchips and is noisy with thuds and cheers and the screeching of metal blades skidding across the concrete floor.

After a five-minute run-down on what to do and not do, the instructor leaves us to it. I can't wait to get started and pick up my first solo axe, but Ben holds up his hand.

"Wait a minute." He trots down to the wooden board painted with a target at the other end of the cage and pulls something from his pocket. I can't see what he's doing until he steps away a moment later, and right there in the centre of the bullseye is a blown-up picture of Josh's face.

"Bonus points if you hit him dead in his weird-creepy eye." And then he laughs before heading back to stand way behind me and let me have at it.

I feel a little bad on the first throw, aiming at Josh's face. But only a little. Anger fuels my throws, and bit by bit, the tension in my body starts to lessen. By the end of our hour, the picture is hanging off the board in shreds, and my temper has been restored. Well, for the most part.

"You're pretty good at this," says a guy in the next cage, nodding to where my final throw has just missed what's left of Josh's two-tone eye. It's quite the compliment coming from a guy who appears to have his own axes and has been hitting the bullseye consistently. "We have a regular tournament if you're interested in joining. Shelley at the counter can give you the info."

"Thanks. You never know. I might think about that." To be honest, I'm not sure I would be quite as good without the added fuel of my anger.

Ben pulls down the photo, and we return our axes to the counter before heading to the craft brewery next door for a beer.

"They make these great fruit-based beers." Ben says as we belly up to the bar. "I recommend the blueberry."

We spend the afternoon testing every beer on the menu, or at least I do, because Ben is driving, and I'm grateful Ben doesn't ask about Josh or mention last night's brouhaha even once.

By the time he pours me back into my flat, I'm drunker than I've been in a long while, and I can't even remember what we talked about all afternoon. But I'm not so drunk I don't know what he's done for me today.

"Thanks, Ben," I slur as he settles me on my bed, pulls my shoes off, and drapes a blanket over me. "I really needed that."

"I got you, little Gee. Always."

And my last thought as I drift off is, *that's nice, I only hope they've also got Josh.*

CHAPTER THIRTY-NINE

JOSH

I wake up the morning after the party with another hangover courtesy of vodka. But I have things to do and people to see, so I rinse and repeat by throwing back three paracetamol, having a long shower and heading to the café on the corner for the hangover breakfast of champions.

I don't even attempt to call Greer. An apology phone call won't cut it. I don't waste my time. First, I head over to the Carters'.

I do it right by ringing the front doorbell, not slipping in round the back like I've been doing all my life. Somehow that seems like an unsavoury metaphor for what I've been doing with Greer, and there will be no more sneaking around.

Mama C opens the door. I'm not sure what I'm expecting, but a teary hug isn't it. Despite what Will said, I at least expected some disapproval or disappointment for the way I've gone about things.

"I imagine you want to see Harry. He's out the back, cleaning the pool. You know how he gets if there's even one leaf in it." She shoos me out before I have a chance to say anything at all.

Harry has his back to me, scooping the already pristine pool as I head down the yard. It's not till I get to the pool gate that he realises I'm there.

"Hand me the bottle of testing strips will you, son?" He points to a little blue plastic tub sitting on the sun lounger. He gives me the once-over as I hand it to him.

"You're looking a bit worse for wear this morning." He takes a couple of steps into the pool and dips the tiny white strip into the water, then holds it up to the side of the bottle to estimate the results. He doesn't say anything more, so it's over to me. It's show time.

"I'd like to apologise for my behaviour last night, Harry. I was rude, and it was unforgivable to cause such an appalling scene in your home." I pause, hoping for something from him, although I'm not sure what.

"And?"

"Of course, I'll apologise to Ethan and Jessie, and Guy."

Even though Will said Harry and Stella are fine with this, the granite look on Harry's face is giving me cause to doubt. Then I realise. If I want Greer, if I'm going to deserve a woman like her, I have to earn her. And as much as I've been fighting it—fighting her—Greer is what I want. More than that, she's what I need.

"I also wanted to tell you I'm in love with your daughter. I'm sorry for the way I went about things. Sorry for the way you found out. I'm not sorry for loving her." I pause to try and read his face, but he's still giving me nothing.

"Go on."

"I realise I don't deserve her, and I've hurt her, but I want you to know I intend to win her back. And whilst your approval—yours and Stella's—would mean the world to me, I will be fighting for her regardless. I hope you can understand and maybe accept me like you've accepted Jessie."

"And how do you plan to do that, son? Because from where I'm standing, you screwed up big-time last night. If there's one thing I know about my daughter, it's that she's got my stubborn streak, and she can hold a grudge like a champ. Winning her over won't be easy."

"Well, to be honest, I haven't quite worked out how I'll get her back yet. But I will. Because I love her. And I won't give up. I'll spend the rest of my life proving it to her, and to you, if that's what it takes."

Harry finally lets out one of his giant laughs. "Well, let's hope it doesn't take that long. Her mother will never forgive you if she doesn't get to plan a wedding."

"It's taken me a while, Harry, but believe me when I say, if there's no wedding, it won't be on my account."

"Would you mind giving me a heads up on when that's likely to be? I lost a couple hundred on how long it would take for this to come out, and I need to recoup my losses. Not to mention regain my dignity. Stella won't let me hear the end of it if she wins again."

I help Harry finish cleaning the pool, and Stella makes us lunch before I head off to Ethan's to apologise to him and Jessie for hijacking their engagement party.

Jessie is not as forgiving or kind as Harry and Stella, and I have to do a whole lot of grovelling before she begrudgingly tells me that if I hurt her friend again, she will cut off my balls and feed them to me for breakfast.

Next stop is Guy. This one I do via phone, not least because I don't fancy getting a fist in the face. I call him from the car on the way to Manly to see the progress on the house. He laughs when I explain I'm in love with Greer.

"No shit, Sherlock. You made that blindingly obvious. You know, you didn't need to tell the entire party I'm a man whore, even if it is true. All you had to do was take me aside and give me a heads-up. I would've backed off."

"I'm sorry. I saw red. And by the way, everyone already knew about you, so ..." We both laugh. "Let's catch up for a beer sometime, yeah?"

"Hmm. Give me a week or two to get over it first, and then sure, let's organise it."

I don't deserve the forgiveness everyone is giving me, but I'm grateful for it anyway.

Now I have to work out how to get Greer to forgive me. What would Matthew McConaughey or Hugh Grant do in this situation?

I mull it over as I head down to Manly to check on the house. Things have moved quickly this week. The painting is finished, the kitchen is in, apart from the splashback and some lighting, and the floors are sanded and ready for varnishing or carpet, depending on the room. By the end of this week, it will be pretty much finished.

As I walk around, I see Greer in every detail, and a bubble of panic starts to rise. What if she can't forgive me? What if I've pushed her too far? She's never said it, but I know she loves me because this feeling can't be one way. It can't be too late. But whatever I do, I know this could be my last chance. It had better be good.

It's one of those middle-of-the-night thoughts. Finally, I have an idea. I know what I have to do. I had told her we were going nowhere. Told her I didn't want Harry and Stella and Will to find out. Well, once I'm done, everyone will know.

I'm in the office at the arse-crack of dawn on Monday, knocking on doors and dragging an emergency crew together. My team are all behind me one hundred percent. The media buyers take a little bit of convincing until I explain why I'm doing what I'm doing. It doesn't hurt that the MD gets wind of it and weighs in on my need to get Greer back. He's a big fan after meeting her at the awards night.

It's going to take a week to get it together, so I spend the next seven days on tenterhooks. I've told Will what's happening because I needed some moral support. Harry and Stella are trying to drag it out of me, but other than those who have to know, and Will, I'm keeping this thing under wraps.

In all the excitement, I completely forget about the Melbourne job until I get a call late on Monday. But my decision is made. No matter what happens with my grand gesture, I'm staying in Sydney. I told Harry I would fight for Greer for the rest of my life if that's what it took, and I meant it. I don't feel even a scintilla of regret or doubt when I tell them no. Sydney is where I belong. With Greer. And the rest of the Carter family. Soon to be my family. Come hell or high water.

CHAPTER FORTY

GREER

The week after the party drags by. Josh doesn't attempt to contact me, for which I'm grateful. No. Really. I am. The last thing I need is him making excuses and telling me yet again why we can't be together.

The one saving grace is I don't have to deal with the Mean Girls anymore. Once Zoe was let go, the other two lost all appetite for tormenting me. And whilst I still see them roll their eyes at me in meetings and hear whispers behind my back, there are no more overt attacks. Which leaves me free to get on with my job. And the new community housing project I'm working on with Jonathan takes up almost all my time.

I miss working on Josh's house and would give anything to see how it's looking. But there's no way I'm going there. I'm not even doing a drive-by. Well, okay. One teensy-tiny little drive-by on the weekend. When I'm sure nobody will be there. The construction fence is gone. The front fence and walkway are repaired, and the carport is finished. The garden is planted, and the façade is painted. It all looks exactly as I imagined, right down to the dormer windows in the new roofline and the restored stained glass in the front door.

I sneak up the front path and peer in the windows. The walls are painted, and the floors are done. There's no furniture, but I guess there wouldn't be since Josh is moving to Melbourne. I wonder whether he'll rent it out or sell it. I hope whoever eventually lives here will love it at least half as much as I do.

I spend the rest of the weekend moping at home. I should be out getting started with my Christmas shopping. It's my favourite time of the year. By now, I'm normally in full present-buying swing. But I can't seem to muster up the enthusiasm.

When the weather is good I like to walk to work which, given the North Sydney traffic, is often faster than catching the bus. As though it's trying to match my mood, Monday morning dawns grey and drizzly, so I resign myself to putting up my brolly and trudge to the bus shelter at the end of my street.

I've been sitting there a minute or two when someone taps me on the shoulder.

"Excuse me. I don't want to be rude, but is that you?" The guy in a three-piece suit points to the end of the shelter.

And right there is a full-colour poster of my face, with the words #joshlovesgreer.

The two teenage girls in school uniforms squeal.

"Yes. It is. It's her. You're Greer." And before I can think anything of it, they're snapping my picture and typing furiously on their phones.

What the hell?

I fish my phone out of my handbag and realise I've had it on silent since my meeting on Friday. At least that explains why nobody called over the weekend.

I'm about to bring up Josh's number when the bus arrives. And there, on the side of the bus, is another photo of me. This one says, *If you see this woman, tell her #joshlovesgreer.*

The girls get on the bus ahead of me and tell their friends, who start taking pics too.

My fingers hover over Josh's number, but I don't know what to say. As we pull up at the next bus shelter, there's yet another pic of me. This time saying *Tell your friends #joshlovesgreer.*

What the actual fuck?

My phone starts blowing up.

There are literally hundreds of notifications on Twitter. I open it up and check Trending. Sure enough, #joshlovesgreer is number one in Sydney, with dozens of photos of me from the bus stop and inside the bus.

Instagram is no different—there's a new page—@joshlovesgreer, where dozens of photos of me are posted.

I look up at the next stop. And the next. Every bus shelter from my flat to the office has a poster of my face, all with the #joshlovesgreer. Everyone on the bus is laughing and cheering and calling their friends to tell them they're on a bus with Greer. I lose count of the number of selfies I'm asked for, until, finally, we reach my stop.

And there is a picture of me. With Josh. I can't even remember it being taken. It's in the back-yard of his house, and we're smiling at one another. My heart, which has been doing backflips and forward rolls since I got to the bus shelter, dismounts from the parallel bars onto the mats with a splat.

Because this one says, *I love you Greer #joshlovesgreer.* And what's more, directly across the road is another bus shelter, with a photo of Josh on his own, looking forlorn, and the caption *If you love me, you know where to go #joshlovesgreer.*

Someone yells out the window of a passing bus. "What are you waiting for, Greer? Go get him." People are whistling and cheering, and still my phone is going crazy with notifications.

I can't stand on the pavement all day in the rain, but I don't quite know what to do with myself, so I head inside and up to my office. Which gets me a standing ovation.

"What are you doing here?" Jonathan asks. "Don't you have someone to meet?"

"I ..." I start before promptly bursting into tears.

I'm shuffled into the conference room and given a hot cup of tea and a box of tissues. Looks like the usual Monday morning Work in Progress meeting is all about me and my crazy love life this week. Nobody seems to mind. They're all talking over each other.

"Do you know where he wants you to go?" "Do you need a lift?" "No, get a cab." "She can't go like that, look at her face." "Come into the bathroom and we'll clean you up first." "Don't worry about work; we've got you covered."

Finally, they run out of steam, and Jonathan takes control.

"Right. I've ordered you an Uber to take you wherever it is you need to go. It'll be here in ten minutes, so go with Catherine to the ladies and she'll fix up your makeup for you. We don't want to see you again today, but we do want a full report by close of business. Okay?"

"Okay. Thank you." I'm laughing and crying and shaking like a leaf as Catherine, who has gone out of her way to make me feel welcome since I started here, leads me off to the bathroom.

Somehow, I find myself in an Uber, giving them the only address I can think of. The rain has made traffic a gridlocked nightmare. We get tangled in the backlog from an accident on Military Road, and by the time we approach Spit Hill, the peak hour is officially over, even though the traffic suggests otherwise. As we crawl down the hill, I see the time. Ten thirteen. No. No. No. Please let us make it. The flashing lights start. Dammit. Right on time for the first bridge opening of the day. I strain against my seatbelt as though leaning forward will somehow propel us over the opening and onto the other side. The bridge deck rises at glacial speed. There's not one but three boats waiting to pass through. Who goes sailing in this weather? It's apocalyptic out there. The boats cruise through like three lazy snails with nowhere to be, and it seems like hours before the deck starts to descend again.

I jump around from deciding to call Josh to resolving to wait to see him in person and back again a hundred times.

Finally, the car is pulling up in front of the house I love so much, and I'm falling out the door. The rain is torrential, and I left my umbrella in the office, so by the time I cross the footpath and make it up the front path, all the hard work Catherine put into fixing my hair and makeup is completely ruined.

The door is ajar, so I slip my sopping shoes off and push it open to find a trail of red and orange and hot pink flowers and petals running down the hall and up the stairs. There's still no furniture until I get to the door of the master bedroom, where an enormous four-poster bed sits perfectly against the wall. It's dressed in fluffy white pillows and a fat white quilt, where a heart of petals has been laid out.

There is no sign of Josh, so I step into the room. On the wall opposite the bed, above the beautiful newly refurbished antique fireplace, is a massive painting. A nude. If I didn't know better, I'd almost say it could be a painting of me.

CHAPTER FORTY-ONE

JOSH

I moved the furniture I might need in over the weekend. The bed and the nude of the woman that looks just like Greer. It crosses my mind she might find it creepy. Too late to worry about it now. If she hates it, I'll sell it. Whatever she wants. If she'll only give me a chance.

I'm there at the house at seven am on Monday morning. In case she's early. And I settle in to wait. The hashtag starts trending on social media just after eight o'clock. My team and the guys in the media department, especially the social media manager, have really pulled a rabbit out of a hat. Twitter and Insta are both blowing up. But I have no way of knowing if she's seen any of it. Until eight thirty when the first 'sighting' of Greer gets posted. Some teens have taken a selfie with her at the bus shelter near her flat and posted it with the hashtag. God bless gen Z. Or maybe they're gen Alpha. Who cares? Bless them anyway.

Greer looks a little shell-shocked. Not angry or unhappy, though, so I take some comfort in that. From there, things escalate quickly. There are sightings and videos right up until nine am when a video of her going into her office building is posted. Then it's radio silence on the visuals, although people are still posting #joshlovesgreer. #whereisgreer and #findgreer are also trending. It crosses my mind this would make a great case study, but that's a thought for another time.

Ten o'clock comes and goes and still no sign of Greer. Maybe she didn't know where I expected her to go. No. She'd know. Maybe she couldn't get away from work? Maybe she's too embarrassed to leave the building? Or maybe she's not coming.

Which I refuse to believe. She'll be here. She has to. Because if this doesn't work I don't have a plan B. Yet.

My heart rate picks up as the clock ticks past ten thirty. I'm about to collapse in a heap when I hear the slam of a car door over the sound of the rain. I peek out the window in time to see Greer coming through the gate. I have just enough time to dart into the second bedroom and push the door almost closed before I hear the soft fall of her bare feet on the stairs and then a gasp as she takes in the bed and the painting.

"You came," I whisper from the bedroom doorway, and she spins around.

"Yes." She sounds the way I feel. Unsure. Hopeful. And more than a little scared.

"Tell me what you need, Greer. What you need to hear from me, what you need me to do, to show you I meant what I said."

"Tell me the truth. Tell me *your* truth."

"My truth? My truth is I've loved you since I hauled that damn red suitcase off the carousel. But I didn't deserve you. I don't deserve you. The problem is, I no longer care. I want you. I need you. And I'll do anything you ask to earn you."

Tears are streaming down her cheeks, mixing with the rain and the mascara leaving tracks on her beautiful skin.

"You don't need to do anything to earn me, Josh. Just love me."

"Oh, Flo. That I can do. That's the easiest thing I'll ever have to do." There's so much more I want to say, but it will have to wait.

Because then she's in my arms, and I realise I'm crying too. She's shaking with cold, having been caught in today's wild summer storm, so I take her into the brand-new ensuite bathroom.

"Do you think maybe it's time to christen the amazing shower my very clever architect specified for this incredible bathroom?"

"Specified? Listen to you using all the technical architecture words. You were listening, after all."

"I've listened to every word you've ever said to me, Flo. And a fair few you haven't." I pull her jacket off her shoulders and turn her around to unzip the shift dress she's wearing under it before turning the hot water on.

"I think I should probably rectify that." She presses her cold, wet hands against my cheeks and looks deep into my eyes. "I love you, Josh. I've loved you as long as I can remember."

It's not until she says those words I realise there's been a corner of my soul I've been holding together with hope and an iron grip. Now I can let it loose, and I finally feel like the hollow space inside me is full. Of love and warmth and the smell of cinnamon scrolls.

I can't get words past the mass of love and relief in my throat, so I drop my lips to hers and continue to strip her clothes. Not kissing, just pressing. Lips to lips. Breath to breath.

As her knickers slip down her thighs, I realise she's been undressing me too, and finally, we're both naked, standing under a luscious cascade of water from jets up and down the wall and along the ceiling.

I thank the universe Greer had the presence of mind to install a seating shelf because I'm quaking with the need to be inside her. Sitting down, I pull her to straddle my lap and thrust inside her without preamble.

Greer gasps. "Condom."

But I can't bear the thought of anything being between us.

"Not today. Just this once. I need to feel you. Just you."

"I'm not on protection."

"Then we're in the lap of the gods."

"Yes," she whispers. "I am." And I smile against her lips as she starts to rock. Slow, steady movements. A rhythm that croons *mine, mine, mine*, until we come, one following the other, although I'm not sure who goes first.

It's hours before I finally come back to earth, curled up with Greer in our new bed, listening to the rain batter windows with another freak summer storm.

"What is it with this house and storms?" Greer asks, running her fingers up and down my chest and belly.

"Isn't rain supposed to mean good luck?" I'm sure I heard that somewhere.

"In that case, it worked."

We're silent again for a time. A comfortable silence, full of the promise that bit by bit, drip by drip, our thoughts and our feelings and our dreams will be told. But there's no rush.

Eventually, I start.

"I bought this bed the weekend I went to the mountains to visit Mum. When I saw it in the shop, I knew it was a serious bed. A bed for a family. For a lifetime. One day, when you're ready, I hope maybe you'll consider birthing our children in this bed."

"Is that why you bought it?"

"Yes. Even if I didn't know it at the time."

"As long as you know it now."

Greer sighs, and I can feel the contentment flowing out of her in waves. "In this bed. In this house."

"Our time starts now."

EPILOGUE ONE

GREER

I'd love to say the weeks after Josh and I finally find ourselves float by in a loved-up bubble of walks on the beach and lazy Sunday morning orgasms. Don't get me wrong, there are plenty of those. But Christmas is coming up fast, and Josh is insistent we hold Christmas at 'our' place this year, so there is also a frenzy of homewares shopping. And while things are still a bit sparse, and there's very little actual furniture, it's liveable.

Officially, I still live in my flat in Kirribilli, and on nights when one of us works late, or has an early meeting, we stay there. But more often than not, we can be found in Manly.

Tyrone's mother has flown off to Europe and left him. Again. So, he'll be spending the summer holidays with us. As soon as the house was finished, Josh asked him to choose a room for himself. He chose the one furthest away from us so he didn't have to hear us having 'gross old people monkey sex' he said. In reality, it was because it's the one closest to the stairs, so he thinks he can sneak out at night without Josh realising. Which hasn't quite worked out for him. Regardless, he seems happy to be here.

The three of us had a great time shopping for furniture, artwork and bedding for him, and even unfinished, it looks much more like a teenage boy's room than the overdone early-Versace vibe at his mother's.

Josh has stuck to his guns about Ty paying him back for the legal fees, so he's been working it off by taking care of the garden for us as well as working with Matt. He complains bitterly, but you can hear him whistling and talking to the plants whenever he's working out there. Matt thinks he might have a future as a landscaper. That's entirely up to him. He's got another year at school before he has to decide.

Susan Kirby was worth her weight in chocolate bars, and managed to get him off with a twelve-month driving suspension and some community service. Josh put her on speed dial, for future reference.

Christmas Day, as often happens in Sydney, dawns cloudy and humid. Ty is up early, making sure there are no leaves in the pool, and the lawn is clear, further proof he loves the garden. Also, he lives to impress my dad, who has strict rules about leaves in pools.

The entire family descends on us right on eleven. Mum, Dad, Will and Ben, Ethan and Jessie. Josh's face looks like it might split; he's grinning so wide. He's thrilled to have the family—our family—celebrating in his first real home ever.

Everyone dumps their gifts under the huge fresh Christmas tree that Josh, Ty and I spent hours decorating with more tinsel, baubles and fairy lights than can be found in Myer. Josh said it had to be perfect, and it is.

"If it's okay with you, Harry, I'd like to be Santa this year," Josh says.

"Well, it's your house, son. Just don't get used to it. You don't have the belly to carry it off once grandbabies come along." Dad pats his ever-expanding waistline and gives Jess and me the side eye.

In a matter of minutes, it's like a feeding frenzy. Presents are passed around, paper is shredded and there a squeals and shouts of delight. Ty bellows his approval as he unwraps the latest wireless VR headset Josh and I bought him and rolls his eyes in mock horror at the high-end gardening tools my brothers chipped in for.

Eventually, there are no presents left under the tree. I look at Josh expectantly. I know he will have bought me something, but it's nowhere to be seen. Which is funny because my present to him is missing too.

Taking my hand, he pulls me up from my seat on the floor.

"Last but not least, Merry Christmas, Greer." He hands me a small, flat, faded velvet box. I know it's not a ring. We've talked about it, and he promised he wouldn't even think about proposing until after Jessie and Ethan's wedding. I snap open the lid, and inside are the most exquisite art deco sapphire and pearl earrings I've ever seen. I make a noise somewhere between a squeal and a gasp because words are beyond me, and Jessie and Mum are up in a flash, looking over my shoulder.

"I bought these the weekend I went to visit my mother." Josh reaches to remove the earrings I put in this morning. "At the time, I convinced myself they were a thank you for all the work you were doing on this house. In fact, they were much more. They were a declaration." He takes one of the earrings and slides it into my ear. "A declaration that you mean more to me than anything or anyone I've ever known. I love you, Greer. I did then, I do now, and I will forever."

The other earring slips in easily, and I feel it sway gently. Behind me, I hear Mum and Jessie sniffling, Dad harrumphing, and Ty and my brothers gagging. But in front of me, there's Josh, and nothing else matters.

"I love you too." I take his face in my hands and kiss him with all the love flowing through my veins.

"Cut it out, Greer," Will interrupts. "Is it time yet?"

I turn and nod, and we race out the back door, across the deck and down the side path.

"Close your eyes," I call. Which is intended for Josh, but when we come back inside, everyone is standing, eyes closed. Although Ty looks like maybe he's cracked one open.

"Sit down and hold out your hands," I tell Josh. I need to get this done quickly before someone breaks cover.

No sooner is he cross-legged on the floor than I'm gently putting his Christmas gift in his lap. Where it wriggles and squirms and leaps up to lick his face. Josh's eyes pop open to take in the fluffy chocolate brown labradoodle.

All he can do is laugh as the puppy leaps at him, madly licking his face, as not just its tail, but its whole back end, whips back and forth.

"I can't believe you got me a dog." He rubs the puppy's head, already totally in love. "Apart from you, this is the best gift ever."

Hours later, when everyone is conked out in a food coma—most especially the as-yet-unnamed puppy, who is sprawled on Ty's lap—Josh finds me admiring my new earrings in the ensuite mirror.

"They're all asleep." He presses into my back and kisses my neck, right below where my beautiful gift sways. "Maybe we could have a nanna nap too. A naked nanna nap."

"I like the way you think." I rub my arse over his ready and willing erection. "How about you lock the door."

And I can't decide which present is best. The earrings or the orgasm. But at the end of the day, neither of them compares to the gift of Josh.

"I think you might need to draw up some more blueprints," Josh says as we lay sweaty and exhausted. "That dog's going to need a pretty special kennel."

"Lucky thing blueprints are my specialty then, isn't it?"

"Very lucky. If it wasn't for your blueprints, who knows how long it would've taken me to pull my head out of my arse?"

Before I can answer, there's a whining and scratching at the door. We look at one another and laugh. Josh lets the puppy in, and it makes a valiant attempt to jump up on the too-tall bed. Josh settles him at the end, and he immediately wriggles his way up till he's between our bodies.

"Yep. Looks like you've got another badly behaved male on your hands."

"What's one more to add to the list?"

EPILOGUE TWO

JOSH

G unners Barracks is a beautiful place for a wedding. All sandstone and chandeliers and harbour views. No. Don't get excited. We're not getting married. Yet. Nick and Lulu are. Although, if we're being technical, they're already married.

I finally met Lulu, the woman Will tried to set me up with, when she and Nick arrived back in Sydney a couple of weeks ago for their 'Australian' wedding. Baby in tow. And I can see why Will might've thought we would be a good match because she's stunning. Beautiful and vivacious. Talented and funny. A lot like Greer, in fact.

I knew there was something up with Nick that day at the sailing club. Turns out, he and Lulu had already embarked on a secret whirlwind romance. It's always the quiet ones.

Lulu and Greer hit it off immediately, and along with Lulu's friend Rosanna, and Nick's sister Claire, have already formed a tight little posse. Which is no surprise, I guess, all being artists of a sort.

The music starts, and we all turn to watch Lulu walk down the garden. Her dress is a work of art, designed and made for her by Rosanna, who is a costume designer. In a departure from tradition, it's the colour of crushed raspberries. Nick's one and only request, apparently. Which was a surprise to me. The Nick I knew back in the day wouldn't even have noticed the colour of a dress, much less cared. There's a story there, I suspect, and one day I'll find out what.

People throw the term glowing around a lot, but Lulu really is. As beautiful as her dress is, it's her face you notice, alight with love as she walks down the garden towards Nick, who is also, well, glowing. And who is holding the cutest little redheaded baby I've ever seen, all kitted out in pale pink satin and tulle. All of which goes to show how much he's changed. I can identify.

I glance over at Greer, who is simultaneously dabbing at her eyes with a crumpled tissue and beaming from ear to ear. Beyond her is Ben, who for some reason, looks like he's been hit in the side of the head with a cricket bat. If we were in a cartoon, his eyes would be spinning around in their sockets and musical notes and hearts would be floating out the top of his head. Weird. I've never seen that look on him before. But I recognise it from my own face in the mirror. I follow his line of sight. Ahhh. The maid of honour.

Standing next to the raspberry confection that is Lulu, is Rosanna. In a cream satin dress that hugs her fantastic curves. She's a beautiful woman alright. It's a shame for Ben, she has a boyfriend.

Their vows are lovely. Funny and heartfelt and mercifully short.

The ceremony ends with cheering and rose petals. Laughing and kissing. The baby, aptly named Isla the Wonderchild, is passed from person to person, giggling, pulling hair and depositing smacking wet kisses on any cheek she can reach. There is so much joy in this garden I almost let out a tear or two myself.

In all the excitement, I take a moment to slip the photographer a fifty to make sure he takes a few special shots of Greer and me. Every now and then, I like to put something up on the @joshlovesgreer account. Gotta keep our fans up to date on what we're up to. It's no longer trending, of course, but we still have followers, and Greer gets a laugh out of showing them bits of our life. The G-rated bits.

By the time dinner is over, baby Isla is asleep, bum up, thumb in mouth in her pram in the corner. I've been joyfully interrogated by Lulu's wild-looking father about my grand gesture and survived a lecture from Nick's mother about Lulu's inappropriate wedding dress.

Nick and Lulu's in-laws are about as badly matched as mine and Greer's will be. When I'm finally allowed to propose. I would've done it months ago, but Greer insisted I wait until after Jess and Ethan have had their big day. Once that's done and dusted, all bets are off and I'm down on one knee.

Nearly a year down the track and we still can't get enough of each other. Life with Greer has been nothing like I ever expected a relationship to be. No dramas. No angst. And certainly no boredom. Just lots of laughter and the best sex I've ever had. Daily.

If you'd told me two years ago I'd be happily settled with the—excuse the corny-ness—love of my life, in a house of my own, I would have laughed. Oh. And a dog. We can't forget the dog.

Finally, Greer, who has been doing the rounds of our friends and family, comes to rescue me, holding out her hand in invitation. She's looking gorgeous in a floaty pink, orange and yellow floral dress that almost skims the floor. I know the bride is supposed to be the most beautiful woman in the world on her wedding day, but for my money, nobody compares to Greer.

"May I have this dance, Mr Markham?"

"It would be my pleasure, Ms Carter." I bow slightly as I take her hand and lead her onto the dance floor.

"Aren't they gorgeous together?" Greer asks as we circle the floor, nodding towards Nick and Lulu, who are forehead to forehead, swaying in time with the band. The way they're look-ing at each other requires a fire extinguisher to be handy.

"They are. Just like us."

Her smile is overflowing with love. "Just like us."

Maybe we need to borrow that fire extinguisher. Only I don't think it would work. And who would want it to?

The End

GLOSSARY OF AUSTRALIAN TERMS

- *Round the Twist* – An Australian kids TV show. Hugely popular in the early 1990's

- Recce – to reconnoitre or investigate

- Hills Hoist – rotary clothesline ubiquitous in Australian yards

- Parti-coloured – refers to eyes that have two distinct colours within one iris

- Tarp – tarpaulin

- Avo - avocado

- Cornetto – the most delicious ice-cream ever made

- Twisties – cheese flavoured snacks essential for movie-going

- Jaffas – orange and chocolate sweets, also essential snacks for movie going

- Smarties – something like M&M's, only with more colours

- Pineapple - $50, so described because of the colour of the notes

- Peppermint - $10, so described because of the colour of the notes

- Myer – Australian Department Store

ABOUT AUTHOR

Carrie Clarke lives in Sydney, Australia and has been writing stories, in her head and otherwise, since she first picked up a Georgette Heyer as a tween. Blueprint for Falling in Love is the second book in the Falling in Love Series.

Five Fun Facts about Carrie:

1.   After writing (and reading), Carrie's favourite thing to do is travel

2.   Carrie loves history, bonus points if it's Egyptian

3.   In Carrie's world the most important meal of the day is dessert

4.   She would love to speak French, but has no talent for languages

5.   Carrie firmly believes sleeping in is the only acceptable use for the mornings

Join Carrie's mailing list at carrieclarkeauthor.com.au to receive advance news about upcoming books, exclusive extras and special content.

ALSO BY

The Art of Falling in Love – Book 1 in the Falling in Love Series

What Happens in Singapore – Short story only available to my
newsletter subscribers

THANK YOU

Every writer needs a team to help them get their words out into the world in a (hopefully) coherent and beautiful package. I am lucky enough to have a great team behind me.

Thank you again to my critique partners Karen, Antonella and Emma, who patiently read through what may have felt like too many versions of this story.

Thank you to Kelly Rigby for her editorial clarity of thought and encouragement, to Jo Spiers for her above-and-beyond proofreading, and to Ryan Gilchrist for another beautiful cover. May there be many more collaborations with you all.

Special thanks to my friends who have been such incredible cheerleaders – Michele, Deb, Lisa, Angela, Mary, Kay, Linda, Michelle and Sue. I couldn't do it without you.

And to my family, who continue to be patient with my regular departures from the 'real' world. Especially to Tech Support, who has the unenviable job of talking me down out of my tree when technology refuses to co-operate.

If you enjoyed this book, I'd love it if you could leave a review on Amazon or Goodreads.

Thanks for reading x

KEEP IN TOUCH

I f you would like to keep you up to date on when the next book in the Falling in Love Series is coming out, receive special bonus content and exclusive offers, including my short story 'What Happens in Singapore', a post-HEA story from my first book The Art of Falling in Love, and lots more, I'd love you to join my mailing list at **carrieclarkeauthor.com.au**.

You can follow me on:
Facebook.com/CarrieClarkeAuthor
Instagram.com/carrieclarkeauthor
Twitter: @CarrieCAuthor

SNEAK PEEK

WHAT HAPPENS IN SINGAPORE

If you loved Blueprint for Falling in Love, keep reading for a sneak peek of What Happens in Singapore. This steamy short story will only ever be available to my newsletter subscribers, so to find out how it unfolds head to my website at **carrieclarkeauthor.com.au** and sign up.

WHAT HAPPENS IN SINGAPORE

CHAPTER ONE - ANNALIESE

The arctic blast of the air conditioning nearly knocks me over as I stagger out of the heat. It took all of thirty seconds to walk from the coach to the hotel, and even in that short time all the moisture in my body rose to the surface of my skin, soaking my already travel-grimed clothes.

I sway on my feet. When I took that last Valium, I hadn't expected we'd get stuck in Singapore. That I'd have to gather all my onboard belongings and get out of the plane. Not to mention having to get on a coach and then stand in the monstrous foyer of a fancy hotel, complete with a full-wall water feature and the dulcet tunes of a baby grand, expertly played by a tiny man in a dinner suit. Hopefully, the cold will wake me up before I reach the reception desk so I don't drool and embarrass myself with the check-in staff. Based on the length of the queue I estimate I have around five minutes to get my act together.

I hate air travel. In fact, it wouldn't be an exaggeration to say it terrifies me. Being trapped somewhere you can't get out of? No thanks. And don't get me started on the middle seat. A London to Sydney flight is a long time to be terrified. Hence the Valium, which I borrowed from my anxiety-ridden mother.

So I don't fall asleep where I stand, I do a bit of people watching. The queue looks to be an eclectic collection of tourists and business people. Two ahead of me is an extraordinarily tall man with broad shoulders and nothing but a laptop case slung over his shoulder. Thank goodness I packed a change of clothes—including underwear—and essential toiletries in my carry-on. My sister laughed at me, but who has the last laugh now? Certainly not the guy with the laptop case. I hope I don't have to sit next to him when we finally get off the ground and he's still wearing today's—and yesterday's—underwear. *Eww.*

It's tall guy's turn, and although I can't hear what he's saying, I can pick up the deep rumble of a warm baritone. Even from the back it's clear from his body language he's doing a bit of friendly flirting with the girl behind the counter. Bet he gets a room with a view.

As he steps away from the counter, I get a glimpse of his profile. Maybe he's an actor or a rock star, because he has the kind of face people stop and stare at. Clean and sharp. His wavy golden hair is almost to his shoulders, and he reminds me of a lion with his graceful movements and burnished colouring. I can't take my eyes off him. Which is unfortunate because he turns and our gazes meet. Heat creeps up my cheeks. But I can't look away. His eyes are golden too. Everything about him is gilded and beautiful. It probably only lasts a couple of heartbeats before he turns and walks away, but I suspect that look will be branded in my memory forever.

Checking in takes no time at all, and is thankfully drool-free. If I wasn't so out of it, I would take a moment to appreciate their efficiency.

"Your room is on the tenth floor. The bar, restaurant and café are on the mezzanine, and here are the details of meals and drinks the airline will cover," my receptionist says, handing me an A4 printout. "Oh, and the pool is on Level 8 if you would like to use it."

My ears prick up. A pool. Exactly what I need to wake myself up a little so I don't sleep all afternoon and lie awake all night. Dammit.

"That sounds lovely. Unfortunately, I don't have a suit."

Sweeping his arm out, the receptionist indicates a wide corridor lined with tiny shops. "We have a shopping arcade with several boutiques where you can purchase anything you might need. Swimsuits, change of clothes, toiletries." He smiles and looks over my shoulder, implying I should move aside and let him get on with things. Okay then.

Rather than go straight to my room, where I might be in danger of falling face-first on the bed, I weave towards the shopping arcade, and step into the first boutique. It's a treasure-trove of essentials for the stranded traveller. I hope they mentioned it to the tall, golden, baritone guy. Someone so beautiful should not be wearing day-old clothes. Ever.

Sign up to my newsletter at **carrieclarkeauthor.com.au** to read the rest of this fun and steamy short story, as well as other bonus content. You'll also be the first to hear about the release date for Book 3 of the Falling in Love Series, A Capacity for Falling in Love, due out late-2023.